"You are stun... **You walked i**... **I was breathless and speechless all at once. Still am, every time I look at you."**

Willow knew the feeling. One more thing to add to her checklist: Nolan set those butterflies to flying inside her.

He considered her. "If I said *grinch* right now, what would you do?"

Her smile came slowly but was unstoppable. "I'd take your hand and sneak away with you."

"Just like that," he said, appreciation in his tone.

Willow nodded. *Just like that, cowboy. Before my heart catches up.*

He approached her, his eyes piercingly clear and never leaving hers. Then he moved right into her space. Closer than some of the couples slow dancing on the back porch.

Those butterflies inside her took flight. And there was nowhere else Willow wanted to be.

He was silent for a beat. Finally, he leaned in. His lips brushed against her ear, his breath warmed her skin and he whispered, "*Grinch.*"

Dear Reader,

Growing up, Christmas was magical. I would lie on the floor, watch the lights chase each other around the Christmas tree and dream. Some were small wishes for a certain toy. Others were more complicated, like wanting a unicorn or finding the gold at the rainbow's end. Funny thing is it was all possible if I believed. I've outgrown lying on the floor (it's the getting up that requires a bit more dexterity now), but I still imagine the possibilities. Only these days, I call those possibilities goals.

In *A Cowgirl's Christmas Reunion*, champion bull rider Nolan Elliot believes the only goals he needs are the ones to do with the arena. Nolan isn't convinced he'll ever settle at his family's Texas ranch—until he runs into a cowgirl from his past. But this cowgirl is still chasing her own dreams, ones that never included him. Now this Christmas, if one determined bull rider and an independent trick rider can unwrap their hearts, they might discover the life they build together is better than anything they ever dreamed on their own.

Happy reading!

Cari Lynn Webb

A COWGIRL'S CHRISTMAS REUNION

CARI LYNN WEBB

HEARTWARMING

Harlequin®
HEARTWARMING™

Recycling programs
for this product may
not exist in your area.

ISBN-13: 978-1-335-05129-5

A Cowgirl's Christmas Reunion

Copyright © 2024 by Cari Lynn Webb

 Harlequin Enterprises ULC
22 Adelaide St. West, 41st Floor
Toronto, Ontario M5H 4E3, Canada
www.Harlequin.com

Printed in Lithuania

MIX
Paper | Supporting
responsible forestry
FSC® C021394

Cari Lynn Webb lives in South Carolina with her husband, daughters and assorted four-legged family members. She's been blessed to see the power of true love in her grandparents' seventy-year marriage and her parents' marriage of over fifty years. She knows love isn't always sweet and perfect—it can be challenging, complicated and risky. But she believes happily-ever-afters are worth fighting for. She loves to connect with readers.

Books by Cari Lynn Webb

Harlequin Heartwarming

Three Springs, Texas

A Proposal for Her Cowboy
The Rancher's Secret Crush
Falling for the Cowboy Doc
Her Cowboy Wedding Date
Trusting the Rancher with Christmas
The Texas SEAL's Surprise
His Christmas Cowgirl

Return of the Blackwell Brothers

The Rancher's Rescue

The Blackwell Sisters

Montana Wedding

The Blackwells of Eagle Springs

Her Favorite Wyoming Sheriff

Visit the Author Profile page
at Harlequin.com for more titles.

To the dreamers—to those who chase them,
change them and catch them. Always have
the courage to keep on dreaming.

Special thanks to my editor, Kathryn Lye.
To my Blackwell sisters—Amy, Anna, Carol and
Melinda—there aren't enough words for how
grateful I am to call you friends. To my family for
cheering me on and holding my hand through
every single up and down. I love you all.

PROLOGUE

ELIAS BLACKWELL, aka Big E, finished parking his motor home, cut the engine and tipped his cowboy hat to a surprised onlooker on the busy downtown Dallas sidewalk. "That is how you parallel park."

"Nicely done, Elias." His younger sister, Denny, gathered her cane and smashed her cowboy hat over her gray hair. "You could give lessons to the car parkers around here. I daresay that little vehicle up ahead is parked sideways."

"We've more important things to deal with than lazy parkers." Big E glanced across the road at Highstreet Treasures, a high-end, luxury department store for the discerning and stylish, according to their website.

Big E had always been more partial to a good pair of jeans and a sturdy flannel shirt. All of which could be found at Brewster Ranch Supply in his hometown of Falcon Creek, Montana. For a fair price and a handshake.

Denny hummed her agreement. "That we do."

"This is our last stop." He and Denny were down to Denny's last granddaughter—the youngest daughter of Flora and Barlow Blackwell and the fifth member of the Blackwell Belles. Willow Blackwell was the final piece of Big E and Denny's plan to bring this fallen branch of the Blackwells back together after a ten-year hiatus. It was past time to do some healing and reaffirm their roots. Big E asked, "Do you reckon Willow will recognize you?"

"I'm willing to bet on it." Denny held out her hand, confidence in her upturned chin.

Never one to back away from a bet or a bull, Big E accepted the wager and eyed his sister. "It might take us some old-fashioned, underhanded trickery to bring Willow to the table."

The table being where they planned to negotiate with Willow Blackwell to get her to agree to one final performance with the Blackwell Belles at the Cowgirl Hall of Fame ceremony, where her mother, Flora Blackwell, and Willow's late aunt Dandelion would be inducted.

"We've certainly tricked a few here and there along the way to get what we wanted." Denny chuckled. "Although I prefer to think of it as creative finessing of a situation."

"That has a nice ring to it." Big E laughed. "We are skilled finessers."

"Exactly." Denny pushed out of the chair, made her way over to the refrigerator and took out a bottle of water. "However, Flora believes she has something her youngest daughter wants. Could be leverage for us."

Big E stood and stretched. "That is peculiar, isn't it?"

Denny sipped her water. "What is?"

"Willow's siblings each wanted something of their aunt Dandy's returned—special items—in order for them to agree to perform one last time." Big E stroked his fingers through his beard. "It would make sense that Willow would want something of Aunt Dandy's too."

"That would be the trend. Aunt Dandy was special to all the siblings." Denny replaced the cap on the water and set the bottle aside. "There's no telling what Willow wants until we get her to that table and ask her."

And that was what concerned Big E. Would Willow Blackwell follow her sisters or prove to be an outlier? Not that Big E ever minded an outlier or a trendsetter. Most days, he admired their grit.

But if Willow Blackwell was so far down blazing her own trail, he worried her family might not be enough to entice her back.

Big E helped his sister out of the motor home and onto the sidewalk. One thing was certain: Big E had some grit of his own left and enough stubborn cowboy in him not to give up until he found a way.

Family was too important. After all, blazing a trail was all fine and well. But standing alone at the end of the blazing trail, well, what good was all that without family to celebrate with?

CHAPTER ONE

ANOTHER SATISFIED CUSTOMER. Willow Blackwell hummed along to the cheerful Christmas tune playing over the department store's speakers and handed the spry widow, standing on the other side of the counter, her makeup supplies. "Now remember, Ms. Davenport, navy blue eyeliner and mascara from now on."

"And apply my blush here to show off my eyes, not my wrinkles." Ms. Davenport smiled wide into the mirror on the glass counter and tapped her cheek. "Willow, you are a magician, and those makeup brushes are your wands."

No. Willow was a licensed makeup artist and just doing her job. Nothing special about that. Still, she appreciated the older woman's pleasure over her makeover. "Happy holidays, Ms. Davenport."

"It will be when I capture a date for my grandson's holiday soiree." Ms. Davenport touched her diamond earring and angled a newly sculpted eyebrow at Willow. "You've renewed me, Willow. I think this is going to be a holiday season to remember. Certainly one for the front page of our personal memory books."

Front page of her personal memory book. Willow struggled to remember a recent holiday she considered front-page worthy and came up blank. Surely that wasn't right? She watched the spirited widow stop to spritz herself with Pink Lilac, the season's hottest new fragrance, on her way toward the evening gown section. Willow sprayed cleaner on the counter, polished the glass and closed that memory book. Nothing good waited there.

"Willow Blackwell."

It wasn't the sandpapery scratch in the woman's voice that Willow recognized. But rather the way Willow's name sounded more like a command than an inquiry. Willow straightened and smoothed her expression into neutral. "Grandma Denny."

Her grandmother's smile was quick and victorious. Her arm shot out toward the distinguished older cowboy standing beside her. "Pay up, Elias. I told you Willow would know me." Gran Denny introduced her older brother, Elias Blackwell, to Willow then added, "Kin always recognizes kin."

And Willow's sister had given her a heads-up text about their extended Blackwell family being in town. Willow had been on the lookout for the past week, waiting for her mother to pounce. Flora Blackwell and her late sister, Dandelion, were being inducted into the Cowgirl Hall of Fame right before Christmas. Flora's five daughters were being asked to attend. Such a simple request on the surface.

If they were a typical family, with run-of-the-mill arguments that homemade dinner and hugs all around could easily resolve. But the Blackwells were far from typical. Flora had seen to that when her five daughters were too young to protest. And if her mother thought one evening together would bring her daughters back and fix her family, well, Flora needed to reread her own memory book in detail.

Willow leaned into her smile. The one she'd perfected with just the right wattage not to be too broad. Or too disingenuous. Just natural enough to deflect someone from her real feelings and emotions. "Well, this is certainly a surprise. What brings you two here?"

"Don't suppose you'd believe me if I said I was in the market for a new red lipstick." Gran Denny tapped a finger on the glass countertop.

Willow shook her head and pursed her lips. "I wouldn't let you buy it either. You need a satin rose or rich brown to bring out your natural glow, Gran."

"Hear that, Elias." Gran Denny adjusted her grip on her cane and jabbed her thin elbow into her brother's side. "My granddaughter says I have a glow about me. Isn't that something?"

"I agree with her." Big E stroked his fingers through his white beard and waggled his eyebrows. "Been told I have one too. It's a Blackwell family trait."

What Big E had was a definite gleam in his eyes.

The kind that spoke of hard-earned wisdom and warned of mischief. Willow liked him instantly.

Gran Denny tipped her head at Willow. "We've come to invite you to dinner."

"Tonight?" Willow hedged.

"If it fits your schedule." Big E watched her as if he already knew Willow's schedule better than she did. "We wouldn't want to inconvenience you."

"But I'd really like to spend time with my granddaughter," Gran Denny added.

And no doubt remind Willow about the importance of family. Of the bond Willow and her sisters shared. Of being there for each other. Yet Willow required no reminders. She knew full well the kind of bond she shared with her sisters. It was no stronger than the barest thread. The Blackwell sisters hadn't been there for each other in more than a decade. On the one night they should've rallied together, they'd all walked away, instead.

Willow's cell phone chimed near the cash register. She frowned and opened the new text from her friend Annie Callow. And her world tipped upside down. Thanks to only two words: Fire. Stables.

Her heart sank to her stomach. Willow stammered, "I'm sorry. I can't..." The text blurred. The letters swam together. Her panic swelled. "I have to leave. Right now."

Gran Denny reached across the counter and touched Willow's wrist. "What's wrong, dear?"

Willow rubbed her forehead and scanned the makeup department for her manager. "There's been a fire at the stable where I board my horses." *Her horses*. They were her family. The ones that mattered to her more than anything. The only ones who hadn't let her down. The only ones she hadn't failed. At least, not yet.

Gran Denny squeezed Willow's arm. "We'll come with you."

"Fires and horses don't mix well." Big E nodded. "We can certainly help."

Willow spotted her manager, reached for her purse and skirted around the counter. "You don't have to do that."

"Situations like these require experience and willing hands." Gran Denny blocked Willow and tapped her cane on the tile floor. "I might be gripping a cane, but Elias and I still have something to offer in times like these."

"Denny can settle a horse like no one I know." Pride curved across Big E's face. "My sister is the best horse whisperer around. Those horses will need to be calmed."

Willow looked from her determined grandmother to her great-uncle. Their willingness to jump in, no questions asked, set her back. She had been going it alone for so long now. Determined not to need anything from anyone. Yet she couldn't deny that pinch of relief inside her. She didn't know what waited at the stables. And for once she was grateful not to be alone.

Willow nodded. "Let me just talk to my manager and then we can leave."

The exchange with her manager was brief. Willow got the rest of the day off, proving her manager wasn't entirely heartless. Yet it came with a firm warning that Willow had officially exhausted her *I-have-to-leave-early* requests. But Willow would have to deal with her prickly manager and her dependability issues another time. Right now, her horses needed her more. Willow returned to her family and pointed at the exit sign. "My car is at the parking garage down the street."

"Then it's good we're parked right outside." Gran Denny linked her free arm around Willow's and steered her toward the main entrance with a determination that belied her petite stature.

Big E hurried ahead and held open the heavy glass door. His smile creased into his beard. "There's our ride now."

Willow paused on the sidewalk and gaped across the street at the dated but well-kept motor home stretching across several parking spaces. "That's an RV."

"Don't let good looks fool you." Big E fished in the pocket of his plaid shirt, pulled out his keys and smiled at Willow. "That RV handles better than most sports cars."

That sounded like a stretch, but Willow flattened her lips together to keep her doubt to herself. Big E looked too earnest, and she wasn't about to disappoint him this early on.

"With Elias behind the wheel, that RV can handle anything." Gran Denny added, pride and amusement swirling around her words. "We've certainly been road testing it the past few months. Hasn't let us down yet."

"That RV has turned out to be more reliable than a bloodhound's nose on a quail hunt." Big E urged them across the crosswalk. "Come on. I'll prove it to you."

Willow followed Big E to the RV that was surprisingly parallel parked more expertly than the compact cars behind it. He swung open the front passenger door and motioned her inside. Willow climbed into the oversize captain's chair and buckled her seat belt.

"Ready when you are, Elias." Gran Denny settled on the couch and tapped her cane on the floor. "I don't need to tell you to step on it, but I will all the same."

Unease washed over Willow. Not that she gave in to it. *Best learn to be better than your emotions, Willow, or you won't have anything more than smeared makeup, red-rimmed eyes and no focus. And that's certainly not the look of success.* Flora, aka Willow's mother, wasn't entirely wrong in her long-standing advice for her youngest daughter. Emotions had always tended to trip Willow up when she'd been a child performer. But she had spent years on her own, mastering her feelings and refusing to lose her focus.

To prove it, she stuffed her worry deep inside her. After all, she needed to be clearheaded if she intended to be the best help for her horses. And Willow Blackwell had been taught that nothing but her best would ever do.

NOLAN ELLIOTT KNEW a little something about breath stealing moments.

Every bull he had ridden over the past decade had bucked the very air from his lungs within seconds. He never much worried about it. He knew he would catch his breath as soon as he and his bull parted ways in the arena. After all, he was a professional bull rider and getting the wind knocked out of him was practically a job requirement.

Yet, right now Nolan struggled to breath. He struggled to inhale air that wasn't soot coated and smoke tainted. And it was more than worry that charged at him now like an aggravated bull. But this wasn't some random arena in any city he was passing through on his way to the rodeo championships. No belt buckle or big payout waited at the end of eight seconds.

This was his stepsister's land. Sun Meadows Stables—the horse ranch Annie had built from the ground up—was in trouble. It was her horse barn that was currently engulfed in flames. Even more concerning, Annie, her teenage daughter, and his stepmother were the only family Nolan had left. Helping and protecting them mattered more than anything else.

So, he dodged his worry, kept his breath shallow and worked his way toward the barn and the fire trucks. A firefighter met him, handed him the lead ropes for two skittish quarter horses, then informed Nolan the barn was empty before rushing back to his crew. Nolan wasted no time escorting the young geldings toward the relative safety of the back pasture.

His stepsister shouted his name and hurried to intercept him. Her fingers were fisted around her cell phone. Her boots kicked up the watery muck and splattered her jeans.

Nolan didn't wait for her to ask. When Annie was close enough to hear him, he said, "These are the last two from the stables."

Only her shoulders sagged. Her face was covered in soot and wholly resolved. "I need to make more calls."

Nolan nodded and adjusted his hold on the lead ropes. "I can handle the horses."

"I need to call. . ." Annie's words drifted away. Her gaze skittered over the geldings, then stuck and widened. That resolve started to splinter.

Nolan stepped in front of her, blocking her view of the destruction. "Annie. We got this."

She blinked and focused on him. Her eyebrows crinkled, then her face slowly cleared. Finally, she dipped her chin sharply. "You, me, and mom. We got this."

"Together," he added and held her gaze. That was how they had gotten through the days after his father's death more than a year ago. *Together*.

It would be no different now. He started walking toward the pasture, forcing Annie to move with him and the horses. "Call your neighbors. See if they have space in their stables for your boarders. Then we can contact your clients."

Her back to the fire, Annie snapped into crisis mode, and tapped on her phone screen. "I'll meet you and mom at the pasture," she said briskly, with confidence.

Phone to her ear, Annie headed away from the noise and toward the shelter of her small house. Fortunately, the wind direction was in their favor and the firefighters were able to keep the sparks and flames away from the home that Annie shared with her daughter, Kendall and more recently, Nolan's stepmother.

While Nolan had been building his bull riding career on the professional rodeo circuit, his stepsister had been building a horse boarding and training facility only a short drive from the working ranch where Nolan and Annie had grown-up. Annie often claimed they both had to leave Sky Canyon Cattle Ranch to chase their dreams. Lucky for her, she didn't have as far to run to find everything she wanted. Nolan quickened his pace, determined that this setback would not alter Annie's goals for her equestrian business.

His stepmother was waiting at the pasture and opened the gate for him to guide the geldings inside to join their other displaced stable mates.

Marla stroked her hand over the neck of one of

the still skittish geldings and removed his halter. "They're safe now, if far from settled."

"Settling will take time." For both the horses and his family. This was definitely not what Nolan had envisioned for the first day of his long-overdue holiday visit. Nolan checked the small herd, offering soothing words and gentle pats for each horse before returning to the gate.

Unfortunately, the pasture provided an unobstructed view of the stable barn. Flames flickered inside the damaged building, despite the fire being contained. Smoke billowed toward the sky, staining the clouds above the barn a deep charcoal gray. Nolan fought back a full-body shudder.

Marla's hand landed on his arm as if the destruction knocked her off balance too.

Nolan curved his stepmom's arm around his, kept his words and steps steady. "It can all be rebuilt. Everyone is safe. That's what matters."

Marla exhaled. Her fingers flexed on his arm. "I'm glad you're here."

"Me too," he said and meant it.

Nothing had been the same since his father had died. The circuit and Nolan's thriving rodeo career had provided him a ready and convenient excuse not to come back. But deep down, Nolan knew it was pure selfishness on his part. The last thing he'd wanted was to step onto Sky Canyon Cattle Ranch where he'd spent his happy childhood. Every good memory included his father, who had become a widower shortly after Nolan's birth, and the family ranch. And when his stepmom and step-sister had moved there, Nolan's life had become all that much better. But now the property reminded Nolan how much he'd lost and how very much he still missed his dad.

Yet, according to his father's last will and testament, Nolan owned Sky Canyon. He still wasn't certain why or how he, rather than Marla, had inherited the property. All his stepmother ever told him was that she was glad the ranch was his. If only Nolan could find the same excitement. If only his heart did something other than ache at the thought.

An RV lumbered up the driveway, drawing Nolan back to the matter at hand. Anything at Sky Canyon Cattle Ranch, sitting ten miles away, could wait until later. Nolan needed to concentrate on his family.

"I don't recognize that motorhome." Marla shielded her eyes with her hand and studied the RV. "I wonder who that could be."

The RV slowed a fair distance behind the fire trucks. Suddenly the passenger door was flung open, and a woman fairly flew out. The woman's boots barely touched the gravel before she dashed straight for the burning barn.

Marla gasped. "Willow."

The familiar name knocked the air from Nolan's lungs all over again and concern seeped in.

"Someone needs to stop her." A tremor worked through Marla's words. "She's going to get herself hurt."

And just like that, Nolan was in motion. He skipped the gate and vaulted over the pasture fence instead. His focus never strayed from the cowgirl on the run.

Willow Blackwell. She was his sister's best friend and a regular at Sun Meadows since she had moved back to Dallas permanently not long after his dad's death. In truth, Willow spent more time with his family the past year than Nolan had.

Willow was also the same cowgirl from Nolan's past that his memories could never seem to outrun, despite a lot of time and distance. The same cowgirl who once stirred feelings in him, ones that he now refused to even acknowledge. And the very same cowgirl Nolan had placed in that all-too familiar *to be avoided* column. Certain that was best for his heart.

But Willow was headed for danger. And like his family, Nolan was driven to protect her.

He pushed himself faster.

His past and present were on a collision course now. There was no turning back.

Nolan could only hope that when the smoke cleared, and he finally regained his breath, his heart had made it out safely too.

CHAPTER TWO

WILLOW RACED TOWARD the stables at Sun Meadows, propelled by panic. She dodged a fire truck, sailed over the hoses stretched across the ground and paid no mind to the shouts and warnings. Only her horses mattered. They were her family. Her everything. And they needed her. *Now*.

She evaded a firefighter's grasp, rounded a second fire truck, and her throat closed. More than half of the stable was in ashes. The remaining roof smoldered. Walls and doors were charred beyond repair. For the first time in years, Willow couldn't swallow her fear and those carefully contained emotions.

Her steps faltered. Her knees buckled. Yet she never touched the ground. Instead, she was swept off her feet and tucked against what felt like a firm wall.

"Willow Blackwell, you know your own horses can tell not all fire is good," a man chided.

That deep voice. She recognized it instantly from her past. Back when she was a smitten teenager in the throes of an enchanting, all-be-it innocent summer fling when his voice spoke directly to her lonely heart. These days, she heard him still, only when she allowed herself to dream.

But this was a nightmare. Willow pleaded, "My horses. I have to. . ."

"Willow." That firm voice captured her mind. "Look at me."

Terrified panic scraped against her throat. "To… find them…"

"Willow." That unyielding yet soothing voice again. "Your horses are safe."

Safe. She curved her fingers around the arms that held her. Yes, her summer cowboy had made her feel cared for and so much more all those years ago. She willed him to be real. *Please*. Willed his words to be true. *Please*. But her fear still swirled. Those tears still fell.

Gentle fingers brushed across her cheek, under her chin and lifted her face upwards. That voice came at her, insistent but gentle. "Look at me, please, Willow. Your horses are fine."

Willow blinked once. Twice. Took in the familiar slate-colored eyes watching her, the full beard and expressive face covered in soot. *Nolan Elliot*.

Her cowboy from long ago. It had been an extremely hot June when they'd met at a rodeo where he'd been testing out his bull riding mettle and she'd been performing with her four older sisters. At that time, being a Blackwell Belle had been all Willow lived for. Back when she had believed all her dreams were destined to come true and that her family was all she would ever need. She and Nolan had been two teenagers old enough to recognize the spark between them, but too young—or perhaps too careless—to understand what it might have become.

Now her best friend's brother was a professional bull rider who made his living on the circuit, not rescuing cowgirls in distress. Willow had stopped calling herself a Blackwell Belle soon after that fateful summer had ended. Mostly because she'd realized the only one she could truly count on was herself.

Being in his arms that spark might have flared. If only Willow didn't have important goals to achieve. If only she didn't know better than to get sidelined by foolish things like an old crush on a handsome, but not-for-her cowboy.

"No—Nolan," she sputtered, then added, "You aren't supposed to be here."

He was supposed to be on the road like always, proving exactly why he was a two-time national bull riding champion. As for Willow, she *definitely* was not supposed to be in his arms. During that long ago summer, Nolan had only ever held her hand. He had never held *her*. Still, she stayed where she was.

"Come on." He brushed his thumb across her damp cheek. "Let's go see your horses and talk where we aren't in the way."

Willow finally noticed the firefighters working around them, moving hoses and clearing debris. Her first step revealed she was far from steady. Leaning into Nolan's side, she told herself she would linger for a moment, just until she was back to rights and standing tall in her own boots once again. Surely that would be any minute now.

After all, leaning on a cowboy like Nolan Elliot for longer than necessary would only lead to certain heartbreak. Good thing Willow had stopped inviting that sort of hurt into her life years ago. After she'd decided that wanting both love and happiness was a bit too greedy, not to mention exhausting. Love and she had parted ways. It was a decision she had yet to regret.

The tall heel of her *department-store-appro-priate-ranch-inappropriate* boot slipped on the wet gravel and Nolan adjusted his hold around her waist. "You good?" he asked.

Good isn't enough, Willow. Prove you have the courage not to settle for good. Only then will you stand out and become someone truly special. Once upon a time Willow had believed not just her mother's words but that Nolan thought she was special. That had been nothing more than a teenage girl's whimsy. *Face forward, Willow. Eyes ahead.*

Willow brushed her hair off her face and nodded. "Fine. Thanks." To prove it, she stepped away from Nolan and her complicated past, then asked, "Can you at least tell me what happened?"

Nolan eyed her for a beat as if assuring himself she was in fact fine. He stuffed his hands inside his jacket pockets and started walking. "I surprised

Annie, Kendall and Marla this morning at breakfast."

"They must have been thrilled to see you," she said.

"There might have been a few tears of joy over pancakes and coffee," he said. "And more hugs than I've had in a long while."

Willow didn't doubt it. Nolan hadn't been home since his father's funeral, which was last July. One month before Willow had moved back to Dallas herself. His family had been eager and open about wanting him to come home.

Willow had been reserved about the idea of seeing Nolan again. Yet, there was nothing tentative about her urge to move closer to him now. So close that she might find herself back in his embrace, giving him one of her own *welcome-back* hugs. She crossed her arms over her chest and kept her boots pointed straight ahead. "Were you here when the fire started?"

Nolan shook his head. "We dropped Kendall off at her friend's house for a sleepover, then Marla, Annie and I stopped at the feed store and the grocery store. When we got back, the storage barn was up in flames and the fire had spread to the loft in the stable barn," he explained. "Annie and I raced to get the horses out while Marla called 911."

Willow shivered. "That explains how you knew my horses."

"I would recognize Phantom in a wild herd."

Same as Willow would recognize this cowboy in a sold-out crowd of thousands at an arena.

"Phantom refused to leave his stablemate," Nolan added.

"That's Stardust," Willow whispered. The newest addition to her small family. Another shiver cut through her. "They've been inseparable since I introduced them."

"They are together now." Nolan unzipped his coat. In seconds he had it draped over Willow's shoulders and was tugging the sides together. "The firefighter I spoke to thinks it's an electrical fire. We won't know exactly what caused it until after they investigate more thoroughly."

"Keep your coat," she said. "You need it."

He ignored her and zipped his jacket up under her chin. He even freed her hair from underneath the thick material and adjusted the collar around her neck as if he always fussed over her.

And Willow let him as if she always welcomed his attention. She should bat his hands away. Return his coat. Put that distance back between them. Instead, she slipped her arms into the sleeves, soaked in the warmth, and barely managed to swallow her own sigh.

Seemingly satisfied, Nolan tipped his head toward the far pastures. "Friends of yours?"

Willow followed his gaze and took in the older pair weaving between the horses while talking to Nolan's stepmom. There among the herd of more than two dozen horses were her two beauties. Stardust kicked at the dirt, while Phantom, her cream-colored quarter horse, trailed after Big E as if he were a dog on a leash. Her shoulders relaxed. "That's my great-uncle, Elias Blackwell. And the woman is my grandmother. Me and my sisters always call her Gran Denny."

Annie hollered a greeting from across the driveway and jogged over to where she and Nolan were standing. Stress made Annie's smile fragile, and the hug she gave Willow felt almost urgent.

"Willow, can we keep Denny and Big E, please?" Annie's voice broke. "They've got a way with the spooked horses unlike anything I've ever seen."

Nolan set his hand on Annie's shoulder as if to support her.

Annie reached up and squeezed his fingers. "I'm okay. There's no time now to fall apart."

Willow watched Stardust walk to Gran Denny and rest her head against Denny's thin shoulder. Willow's grandmother simply shifted her weight and stroked her fingers under the mare's black mane. The mare calmed instantly. Big E had not exaggerated Gran Denny's horse whispering skill.

Suddenly Willow wanted Gran Denny and Big E to stay too, if only so she might learn more about the duo. Although, she hesitated to step back into the family fold again. More than a decade had passed since the Blackwell Belles' final performance that had splintered her family. Time had not dulled Willow's hurt or her regret for the pain she had unintentionally caused her older sister, Maggie. Willow feared stepping toward her family if they only turned away from her again. She wasn't certain she could handle that. Best to keep on as she was—on her own and better for it.

Willow hurried to greet her horses, who were the only family she needed. "I'm not sure how long Gran and Big E plan to be in town."

"Well, I'm grateful they're here today." Annie walked with Willow and Nolan to the pasture fence.

Willow introduced Nolan to her grandmother and great-uncle then whistled, calling both her horses to her.

"You know..." Annie leaned her elbows against the fence post and slanted her gaze toward Willow. "Whenever I used to beg Nolan to let me wear his clothes, he always told me no."

Willow sank her fingers into Stardust's thick mane and waited to see where her best friend was going with that observation.

"Annie," Nolan chided and leaned around Willow to peer at his sister. "We were kids. You refused to share your hidden stash of candy with me, so I refused to let you borrow my things."

"Well, we are grown adults now, not petty kids." A trace of amusement twitched through Annie's words. "Nolan, can I please borrow your jacket?"

Nolan shook his head. "It is Willow's for as long as she needs it."

Annie bumped her shoulder against Willow's. "I believe I told you before that you are his favorite."

Perhaps Willow had been Nolan's favorite for a

brief time one summer long past. When Willow had believed everything was possible and nothing could stop her from having it all. However, time had honed her focus. Now she wanted only one thing—to find her big break and finally prove she could be someone truly special after all.

Still, Willow's cheeks warmed at Annie's claim, and she reached for the zipper under her chin.

"Keep it on, Willow." Nolan brushed her hand away. "You need my jacket, and it suits you."

There had always been something about her cowboy that suited her. Good thing Willow chose to concentrate on things she excelled at these days. Fortunately, love and relationships were not on that list. Otherwise, she just might be curious to discover what it meant to *be* Nolan's favorite now.

Annie pointed back and forth between Willow and Nolan. "Well, this suits me."

Willow's eyebrows climbed higher on her forehead. "Annie, what are you getting at?"

"Nothing much." Annie's words were casual. "It just feels like a good start toward you two finally going on that long overdue date."

Date. With Nolan. The air around Willow thinned. Awareness flared for the cowboy that stood not an elbow nudge away. And something else—something like interest—pulsed inside her.

No. No. No. Warning bells clanged.

She was not interested in a date with her former cowboy crush. She was not intrigued either.

Nor was she the least bit curious if Nolan ever

imagined what their first date might have been like. Curiosity would only lead her down paths better left untraveled.

Willow curved her fingers around the fence post and readied her rebuttal. But the best she came up with was, "We aren't seriously talking about this now, are we?" As if she'd intended to talk about it later. Well, that wasn't happening.

"Humor me." Annie tugged her phone from her back pocket and tapped on the screen. "I need something happy. My barn just burned down."

But there was nothing funny about dating Nolan. Willow held herself still, wanting to keep from accidentally brushing up against her cowboy. Yet, she felt his presence beside her. That awareness threatened to spike.

Desperate for a diversion, Willow lifted her gaze and took in the all-too-attentive trio watching from the other side of the fence. Marla's mouth tipped into one of those secret smiles as if she'd enjoyed the entire exchange. While Gran Denny and Big E shifted their shrewd gazes between Nolan and Willow.

Willow opened her mouth, fully prepared to stop their speculation.

But Annie cut in and thankfully drew everyone's attention. "Looks like I've found stable space for our boarders."

"That's good news," Gran Denny said, approval in her words. "Quick work on your part, Annie. Always nice to see folks pulling together to help their neighbors."

"The horses will definitely calm once they are out of the smoke and settled for the night." Big E gave a quick nod.

Willow noticed Annie's deepening frown. "What's wrong?"

"Phantom and Stardust need to be split up. There isn't enough stable space available." Annie winced. "Or they can stay turned out."

"The weather is due to take an unexpected dip in the next day or so." Gran Denny leaned both hands on her cane and lifted her face toward the afternoon sky.

"Don't suppose Phantom has spent many winter nights turned out," Big E mused.

"None. Not in winter or summer," Willow admitted. Even when the Blackwell Belles had traveled the country for their performances, Willow always provided a make-shift stall for her horse. After Phantom's years spent performing, he had more than earned some pampering. Willow was happy to indulge him. "Stardust needs to be stabled for three more days. Doctor's orders. She's still recovering from her eye infection."

"There's no need to split up Willow's horses. Or keep them turned out." Marla aimed her smile at Nolan. "There's more than enough space at Sky Canyon, isn't there Nolan?"

Stable her horses with Nolan? Put them in the cowboy's care? Trust him with her... Willow turned toward Nolan and blurted, "I'm sure I can make other arrangements."

"But your horses will be in climate-controlled stalls," Marla insisted. "Sky Canyon has some of the best stables around."

Nolan ran his fingers over his bearded cheek. His gaze never left Willow's. "Your horses are welcome at Sky Canyon where they can stable together."

There was a time when all Willow wanted was to be together with her summer cowboy. *You can't follow your heart and chase your dreams, Willow. But make your dreams come true and you can have anything your heart desires. Your choice.*

Willow had chosen and was still determined to make her dreams come true. Even if those dreams seemed a bit further out of reach these days. Nothing a tweak to her resolve wouldn't correct.

She took in the cowboy before her. Nolan had made his own dreams a reality. He was the current national bull riding champion. A resounding and undisputed success on all counts. The same as Willow wanted to be one day.

Standing with her cowboy, she felt undeniably drawn to him all over again. But she knew what she wanted. She had always known. And surely what she wanted would not be found following her misguided heart and reaching for her cowboy. Even if she couldn't help wondering what if.

"We best get Willow's horses loaded into the trailer so Willow and Nolan can be on their way."

Marla opened the gate for Gran Denny and Big E to join the rest of them.

Willow glanced at Marla. "I can load my horses. We can follow Nolan in Big E's motorhome."

"You'll have to ride with Nolan." Gran Denny stepped up beside Willow.

That sounded like Gran Denny intended to leave her alone with her cowboy. Willow wheezed. "Why?"

"Elias and I need to help Marla and Annie with the other horses." Gran Denny thumped her palm on Willow's back.

"We're going to show Marla how to rub ointment in the spooked horses' nostrils," Big E explained. "The strong smell will mask the scent of smoke and help soothe the horses."

But Willow was suddenly less than calm herself. Her words rushed out. "What about that dinner the three of us were supposed to have tonight?"

"Elias and I will swing by to pick you up for dinner when we're done here." Gran Denny grinned.

"You and Nolan might consider discussing when to have your own dinner date while you're seeing to your horses." Big E's eyebrows lifted, revealing the gleam in his clever gaze. "It's the holiday season and social calendars tend to fill up real quick this time of year."

Social calendars. Willow blanched.

"That they do," Marla added cheerfully. "Best to start making plans, you two."

Big E gestured to Marla. "Perhaps we should

find that ointment and get to the other pasture. Let these two discuss their upcoming night out."

Upcoming night out. Willow lost her next words. Same as her family seemed to be losing their senses.

"I was always partial to moon-lit strolls," Gran Denny offered.

"Been on a few of those myself a time or two." Big E's sigh drew out a small grin. "Still get out with my wife even though our pace is a bit slower these days."

Gran Denny smiled wistfully. "I always found Christmas to be a good season for strolling."

Willow gaped at her grandmother, who, as far as Willow knew, had been single ever since the father of her twin sons had passed away when the boys were still toddlers. According to Willow's dad, there had never even been a whisper of Gran Denny dating anyone after, let alone going for a Christmas stroll.

"I recommend strolling after a candle-lit dinner." Marla's gaze sparkled before she eyed Nolan. "Do not forget the candles. Your father would be disappointed."

"Yes, ma'am." Nolan sounded quite serious as if he was jotting down their date night suggestions.

Willow slanted an alarmed look at Annie.

Annie caught her chuckle behind her hands, then grinned. "I knew this idea had merit. Everyone clearly agrees with me."

They were talking about Willow going on a date

with Annie's stepbrother. There was no merit in that. General curiosity, definitely.

"Be more creative than a simple pizza parlor date, Willow. It's the holidays, embrace the magic of the season." Gran Denny thumped Willow one more time as if to jump-start Willow's social butterfly. Her grandmother sauntered off with the others.

Willow's mind raced but it wasn't her holiday social calendar she was worried about. It was her heart.

Because one date with her cowboy could have her heart strolling toward things like a relationship and all those better-left-unspoken wishes. After all, love expected too much and came tangled up in entirely too many conditions.

"You know…" Nolan's slow drawl pulled Willow's gaze to him. "We don't have to take their advice."

Right. She had not asked him to go on a date. Nor had he agreed to take her on one. Talk about jumping ahead. No harm done. After all, falling for her cowboy was not a choice Willow would ever allow her heart to make. Willow smiled at him. "I couldn't agree more."

CHAPTER THREE

NOLAN CONSIDERED HIS cowgirl and refused to feel anything but relief at her quick agreement with his comment.

He had absolutely no business even considering taking Willow out on a date when he knew it would lead nowhere. After all, his relationship resume included a failed marriage and a disconnected heart. These days he stuck to what he knew best: bulls, rodeo and how to be alone.

However, he was very much considering a date, when he should be taking his own advice and walking away from his cowgirl.

Instead, he moved closer to her. He had always been compelled to be near her. Back then and even now it seemed. "We should load your horses. You can get them situated at the ranch while I come back to collect Annie's horses."

"Sooo, we'll just forget about us going on a date, right?" She was trying to sound disinterested, but it wasn't quite working.

One side of his mouth curved up and to his delight seemed to catch her full attention. Not quite so indifferent, he thought. He kept his full smile in check. "There will be time enough later to discuss a possible date, if you want."

Her gaze lifted to his and held. "But I've already forgotten about it."

In the pause that hovered between them, her dark eyes gave her away, hinting at an interest she fought to hide. Before he got lost in her and ignored all the logical reasons a date was a bad idea, he tugged her toward the pasture gate. "Come on. Let's look after Stardust and Phantom."

Fortunately, the horses required their full attention and there wasn't time to linger on any date-night discussion. Unfortunately, not even Phantom's easygoing demeanor or Willow's soothing words were enough to convince a still-spooked Stardust and Annie's pair of high-spirited and equally stressed geldings to enter the unfamiliar trailer. Eventually he and Willow got the horses into the trailer. The twenty-minute trip to Sky Canyon Cattle Ranch was mostly silent. Nolan concentrated on keeping the drive as smooth as possible, to not disturb the horses and to keep his eyes off the cowgirl next to him.

At Sky Canyon stables, their focus returned to the horses. They guided each one into a separate stall. Willow filled water and feed buckets and kept up a constant one-sided conversation with the foursome. Nolan left to pick-up Annie's three senior horses and one pregnant mare. Then it was brush-downs. Final stall checks. And, at long last, Willow and Nolan walked out of the stable.

Dusk was overtaking the afternoon sky, and the sun was preparing to start its descent. Evening used to be one of his favorite times on the ranch. Recently, however, nightfall seemed to sharpen his memories and the edges of his grief. When he was at Sky Canyon, regret always hit that much harder too. That was why he had kept his distance from his home over the past year. Yet no matter how many miles he put between him and Sky Canyon, his feelings always kept pace.

Willow checked her phone. "Looks like Gran Denny and Big E are on their way to take me to dinner."

"I could have driven you back to Annie's." And avoided facing those memories of his dad a little bit longer.

"It's not a problem." Willow raised her hands. "Although I could use your bathroom to wash up."

"Sure thing." Nolan studied the ranch house yet didn't move. "The house should be open." At least according to an earlier text from Wayne Raskin, his ranch manager.

"I also wouldn't mind a glass of wine if you have that." Willow rubbed her forehead. The grin she aimed his way was weak and brief. "The strain of the afternoon has found me."

Nolan took in the exhaustion behind her eyes. "I'm sure there's something inside the house."

At least he hoped this time he found more than

heartache and an uncomfortable emptiness. On the back porch, Nolan motioned Willow into the mudroom and held his breath. Waited for his father's booming voice to shout a welcome and hearty come on in. But only silence greeted him.

"Nolan." Willow touched his arm. "You okay?"

Maybe it was the concern in her brown eyes. Or the worry on her face. Or that Nolan was glad not to be alone for once. Whatever it was, he confessed, "It's hard to be here." *Total understatement there*. "Without my dad, it's like I don't know this place anymore."

In truth, he didn't know where he belonged. He felt like an imposter in his father's house. Worse, he couldn't quite shake the feeling that he had won big yet lost something on his last bull ride at the national finals. But if he wasn't meant to be in the chute, adjusting his seat on a fifteen-hundred-pound bull, then he wasn't sure where he wanted to be.

"But this is your home." Willow's eyebrows drew together. "You grew up here."

"I grew up in the old ranch house on this land," Nolan corrected. The prior house had been converted into the ranch manager's office and home several years ago. "My dad and Marla built this place after I moved out, and I didn't stay longer than a night or two whenever I came back." Those visits were infrequent at best. And for the first few days after his dad's funeral, he stayed at Annie's place before he'd headed back out to the circuit.

This house was all part of his father's legacy handed down to his only son. A legacy Nolan was tasked to continue. Except Nolan wasn't certain he had the passion or the desire to keep the ranch without his dad there to guide him. Now he was home to see his family and ultimately decide Sky Canyon's future.

"It seems like we could both use a cocktail." Willow faced the connecting doorway leading into the main part of the house.

"There's only one way we're going to get what we need." Nolan stepped around Willow to head inside and flipped on the lights over the large butcher block island. "How about we wash up first and then find that wine?"

Willow nodded and followed him through the family room to the pair of guest bedrooms on the first floor. Nolan opened the first door for Willow, then moved to the next room. As he suspected, it was elegantly appointed as if inviting visitors to stay. That was so Marla.

Nolan had often promised to visit soon, but he always headed off for another rodeo. Another eight second ride. So certain there would be time to come back. How wrong he had been.

He heard Willow's boots on the hardwood floors in the hallway. He dried his face quickly and went to join her, stopping briefly at the wine closet under the staircase. The very one Marla and his dad had custom built.

His dad had called Nolan to encourage him to

join himself and Marla on their springtime California vineyard excursion to stock their new wine closet. They had planned to open their completed dream house for the first time to friends and family at their Fourth of July party.

Nolan had turned him down.

Soon after that phone call, Nolan's dad had gotten sick. The wine country trip was postponed, replaced by more urgent trips to the hospital. Then all too quickly the July Fourth party became a celebration of life for the best man Nolan had ever known. Then the house was closed before it had ever been fully opened.

Thankfully there were a handful of wine bottles in the closet. Nolan grabbed one and escaped his memories to join Willow in the kitchen. He lifted the bottle. "Found something, if you are okay with white wine?"

"Definitely." Willow turned from the counter and held a very familiar horseshoe picture frame. "I can't believe how much you look like your dad without your beard."

Nolan knew what she was looking at. He had the same horseshoe frame and picture in his fifth wheel camper. "That picture was taken after I won my first buckle on the professional circuit."

"I can't tell who looks happier." She studied the picture. "You or your dad."

"My dad," he said, even though he knew they both wore matching ear-to-ear grins that day. "Dad was always my biggest supporter. I gave him that buckle."

Willow nodded. "I'm sure he wore it."

"All the time according to Marla." Nolan's shoulders loosened and he grinned despite the sadness crowding his chest.

Willow trailed her finger over the curve of the horseshoe. "I've never seen a picture frame quite like this."

"My dad had two frames custom made from old iron horseshoes worn by my great-grandfather's horse." Nolan set the wine bottle on the island. "Dad kept one frame and gave me the other one."

Willow's smile was gentle as if she understood he was stepping gingerly into his memories.

"Dad said it was a way to keep a piece of him and our family roots with me on the road." Nolan smiled. It was quite possibly his most prized possession. "The picture always reminded me what I was working toward. What I wanted." Another win. Another buckle to give his dad.

"And your dad got to keep a piece of you here with him." Willow carefully returned the frame to the open shelf, where it could be seen from every angle in the kitchen. "I'm sure the picture lifted his spirits in the best way when he looked at it."

"I hope so." Nolan liked the idea that his father had good memories to fill him when Nolan was not there. He opened a drawer with a collection of assorted kitchen devices and picked up the manual wine opener.

Willow set two glasses on the large island. "Can I ask where you're staying, if not here?"

"I'm at Sun Meadows. My niece very kindly gave up her room for me and is bunking with Marla." Grateful for the conversation change, Nolan pulled the cork from the bottle and added, "Kendall is going to be devastated about the fire. I promised I would help her decorate the stables for the holiday."

"Maybe you could decorate here, instead," Willow suggested softly.

Nolan took in the L-shaped sofa in the sprawling family room and the logs stacked inside the stone fireplace. It was all very homey. But it should be his father lighting the fire. His dad directing the decorating like always. Nolan had grown up believing his father had a direct line to the North Pole. After all, his dad had Santa Claus's laugh and the same over-abundance of holiday joy.

Nolan could not claim the same. He always considered Christmas decorations nothing but a hassle in his fifth wheel camper. As for that holiday joy, well, that seemed to fade more with each passing winter. He supposed that made him a grump at best or a grinch at worst. Hardly the legacy his dad wanted him to continue. He frowned. "Annie's extra Christmas decorations were stored in the stable loft. I doubt any of it survived the fire."

"Well, it was just an idea. You don't have to decide tonight." Willow handed him a wine glass. "Come on. I've wanted to sit on the sunporch since Marla texted me pictures of it. The view looks amazing."

"Not sure you will find one better." Nolan knew

that firsthand. He had designed and helped build the sunroom as a surprise birthday gift for his dad, who'd been delighted with it and declared it would be the place where they planned their fishing excursions.

Unfortunately, there hadn't been a first fishing trip for father and son. Nolan pushed aside those memories not made. The ones he had always pushed off until after he'd reached his goals. But when was that, exactly? "Dad used to call and check in when he was watching the sunset. I haven't been in the sunporch since he passed."

"We can try it out together." Willow slipped her free hand into his and glanced at him. "Or, if you want to leave, we can."

He considered their joined hands. Marveled that such a small thing steadied him like nothing else. He should let go. Find his own way like he always did. Instead, he tightened his hold and lightened his words. "Marla and Dad claimed it was the best room in the house."

"We can be the judges of that." Willow chuckled. "It'll be tough, though, because the kitchen is spectacular. I wouldn't mind napping on the sofa. And the guest bedroom is nothing short of whimsical."

"Marla is a great decorator," Nolan said.

"Not just Marla. I heard your dad had quite a hand in the décor." Willow nudged her shoulder against his. "And I recall Marla mentioning that she got your opinion on things as well."

"They called it a family affair." Nolan smiled again.

Willow sat on the small sofa that faced the floor to ceiling windows overlooking the pond and extensive pastures. "They wanted you to be included."

"Every step of the way. There were texts and emails and video chats for everything." *We just want your opinion, Nolan. We can't decide, Nolan. Break the stalemate, Nolan.* He leaned back into the plush cushions, pleased to discover the memories didn't sting quite like he'd expected.

Willow slipped off her boots and tucked her feet under her, then shifted toward him. "So, wat do you think?"

"Dad was right." Nolan relaxed even more and kept his focus on Willow. "One of the most memorable views I've seen in a long time."

"I agree." She tapped her wine glass against his before looking around. "This room just might be vying for my top spot."

His favorite spot could be right beside his cowgirl. If he wasn't careful.

But that wasn't likely to happen. If nothing else, his whirlwind of a marriage and his even swifter divorce had taught him the value of caution in relationships. And the practicality of sidestepping all things inspired by love.

Willow sipped her wine. "Can I ask you something?"

"Sure." *Except don't ask me about this house or my heart. Because I don't want to feel anything about either one*. Yet being with her again, he felt almost like he was. . . He cut off his next thought and locked his gaze on the windows, despite the view suddenly seeming unclear.

"Have you ever wondered what our first date would have been like?" Her words were measured as if she feared revealing too much.

He lifted one shoulder. "Haven't *you* ever wondered what if?"

"That's not a habit I try to let myself indulge in," she said. "And you didn't answer my question."

Neither had she. The stalemate was more than clear.

There was something about her that he had never forgotten. On the nights when his body ached, and sleep eluded him, he certainly wondered about her. When he forgot that he was better off alone, he wondered about them.

Foolish fantasies, he supposed. Daydreams, no doubt.

But sitting here right now with Willow, it seemed like a connection between them could be very real. That was dangerous. And a notion best kept to himself. It was never wise to confuse silly illusions with truth.

And the truth was simple. Love wasn't a good fit for him. And a cowgirl like Willow was too good for a cowboy like him with his disconnected heart.

He straightened and tipped his head. "I believe your ride is here."

Confusion crossed her face seconds before the

rumble of a vehicle filled the silence. There was a distinct toot-toot of a horn. Willow set her wine glass on the coffee table. "How did you hear that?"

I was desperate to hear something other than the heavy beating of my heart. He winced. "Dad always claimed I could hear a mouse outside in the hay loft."

"Thank you for taking in my horses and for the wine." Willow slid her feet into her boots, stood, and walked with him to the front door. "I'll stay out of your way when I'm around here."

"You're certain to be here more than me." He joined her on the front porch and waved a greeting to her family. "The stables and even the house are yours to use as you need."

"Then I guess I'll see you around." Willow headed for the motorhome idling in the driveway.

"Willow," Nolan called out and waited for her to turn around. "I've already planned every detail of our first date."

She paused and considered him. There was a hesitancy in her words as if she didn't know what to make of him. "You're serious?"

He'd caught her off-guard. He grinned, albeit close-lipped. "Is that a problem?"

"That depends…" Her hands settled on her hips.

Her deep brown gaze sparked. At least, he hoped that's what he was seeing. He'd always liked it when she seemed to shine bright from the inside, like one of those shooting stars he used to spend hours searching for in the sky. "On what?"

"On whether you planned the date for the cowgirl I am now or the girl I once was?" Her smile was slow to arrive. When it did, triumph spread from cheek to cheek.

Just like that, Nolan was more enchanted than he had been in far too long. He crossed his arms over his chest. "Is that a challenge, Willow Blackwell?"

"Only if you accept," she countered, then tapped her forehead as if tipping her imaginary Stetson at him. "Night, cowboy."

That was when Nolan suspected he might have a problem. The cowgirl kind.

Because looking at Willow in that moment, her pretty brown hair falling around her shoulders, framing her beautiful face and appealing brown eyes, he already knew there would be messy complications—the good kind—after just that one date with her.

Luckily, he'd always accepted the risks and pressed ahead, anyway. Often to his father's dismay. *Sorry, Dad. If I get hurt from this ride, you won't have to tell me I told you so.*

He waited until she reached the door of the RV before he called out, "Hey, cowgirl! I accept."

CHAPTER FOUR

WILLOW BLACKWELL, you have seriously misplaced your senses. Flirting with cowboys will get you nothing but dust-coated kisses and dents on your heart. Trust me, that is not the look we want if we intend to make you a star.

Willow rushed toward Big E's RV and forced herself not to look back. Still, she felt Nolan watching her. Knew what he thought he saw. A chic cowgirl in flared faux leather black pants, a cream-colored cable-knit sweater layered with a statement silver blue faux fur vest, and fashionable boots. Albeit now covered in horsehair and ashes, and sporting a distinct, smoky scent.

It was all just an image. Easy to create with perfectly on-trend attire, appropriate styling, and his memories of the girl he once knew. The truth was that these days Willow Blackwell was no more a cowgirl than Santa Claus was a grinch who ruined Christmas.

Willow lived in a studio apartment in downtown Dallas. A cosmetology license sat alone on her shelf, not a collection of belt buckles. She spent more time gripping a blush brush behind the makeup counter at Highstreet Treasures or backstage with the cast at the small community playhouse on the fringe of the downtown theater district than she did holding the reins of a horse. And she had tallied more audition fails than victories for parts on the big screen, small screen and live stage in search of that all-important break over the past decade.

Only stars that shine the brightest make the biggest difference, Willow. If you stop trying, you will most definitely stop shining. You can fade out or get back on the horse. Willow had always gotten back on her horse. There hadn't really been a choice. Disappointing her mother had never been an option growing up.

She had yet to give up. But now it was about proving Flora Blackwell wrong. *Without her act, Willow is just another pretty face. What's special about my daughter then?* Willow pressed Mute on her mother's callous words and her past, then climbed inside the RV.

Reaching for the door, she caught sight of her cowboy standing on the porch. Still tracking her. No, she wouldn't give up. She would find that one break and shine brighter than anyone imagined. Perhaps then she would finally be a cowgirl fit for a successful cowboy like Nolan Elliot. *No. Strike that.* She wasn't looking to be Nolan's anything.

She was perfectly fine making her way in her life on her own terms. One glass of wine on a cozy sunporch sofa with a handsome cowboy would not so easily steer her off course. Neither would a date with the same handsome cowboy. After all, catching a cowboy had never been *the* dream.

Willow flopped onto the surprisingly comfortable couch in the RV and flung her arm over her forehead.

"All good back there, dear?" Gran Denny called out.

No. But I will be. When I figure out how to shine. Willow lifted her arm from her face and said, "Sure. Ready to roll."

Big E drove around the circular driveway, passing the stable barn and adjoining pastures. He asked, "Any problems getting everyone settled in at Nolan's place?"

"Nothing we couldn't manage." If she excluded one problem in particular. The one where she was decidedly *un-settled* by the fact that she could've curled into that sunporch sofa. Right into Nolan's side and been happy for the rest of the night. Willow plucked horsehair from her sweater. "Are you certain I don't need to change for dinner?"

"Positive," Gran Denny replied. "This is one of those come-as-you-are sort of places."

"Always preferred those myself," Big E mused.

The ranch house at Nolan's felt like that. Despite the chill from being unoccupied, the house had a certain inviting energy inside. Or perhaps that was simply Willow's imagination. She had always wanted a large house for family and friends to drop by unannounced and stay for dinner or the weekend. A house where boots were propped on the coffee table as often as glasses of homemade lemonade. And it was always come-as-you-are. *Just as you are. That's enough for us.*

Willow brushed more horsehair from her vest, tucked her naive childhood wishes away and straightened her clothes. "Where did you say we were going again?"

"I can't recall the exact name. My mind is more like an eraser than a tack these days." Gran Denny tapped her forehead. "But I've heard good things about the food."

Perhaps that was all Willow required. A good meal to get herself and her thoughts back in alignment. She'd had an early lunch before her shift at the department store and nothing since. Hunger tended to make her somewhat melancholy and sleepy. No wonder she had wanted to curl up next to Nolan. That was clearly a side effect of low blood sugar. Willow stretched out on the couch.

Gran Denny peered around the captain's chair. "You look plumb worn-out, dear. You should close your eyes and rest before dinner. We've a while to go yet."

Willow plumped a pillow behind her head. "How far away is this restaurant anyway?"

Gran Denny cast a glance at Big E. "Not far," she said, her words suddenly hesitant.

"Can't take the turns as fast in the evening," Big E announced. "Have to slow my pace. Never know what we might encounter on the roads at dusk."

Willow yawned.

Gran Denny added, "We'll wake you when we get there."

Willow wasn't certain if she had slept twenty minutes or more than an hour. All she knew was that Gran Denny and Big E were standing outside the motor home. She was suddenly wide-awake and fully alert. Her gaze skipped from the faded brick single-story house to the fenced pasture bordering one side of the driveway.

A pair of very familiar quarter horses, one a blue roan and the other chestnut, stood at the wooden gate as if eager to greet the new arrivals. No surprise there. Wildfire and Skylark had always been by far the most curious and outgoing of the Blackwell Belles' performance horses. Age and time had not seemed to dilute those traits.

"This is not a restaurant." And it was no place Willow wanted to be. She knew exactly where she was, even though she had never been here before. The crafty duo had set her up quite neatly. A dinner offer turned ambush reunion. Willow crossed her arms over her chest. Accusation clipped her words. "This is my parents' property." She wasted no time striding from the RV.

"It's not exactly what I had in mind," Big E mused, then lifted his hand toward the plain house. "Given Flora's natural flair."

Gran Denny leaned on her cane and studied the bland front porch. "It is rather subdued."

Subdued or not, Willow would not be going

inside. She should have stayed on that sofa with Nolan. She would gladly take dozens of dusty kisses and more dents in her heart over a confrontation with Flora Blackwell. Willow clamped her teeth together.

"Nothing some shimmery garland and colorful lights wouldn't remedy." Gran Denny patted her brown cowboy hat into place as if preparing to lead the decoration charge.

Yet twinkling lights, holiday inflatables and all the Christmas spirit of the season would not change Willow's mind. She started to turn around to head back inside the motor home. Behind her a screen door slammed shut. Footsteps sounded on the paved driveway. Then came her father's boisterous words. "Willow-bee, don't think about sneaking off. You still owe me a hug from last Christmas."

Willow paused and squeezed her eyes closed. Her dad had told Willow that was all he wanted for Christmas last year: *one genuine hug from my youngest daughter.*

Her father's words were closer and softer. All the more heartfelt. "I mean to collect on that hug, Willow-bee."

Only her dad ever called her Willow-bee. Only her dad ever called her. She should have outgrown the nickname. Outgrown his hug. But she hadn't. She doubted she ever would. Willow spun around and launched herself into her father's arms. "Hey, dad."

Her father squeezed her tight, then peered into

her face. Worry flattened his smile. "What's this I hear about you racing into a burning stable?"

"The fire was out when we arrived." Although her knees ached from running in her heeled boots. Not the wisest choice. Yet she would do it again. Willow pressed her finger into her father's chest, pleased to watch the usual twinkle in his hazel eyes return. "I had to get to my horses. You would've done the same."

Her father grinned.

"I would've beat Willow to the stables myself if it wasn't for my cane slowing me down." Gran Denny stepped into her son's side for a one-armed embrace.

Big E shook Barlow's hand. His smile lifted into his white beard. "I'll tell you this, Barlow. Your daughter has both grace and speed. And a way with the horses that rivals her grandmother's."

To be like Gran Denny in some small way meant the world to Willow. Her gran was strong, independent and the kind of cowgirl Willow wanted to be: unstoppable.

"Speaking of horses." Her father tipped his head toward the pasture. "I think those two are waiting for you, Willow. They've missed you. We all have."

Willow bit the corner of her lip. She missed her father, too. Her sisters. The horses. But her mother, well, that was complicated. Besides, Willow wasn't quite sure her mother missed her all that much either.

Are you washing your hands of me, mother?

Silence—the kind that chilled the very air—had jammed the phone line on their last conversation more than five years ago. Finally, Flora had replied: *Remember your words, Willow.* Seconds later, Flora had disconnected their call. Mother and daughter had not spoken since. Willow cleared her throat. "I'm going to greet Skylark and Wildfire."

"I'll join Willow." Big E raised his eyebrows at Willow as if daring her to deny his company. "I'd like to meet your show horses. I've heard stories of your performances. Seen the videos."

Gran Denny smiled. "Barlow and I will go in, check on Flora."

"Don't be too long." Her father squeezed Willow's shoulders. "I've made your favorites for dinner."

If only her father was not an endless well of kindness and compassion. If only Willow could thank him and leave with no regrets. She managed a nod yet still wasn't ready to walk inside and face Flora.

At the pasture fence, Willow propped herself on the top rung, ignoring the slight twinge of protest in her left knee. She wrapped her arms around Wildfire's neck and held on tight. "Big E, you can go on in. I'm perfectly fine right where I am." Willow peered at the older cowboy. "You have the keys to the RV, so it's not like I can make a hasty getaway."

"That I do." Big E patted the pocket on his plaid shirt, then reached up to stroke the long white blaze on Skylark's face. "You should come in with me. After all, you've already come all this way."

"Not by choice." Willow parted Wildfire's mane and began braiding the deep black strands.

"You won't be getting an apology from me or your gran," Big E said, no remorse in his words or expression. "We made a decision in the best interest of family. That's how we've been making most of our decisions these days. Some just happen to be more uncomfortable than others."

Willow shifted on the fence post and concentrated on weaving Wildfire's mane into a more intricate braid. Her family situation might be messy, but that hardly meant their horses couldn't look pretty and tidy. She frowned. "We haven't been family in years."

"Doesn't have to stay that way," Big E countered. "It is after all the season for compassion and goodwill."

But one dinner would not mend their family this season or any other. Besides, the holidays had always been about performing, not gathering around a Christmas tree decorated with handmade ornaments and popcorn garland. Her parents' dreary porch was proof that Flora lacked the holiday spirit. The season was simply something Willow worked through until the auditions began again in the new year. She argued, "Maybe it's better that things don't change."

"What do you have to lose by going inside?" Big E lifted one shoulder. "At the very least you enjoy a good meal and leave with a full stomach."

"And make my father happy," Willow added.

"That too. Don't think your father hasn't suffered in all this," Big E said, his words straightforward. His expression earnest. "It's one dinner. Perhaps even a little bit of conversation."

Except conversations with Flora were more frustrating than satisfying. *Get back to your horse where you belong, Willow. Where I taught you how to truly shine. Dreams are realized in the arena. Listen to me before it's too late. You don't want to be nothing more than a has-been, do you?*

Willow pressed her forehead between Wildfire's dark ears and inhaled.

Yet those last harsh words between mother and daughter blared inside her mind. *Then I would be just like you, Flora. That is what you always wanted.* Her mother's voice across the phone line had been stoic. Cold. No compassion. No tear-soaked words. Flora had said simply, *It appears we are finished here.*

Her mother had not reached out since. Willow had kept in touch with her father and relied on her dad to be the middleman between herself and her mother. *Tell mother Happy Birthday. Tell mother Merry Christmas.* Season after season. Year after year. Her father never lost his patience. Never pressed Willow to make things right. Never ambushed her. Not once. She owed him.

This is for you, Dad. Willow's stomach rumbled as if in agreement. She carefully climbed off the fence, stepping first onto her right leg and her less sore knee. Brushing off her faux leather pants, she sighed. "Fine. I'll eat, but I'm not staying for dessert."

"Fair enough." Big E linked his arm through Willow's and walked with her back to the house. His gaze gleamed in the porch light. "Remember, if we like the dessert, there's nothing stopping us from taking it to go."

Laughter built inside Willow for the first time that day. Perhaps with Big E, Gran Denny and her dad, dinner would be a simple enough affair to get through.

Five minutes later, Willow was inside her parents' house. Her dad escorted her to the chair beside Gran Denny at a rectangle glass dining table with a rustic wood base. No sooner were Willow and her dad seated than Flora made her entrance. Her mother's camel-colored duster, matching turtleneck sweater, winter white jeans and leopard-print ballet flats proved time had not dulled Flora's impeccable fashion sense.

But her mother's false eyelashes, which appeared one good blink away from falling off, might have given Willow pause if not for the grumbling brown fur ball in Flora's arms. It looked like a cross between a dog and a faux fur hand muffler.

Her mother floated onto the bench seat across from Willow with a flourish and settled the muffler dog beside her. Then she gushed over the rumbling brown pooch and adjusted the pearl collar around the dog's thin neck. To her youngest daughter, Flora simply offered a brief greeting that consisted of only a single, short syllable.

Willow rubbed the back of her neck. Her mother had never gushed over Willow or her sisters like she was fussing about the dog. When Flora had adjusted their sequined costumes backstage at a performance, it had been with a critical tug and more tsks than praise.

Gran Denny bumped her elbow into Willow's ribs. "That's Zinni. She vocalizes more than an off-key children's band concert."

Big E chuckled from the end of the table. "You'll get used to her eventually."

As if testing that claim, Zinni snuffled a low sort of noise. Flora smoothed her finger between Zinni's ears and slanted her gaze at Willow. Her false eyelashes flapped then steadied. "Zinni and I are very in tune. Zinni senses my emotions and becomes very vocal. It's her way of protecting me."

Or perhaps the scrawny dog was starving and simply craving a bite of the thinly sliced tri-tip steak from the platter Willow's father had set in the middle of the table.

"We should eat while it's hot," Barlow declared and handed Willow a basket of warm biscuits. "I seem to recall these used to be your favorite."

"That depends." Willow pulled out a biscuit and grinned at her dad. "Did you make your signature honey butter?"

"Double batch of both." His smile widened. "Thought you might like to take some home."

Willow nodded. "More than happy to do that."

"Just be sure to have a balanced meal with those biscuits and butter," Flora added, her words polite.

Willow smeared more butter on her biscuit, determined not to let her mother get under her skin so quickly.

At the sudden quiet, Flora continued, "I simply meant for Willow to add protein to her meals. Willow needs the protein to keep her energy up for her training and performances." Flora lifted both hands, her expression innocent. "Even Zinni here is on a high-protein diet. It's important for Zinni to feel her best."

Same as it had been for Willow to *be* the best. Determined to take on her mother with a full stomach, Willow concentrated on polishing off her tri-tip steak and fresh corn and green bean salad at a rapid rate. Fortunately, her last green bean was speared on her fork when the dinner took that turn Willow had known well enough to anticipate.

"We should toast to Aunt Dandy and my induction into the Cowgirl Hall of Fame in less than two weeks." Flora lifted her wineglass and swirled the red liquid inside.

Everyone picked up their glasses.

"Of course," Flora started and arched an eyebrow at Willow. "We could have a toast with the entire family after the ceremony. That is if Willow agrees to attend."

"We should probably toast now." Willow watched her mother and lifted her wineglass further across the table, closer to Flora's. "I'm not certain what my work schedule will be that night."

"That's a shame." Flora's lips twitched. "Your sisters have all agreed to not only attend, but also perform at the ceremony."

Willow slowly lowered her glass. "You can't be serious."

"Why not?" Flora batted those false eyelashes and sipped her wine before fluttering her ring-be-decked hand around the table. "Ask your grand-mother. Or your father. Or Big E."

Willow skipped her gaze from one family mem-ber to the next. At their collective nods, she re-turned her attention to her mother. "How did you get my sisters to agree?"

"I asked," Flora said, satisfaction in her smile. Then she added, "Well, Big E and Gran Denny also asked."

"It's true." Gran Denny touched Willow's arm. "Elias and I have spent the past few months vis-iting each of your sisters. And we've come to an agreement."

"To perform at the Hall of Fame ceremony," Wil-low stated. Her gaze tracked to Big E.

Before her great-uncle could respond, Flora cut in, frustration in her words. "Yes, Willow. There's no need to keep repeating yourself."

There was every need. The Blackwell Belles had splintered after the disaster with Maggie. Not for a few hours to cry through their fright and subse-quent relief that Maggie would recover. Or even a few days to cool off. But rather for more than a decade they'd gone their separate ways.

Now Willow was supposed to believe that her sisters had simply decided to get back together and perform. That was like saying Flora Blackwell baked more cookies than Mrs. Claus at Christmastime.

But Flora had never cooked in her life. Her mother's favorite part of the season was a holiday parade that featured her on the main float. Flora was no Mrs. Claus.

But her mother *was* the woman who had insisted Maggie accept the blame for getting herself shot by an arrow. Willow's arrow. All during a Blackwell Belles performance. Even though it hadn't been Maggie's fault. It was entirely Willow's. And everyone knew it. That was why Willow's sisters had abandoned her after that fateful night. They couldn't trust Willow would not injure them too or worse…

Willow exhaled around her memories. No sense poking at that wound now. This was certainly not the place for healing. Willow doubted there was such a place.

Yet the reminder was enough to alert Willow to the calculating gleam in her mother's gaze. The one even Flora's false eyelashes couldn't quite conceal. *Got you, Mother.* Willow straightened in her chair and eyed Flora. "What do you really get out of all this, Mother?"

"Can't it be about joy?" Flora wiped a napkin

across her mouth. Her features, delicate and time-less, gave nothing away. "Can't it just be about the joy of seeing my five daughters perform together again?"

"No." Willow braced her hands on either side of her plate and shook her head.

It was never about joy or family bonding or sisterly affection. If it had been, the family would not have fractured so irreversibly after the disaster. They would have pulled together through their worst time. Instead, they'd fled and never looked back, as if those family ties were as temporary as a snowman caught in the full sun.

Flora folded her napkin into a neat square, set it carefully on the table, then smoothed out the wrinkles.

"I will ask again." Willow refused to back down. She had to know what this was and what this wasn't. She had to know if she should encourage that flicker of hope inside her—the one that missed her sisters terribly. The one that hinted of long-overdue apologies and possible forgiveness. The one she was afraid to acknowledge for the briefest second in the deepest hours of the night. Or was it finally time to snuff out the last of her hope completely? She pressed again. "What do you really get, Mother?"

Her father set his hand on Flora's arm and frowned a warning at his daughter. "Willow."

"I'm done." Willow pushed her chair back, stood

up and started for the back door. "I can see myself out."

"Fine," Flora stated, and her voice stopped Willow's retreat. Her mother continued, "Do you know what I get? One night. One night to pretend I have a legacy."

A legacy. Willow turned around to hear her out.

Flora lifted her chin. Her gaze glittered. Then she rose as if intending to meet Willow eye to eye. Her words were steel-wrapped. "I get one night to pretend everything Dandy and I loved will live on. One night to pretend everything we worked for and believed in didn't die with my only sister. That is what I get."

Silence washed over the dining room. Broken only by the steady ticktock of the grandfather clock in the family room.

Flora sank back onto the bench and seemed to all but wilt before Willow. Zinni jumped into Flora's lap. The dog's tiny body quivered as she eyed Willow over the glass tabletop. Willow wanted to wail, too.

Aunty Dandy had been the cornerstone of the Blackwell Belles. Their loudest cheerleader. Their biggest champion. Their cherished coach. Aunt Dandy had been Willow's sunshine in a field of constant criticism from Flora. Willow liked it when her mother was proud of her. But Aunt Dandy was the one Willow always wanted to make proud. She still did. That hadn't changed with Aunt Dandy's unexpected death. Willow gripped the back of her chair. "I'm not saying I'm agreeing to perform. But if my sisters and I perform, we do it our way, Mother."

Flora placed a finger against the corner of one eye and lifted her head. No hint of tears on her cheeks or in her reply. "Of course."

"I mean it, Mother," Willow warned. "No interference."

Flora nodded. "Violet and I have already been working on our part of the act."

"Then Violet really intends to perform?" Willow asked, confusion coating her words. Her older sister, Violet had texted Willow about the Cowgirl Hall of Fame ceremony and their family being in town. But she had never mentioned possibly performing. Not even a hint. The foursome at the table suddenly looked everywhere but at Willow. Her frown deepened. "What have I missed?"

Gran Denny tapped Willow's chair. "You should probably take your seat, dear, for the rest."

There was more. Always. Not surprising when Flora was involved. Reluctantly, Willow returned to her chair.

"Maybe we should have that dessert now," Big E suggested and touched his stomach. "A little sugar tends to sweeten things right up. I find that's never a bad thing."

Barlow stood and touched Flora's shoulder. "You stay and talk. I'll serve dessert. It's double-chocolate pecan pie."

Another one of Willow's favorites. Her father was pulling out all the stops.

"Double servings, Barlow," Gran Denny said. "This feels like a double whipped cream, double slice kind of conversation."

Her father's smile was sincere. "Coming right up."

"You might as well just come out with it," Willow said.

Flora handed Zinni to Big E, who passed the fluffy brown muffler to Gran Denny. Her grandmother promptly deposited Zinni into Willow's lap as if Willow was in need of warmth and comfort. Zinni grumbled a wheeze and used her paws to fluff Willow's vest, circled twice, then curled into a tight ball against Willow.

Gran Denny looked at Willow, but her smile didn't reach her eyes. She said, "Your sisters have each agreed to perform. But they have conditions."

Willow expected nothing less from her sisters. After all, she had her own. Willow nodded.

"Their terms are a bit more complicated than no interference from me," Flora added.

Willow ran her fingers over Zinni's back. The dog shivered, sneezed a sigh and cuddled closer.

"Maggie wants Ferdinand back," Gran Denny started.

"But Violet won't give up the bull until Iris gives back Aunt Dandy's saddle," Big E explained.

"Iris really does need that saddle for our act,"

Flora mused. Confusion colored her next words. "But Ferdinand is much too old to perform again."

But it wasn't about performing for Maggie. Ferdinand and Maggie had a special bond. The same as Willow had with Phantom, her longtime show horse. That bull was family to Maggie. And her sister wanted her family back. Willow rubbed her forehead. "Let me guess, Iris won't return the saddle unless J.R. gives her…"

"The charm bracelet," Gran Denny finished.

"And that brings us to you." Big E picked up his cowboy hat that he had propped on the chair back and set it on his head. Then he tapped the brim. "J.R. would like Aunt Dandy's cowboy hat returned to her."

"Do you know which one?" Gran Denny eyed Willow.

Of course, she did. It was the same white cowboy hat that Willow wore in her headshots. The same one she had worn to the few auditions where she had managed to land small roles. The same one that had each of the sisters' flowers embroidered on the rim by Aunt Dandy herself. The very same cowboy hat Willow never had any intention of handing over to anyone, least of all her oldest sister, J.R. Who never in her life wore white, despite having the coloring to look stunning in a winter white ensemble. Beyond that, J.R. would most likely get the cherished cowboy hat trampled by one of her prize bulls on her ranch. Willow crossed her arms over her chest.

Her father returned and passed out plates of pecan pie with those promised extra scoops of whipped cream.

"If you simply return Dandy's cowboy hat, then the others will do the same." Flora picked up her fork and aimed it at Willow. "Then we can concentrate on what matters."

But those very specific—family heirlooms, some would call them—mattered. Very much. Yet in typical Flora fashion, her mother missed the point. Willow saw the game with a new clarity now. Her sisters had chosen items that they did not believe would ever be returned. That in turn got each one of them out of performing. Clever. Very clever indeed. Willow watched her mother. "What is it that matters exactly?"

"The Hall of Fame ceremony," Flora said, the exasperation once again thick in her words. "The very reason you are here."

Right. This was not a reunion. Not an apology. Not her mother missing her youngest daughter. Most definitely not a time for hope. Time to douse that here and now. And keep her emotions in check. They had no place at this family dinner table. *Get emotional if you must, Willow. All you'll end up with is eyes too swollen to face the truth of the situation in front of you. Best keep your eyes dry. Your mind clear. And your thoughts focused.*

She was clearheaded now and she saw the Hall of Fame performance for what it was. An illusion for the public. A way to make Flora Blackwell look good.

It could be something else, too. If Willow dared. She sipped her wine and eyed her mom over the rim of her glass. "What's in it for me if I return Aunt Dandy's cowboy hat to J.R. and agree to perform?" Selfish. Very selfish. Like mother, like daughter, after all.

Flora never flinched, as if she fully expected her youngest daughter to have demands. Her bold smile bordered on triumphant. "I've sent a personal invitation to Royce Chaney and his family to attend the ceremony."

Now it was Willow's turn not to flinch. Not give away that she was even remotely impressed. Even though she was.

"Your father and I met Royce and his family at a charity event several years back. We've become personal friends of sorts," Flora continued and waved her fingers as if dangling her bait. "If you perform, I promise a personal introduction. He was just telling me at dinner a few weeks ago about his production of *Glass Ceilings and Petticoats*. It's going to be quite the immersive live theater experience. He plans to start casting early in the new year."

Oh, Flora Blackwell was so very good. Willow had to hand it to her mother. Flora knew exactly what this was, too. It most definitely was not about reconciling with her sisters. Family bonds. Or sentimental holiday reunions.

Yet it wasn't that simple. Willow was not returning anything without a guarantee that her sisters would perform for one night. She hedged, "I need to talk to my sisters first."

"But." Flora's smile dimmed.

Gran Denny cut in. "I believe that is a fair enough start."

Big E nodded. "I believe we should enjoy this delicious pecan pie and let Willow work out the details, don't you, Flora?"

"That suits me." Willow cut off a bite of pie with her fork. But the fluffy whipped cream and decadent chocolate and candied pecans did nothing to sugarcoat her sudden unease. The details were a bit murky. In truth, she was not quite certain where to start. Or rather which sister to start with.

Still, Willow could get her sisters exactly what they wanted if she returned the hat to J.R. and thus initiate the giving back of the other items to each sister in turn. But only if Willow got what she wanted. And that was an introduction that could finally give Willow her big break.

True, she meant to use the family heirlooms against her sisters. Not her proudest moment. But she only needed one night from her sisters. Then they could all resume their regularly scheduled lives without each other.

Because despite the season of goodwill and peace being in full swing, Willow had stopped believing in Christmas miracles long ago. It was about the same time she had accidentally shot her sister with an arrow during what turned out to be the sisters' final performance, thereby rupturing her family. When it had become every Blackwell Belle for themselves.

Not even Santa Claus had enough Christmas magic to ever change that.

CHAPTER FIVE

NOLAN RINSED THE wineglasses in the sink and set them on a towel to dry. The unfinished wine in the open bottle he considered pouring down the drain. There was no sense keeping it. He wasn't inviting Willow back to finish it, even though he very much wanted to.

With Willow beside him, Nolan had not strained to hear his father's laughter. He had not glanced at the dark mudroom, waiting for his dad to come bounding inside, ready to welcome his son home with open arms and more affection and pride than Nolan deserved. For those few moments with Willow, Nolan had not felt quite like a stranger in the house his good-natured father had so easily transformed into an inviting home.

I miss you, Dad.

Nolan propped his hands on the farm-style kitchen sink and stared out the wide window at the land that extended so far it looked as if the open pastures collided with the dusk-tinted sky. According to his father, the view had inspired the original owners to call the property Sky Canyon Ranch. And the same view had inspired Nolan's great-grandparents to purchase the property for their retirement.

Yet it had been Nolan's dad with the vision and a passion for a working ranch. Nolan's dad who had expanded the name to Sky Canyon Cattle Ranch. Nolan's dad who had wanted to build the property into something that would thrive for generations.

But Nolan had different goals. Ones that took him on the road, away from the ranch and that legacy building. Despite promising his dad that he loved the ranch and the land as much as his father did.

I'm sorry, Dad.

Nolan squeezed his eyes closed. Blocked out the view that had inspired his ancestors but only left him feeling adrift.

He was a two-time national champion bull rider. His goals had been achieved. He had reached the pinnacle of his professional rodeo career. Yet he felt oddly like he was in an uncertain freefall, not a celebration.

The rodeo circuit beckoned, ready and willing to take him back. The land waited, impatient for him to take charge. Yet without his father, Nolan seemed to have lost his footing. And his direction.

But that was why he had finally returned. Sky Canyon Cattle Ranch was not going anywhere. Now Nolan had to finally decide if he was. *Settle or sell, Nolan. Time to decide.*

Those had been the words of Wayne Raskin, Sky Canyon's longtime ranch manager and his father's close friend. After Wayne had told Nolan he intended to retire in the coming year. And before Wayne had wished Nolan a Merry Christmas.

Now Nolan was home to decide. Wayne was in Colorado helping his friend recover after hip replacement surgery. Wayne had asked his son, Ryan, to watch over things at Sky Canyon in his absence. Still, Wayne had been clear that he expected an answer from Nolan when he returned to Sky Canyon the day after Christmas. That gave Nolan a little more than two weeks to make his choice. *Settle or sell.*

A commotion on the back deck disrupted his silent debate. He grinned. For a moment thinking perhaps his cowgirl had returned. And wouldn't that be a welcome diversion.

The mudroom door swung open. A figure in a bright purple beanie hat and tall fur-lined boots burst inside and sailed straight for him. "Uncle Nolan. Uncle Nolan."

Not his cowgirl. Still, his disappointment was no more than a passing thought. After all, his niece was as good a distraction as any. Nolan caught Kendall and lifted her into a bear hug. He squeezed the petite teenager until her bright laughter filled the kitchen and elbowed his own disquiet aside.

"That's entirely unfair, you know." Annie stood in the mudroom doorway, her hands on her hips. A frown on her still-soot-smudged face.

Nolan squeezed Kendall once more and set her back down. "What is?"

"That my fourteen-year-old daughter only laughs for you." Annie arched an eyebrow at them.

"I laugh, mom." Kendall swiped her gloved hand under her nose and rolled her eyes at Nolan. "Of course, I might laugh more at home if my mother treated me like a part of the family and not an afterthought."

Annie swiped her palm over her face, smearing the soot below her chin, then groaned. "I have never treated you like that."

"What about today?" Kendall perched her hands on her hips and mimicked her mother's earlier stance. "Total afterthought."

Annie flung her arms out, turned a pleading gaze at Nolan, then ordered, "Please explain to my daughter, Nolan, that I didn't want her to worry. That I wanted her to enjoy her sleepover with her friends. And that is why I didn't tell her about the fire today."

"Uncle Nolan." Kendall tapped the toe of her boot. "Please tell my mother that I had to hear about it from Charlotte, whose own mom was thoughtful enough to text Charlotte about *our* fire."

Nolan covered his smile at his niece's overly theatrical stance. He knew enough about the mother-daughter duo to understand that revealing any kind of amusement would not get a good response from either one.

"If we want to discuss afterthoughts, how about we talk about your poor grandmother over here?" Marla squeezed around Annie, dragging a rolling cooler behind her. "And about how I could use some help unloading the truck."

Nolan rushed to Marla and took the cooler handle from her. "What exactly is going on?"

"Uncle Nolan, you are supposed to be telling Mom to treat me like a real part of the family," Kendall said, her words having the same commanding edge as her mother's. "I'm old enough not to be excluded."

"I'm not getting involved in this." Nolan lifted his hands up. "I'm what you would call neutral territory."

"Good luck, Nolan." Marla chuckled and unzipped her knee-length jacket. "They will get you to take sides and fate help you then."

Annie frowned at her mother. "I still can't believe you sided with Kendall on this one, Mom."

"I can always count on Gigi-M to have my side." Kendall beamed and wrapped her arms around Marla, then she cast her clever gaze at Nolan. "And my favorite uncle, too."

"Only uncle," Nolan corrected, then motioned to the oversize red cooler he'd parked near the refrigerator. "Now back to my original question. What are you doing here?" Taking in the trio's sudden and coordinating consternation, he quickly added, "Not that I'm not happy to see you all, of course."

"Oh, I get it." Kendall's face cleared and she gave a little clap. "Mom didn't tell you? Guess she didn't want you to worry, either, Uncle Nolan."

Unease washed over Nolan. "Worry about what?"

"It's nothing." Annie unbuttoned her jacket, then buttoned it back up as if uncertain whether she was coming or going.

Marla frowned and brushed her salt-and-pepper-colored bangs off her forehead. "No power is not nothing, dear."

"You don't have power." Nolan frowned at his sister. "What about the generator?"

"Damaged in the fire." Annie winced. "I can get a new one tomorrow."

"But the only one in stock won't even power the small kitchen appliances let alone warm the whole house." Kendall tugged off her beanie, revealing her dark braids twisted into an intricate bun on top of her head.

"I was going to call you, Nolan." Annie chewed on her lower lip. "But Kendall was hungry and cold."

"And mad." Kendall stuffed her hat into the deep pocket on her jacket. Her words lacked any real heat. "Don't forget that."

"I just tossed all our luggage, including yours, Nolan, into the truck bed, piled everyone inside and came here." Exhaustion rimmed Annie's green eyes. Stress made her shoulders sag. Yet there was compassion and concern in her gaze. "We can stay at a hotel if it's…"

"Why would we do that?" Kendall thrust her arms out. "Uncle Nolan has this whole big, huge house. So many empty bedrooms we could sleep in a different one each night."

Annie held Nolan's gaze and his confidences.

And for that, Nolan was grateful. Even more his sister had his loyalty. Always. He wouldn't send his family to a hotel. That went against everything his father had taught him. No, he wasn't kicking them out. Not tonight. Or any other. Even if staying in his father's house felt entirely wrong. Like he was intruding on a life he had not fully committed to. Not the way his father had. Not in the way his father wanted his only son to. Nolan massaged the back of his neck and finally said, "We can all stay here."

"I knew it." Kendall danced around the kitchen, unable to contain her excitement. "I told you Uncle Nolan would let us stay, Mom."

Annie searched Nolan's face, seemingly not as convinced as her daughter.

Nolan scratched his fingers through his beard and collected himself. Decisions needed to be made. But not tonight. Tonight was about his family and providing what they needed. "I can help with the cold, but not the food."

"That's all right." Kendall hugged him quick. "Mom has the app for Crispy Olive Pizzeria on her phone and free delivery."

Marla nudged her boot against the cooler. "Also, we cleared out Annie's refrigerator and brought the groceries we bought earlier today."

"The electric company thinks it might be four to five days before full power is restored," Annie said. Defeat and distress surrounded her words. "The transformer was blown. With the approaching holiday and colder than normal temperatures, staff is short and parts harder to get quickly."

"No problem." At least, he would not let it be. Nolan stepped over to Annie and wrapped his arm around her shoulders. "We can stay here as long as we need."

Annie leaned against him and whispered a quiet "I owe you."

Nolan gave her shoulders a quick squeeze to let her know he heard her, even though she was wrong. He owed his stepmom and stepsister far more. The pair had been there for his father more than Nolan had in recent years. They'd been his dad's support while his son had been off pursuing his own goals, convinced there would be time enough to reconnect. Nolan had not always been there for his father. But he could be here now for Annie, Marla and Kendall.

"We just might need to stay awhile, Uncle Nolan," Kendall said, sounding more pleased than upset by the idea. "Our house sure does smell like smoke. It's bad, isn't it, Gigi-M?"

"It certainly has a distinct smoky scent, even though the fire was at the stables," Marla admitted.

"Your house smells okay, Uncle Nolan." Kendall peeked into the family room. "But you should have Gigi put together her special apple cider and spices on the stove like she does. Then it'll smell like Christmas in here."

Nolan could not quite remember what Christmas smelled like other than salty air and humidity. He had not been back to Texas for the holidays in years. When he had been married, his then wife, Victoria, had preferred to spend Christmas with her family at the beach. Nolan's father had only ever been gracious. *I get to see you ride in person, son. Spend the holidays with your in-laws.*

Nolan's dad had watched from the stands in as many arenas as he could drive to over the years. Nolan had been better knowing his dad was there. Yet Nolan hadn't been as focused on his father as he should have. He inhaled around those endless if-onlys and tough regrets that proved ever difficult to dislodge.

"Can we decorate?" Kendall spun around, rushed to Nolan and tugged on his arm. "Please, Uncle. You promised we would decorate the stables and now we can't."

But he had decisions to make that didn't include how tall the Christmas tree should be or whether silver or red garland popped more on the fireplace mantel. He couldn't get wrapped up in the holiday chaos. Besides, letting his family stay fulfilled his brotherly duties. Surely that was enough, wasn't it?

Nolan took in the wide-eyed plea of his rambunctious niece and lost his resolve. "If you can find decorations, we can put them up."

"Yes!" Kendall cheered.

"Come on, Kendall." Annie turned and headed into the mudroom. "Let's grab your bags from the truck and you can pick your room."

"I already know which one I want." Kendall

raced after her mother. "The blue-and-silver room. It's like standing inside one of those super fancy Christmas ornaments. I always wanted…"

The mudroom door slammed shut on the pair, cutting off the rest of Kendall's excitement.

"My granddaughter became a teenager and turned into a handful." Amusement flitted across Marla's face. "I remember when Kendall barely whispered a word and we worried. Now it seems she's a fountain of opinions that she can't resist sharing."

"I seem to recall being called a handful a time or two growing up." Nolan lifted the cooler lid and peered inside. "Or was it Annie who you and dad called a handful and me who you referred to as a gem?"

"You two were more than handfuls and you know it." Marla chuckled and opened the refrigerator door.

"But we turned out all right." Nolan handed Marla the milk jug and the butter container from the cooler. "Thanks to you and Dad."

"Still, we worried all the same." Marla accepted the items, then touched Nolan's arm. "I still worry, even though you're grown. Are you okay with this arrangement?"

Nolan's chest squeezed. Marla had been worried about him and his feelings since her first date with his widowed dad decades ago. Nolan had been seven years old, and Marla had taken him aside and personally checked in with him. He had liked her instantly and loved her more now. As stepmoms went, Marla was the true gem.

Yet this had been Marla and his father's dream house. They had built it together. Marla had moved out less than a month after her husband's funeral. According to Annie, Marla's visits to Sky Canyon were as infrequent as Nolan's. He set his hand over hers still resting on his arm and said, "I'm okay. What about you? Are you okay?"

Her fingers flexed under his. Her grip tightened as if she was finding her own balance. Her eyes closed briefly. "I miss him so very much."

Nolan nodded.

"But your dad would never have wanted this house to be empty." Her smile was tender, her expression sincere. "He built it for family."

Nolan agreed. He just wasn't sure the house was meant for him. As he was. If this was the last time he was in the house, it felt right that they were all there together. Nolan squeezed Marla's fingers. "Come on, let's get this cooler unloaded and get you guys settled. You can stay in your old bedroom."

"That's not necessary. I had the primary suite completely refurnished after I moved out." Marla shook her head and set the egg container on the shelf in the refrigerator. "This is your home now, Nolan. That suite is for you."

His home now. How simple Marla made that sound. As if it was so easy to accept. Nolan wrapped his fingers around the ice cream carton. His dad and

Marla had always provided Nolan a home growing up and one to return to whenever he wanted. Lately he considered the road to be the place he belonged. Stepping into his father's shoes seemed impossible. He wasn't certain he even knew how to create a *home* for himself. Perhaps it was better to get back to that road after the holiday. Stop pretending his boots were ever meant to stand still. He shifted, widened his stance as if testing his direction.

"Besides, I already know what guest room my granddaughter wants." Marla chuckled and took the ice cream from Nolan to put into the freezer. "I do believe we should bargain with her. The blue-and-silver room if she agrees to dinner cleanup duty while we are here. What do you think?"

I think I need more time. I think I'm not ready to let go and leave just yet. He leaned down to unpack the last of the cooler. Then he grinned at Marla. "Blue room for dish duty. I like the way you think, Marla."

"It wasn't that long ago when your father and I struck more than one bargain with you and Annie for chores like vacuuming and window washing." Marla closed the refrigerator doors.

"Don't forget cleaning stables and the hen house." Nolan dropped the lid into the empty cooler and grabbed the handle.

"You and Annie used to argue something fierce about the chicken coop," Marla said.

"It wasn't the chickens," Nolan countered. He rolled the cooler into the mudroom and smiled at the memory. "Dad always seemed to find the meanest roosters in the county. They would peck your ankles something awful."

"Why do you think he always passed that chore off to you and Annie?" Marla laughed at Nolan's surprised expression. She wrapped her arm around his waist and patted his chest. "Your dad would be thrilled you are here. I know I am."

He wasn't certain how long he would be in town. But he wasn't about to ruin the moment. They went to join the others.

"Gigi-M, we have a big problem." Kendall stood in the driveway, her arms wrapped around a large, square, pink fuzzy pillow. Worry widened her eyes to owlish. "Mom says we have to cancel the annual holiday open house."

"What is a holiday open house?" Nolan joined his sister near her truck.

"Nothing fancy," Marla said, her expression reassuring. "Just a simple gathering of our friends and family."

"This year is a give-and-get theme," Kendall explained. "Guests bring something to donate to the local animal shelter or to the local toy drive. And they bring a favorite must-have item for the kitchen to put in the gift exchange." Kendall tipped her head at Nolan. "That's the get part of the give-and-get party."

"Got it." Nolan grinned at his niece.

"The giving part was Kendall's idea," Marla said,

pride in her words. "We also have a game portion of the evening and a cookie swap."

"That's the tastiest part. Gigi and I ordered special boxes for everyone to take their cookies home in." Kendall squeezed her pillow. "They are so cute. They look like colorful gingerbread houses."

Games. Gift exchanges. Gingerbread to-go boxes. Their so-called simple gathering was getting more complicated.

"But Mom is canceling the party." Kendall frowned.

"It's just with the fire and now the power outage." Annie opened the tailgate on her truck. "We can't host it at our place."

"We could have it here." Hope filled Kendall's face. "Couldn't we, Uncle Nolan?"

"I don't know." He knew nothing about party planning. And no one opted for the grinch to host ever. He embraced his inner holiday grump. "I'm sure everyone will understand if you cancel."

Kendall's frown deepened. Her eyebrows slammed together. Dismay worked across her words. "But Uncle, invitations were already sent out. I started an RSVP list. Practically everyone has said yes. We can't disappoint *everyone*."

He rubbed his chin and tried to ignore the disappointment he was clearly causing his niece.

Marla shook her head. "There surely isn't any holiday cheer in canceling," she said, a forlorn note to her words. "Given all that has happened, we certainly need as much happy as we can find this season."

Not his stepmom, too. But holiday grumps were supposed to be impossible to sway, weren't they? He knew who he was. And he was not going to board the holiday express train. Nolan kept silent.

"We should really listen to Gigi-M. She does know best." Kendall perked back up. Her smile brightened her eyes. "Gigi is like our own personal Mrs. Claus. And I'm her favorite head elf. We can take care of everything."

"We will handle the party prep," Marla added, her smile encouraging. "All you have to do is make time to have an evening of fun."

There it was. *Time.* What Nolan wanted back. What he wanted more of with his dad. That was not possible. But he had the next few days with his family. Still, a holiday party was not exactly his first choice of family activities.

"We are seriously outnumbered." Annie bumped her shoulder against Nolan's and kept her words low. "You might as well concede. Those two are quite the force when they team up."

"It's one evening," he said under his breath to Annie. *Toot-toot. All aboard.* "How bad could it be?"

"That's the spirit," Annie whispered.

But Nolan hadn't returned to locate his misplaced Christmas spirit. He was there to settle or sell. Not deck the halls or join the reindeer games.

Still, he smiled at Marla and Kendall. "You can have the open house here."

"Gigi, I'll make a list of decorations we must have." Kendall spun in a circle, her enthusiasm bubbling out of her. "Because we cannot host a holiday open house here without the *holiday*."

"I do believe this is going to be a wonderful Christmas after all." Joy filled Marla's face from her sunny smile to her sparkling eyes. "I get to share an evening with friends. I'm surrounded by my family. Nolan has a girlfriend. Now he and Willow can really build something special together."

Girlfriend. Willow was not that. Nor was he building anything with her either. It was more like he was finding the answer to his long-standing curiosity. Would a date with Willow Blackwell be as memorable as he had always imagined it would? Not that a date should be his priority right now.

"My heart is filling again. I won't deny it's a very welcome feeling." Marla pressed her palm over her chest. "I just want you two and Kendall, when she's older, to experience the kind of love Duncan and I shared with each other." Marla fixed her gaze on Nolan. Her smile turned luminous. "Willow is the cowgirl of your heart, Nolan. I just know it."

Willow wasn't his cowgirl. Of the heart or otherwise. He adored his stepmother, but he had to set her straight. Nolan opened his mouth to correct Marla.

Annie reached over and squeezed his arm until he slanted his gaze toward her. She gave him a subtle headshake. Then seemingly satisfied he intended to remain silent, she pulled a suitcase out of her truck bed. The first she handed to Marla. The second to Kendall before telling them that Nolan and she could handle the rest. The pair headed inside without a backward glance, already absorbed in their party planning details.

As soon as the back door slammed shut behind the pair, Annie rounded on Nolan. "Do not ruin this."

Nolan crossed his arms over his chest. "Ruin what?"

"Don't pretend with me." Annie tugged his duffel from the truck bed and tossed the bag at him. "You were going to tell Mom that there is nothing going on between you and Willow."

"But there isn't. And Willow is definitely not my girlfriend." He caught the bag but kept his gaze on Annie. "As you know full well."

"Can't you just give Mom this?" Annie yanked her suitcase out and closed the tailgate. "This is the happiest she has been after Duncan's passing. Let her believe you found someone. You heard her just now. That has always been her biggest wish for us."

Nolan was beginning to wish he had taken them all away again this season. Just as he had done last year for their first Christmas without his father.

"It's the holidays," Annie pressed on and walked beside him toward the house. "You know this time of year is the hardest for her. Please give her this. After the fire today, we need this."

"You need me to pretend-date Willow?" Nolan held open the back door and waited for his sister to step inside.

"I need that." Annie pointed to the kitchen where Kendall and Marla stood shoulder to shoulder at the island, laughing. The merry sound spilled around the room like so much spun sugar. Annie added, "I swear this is the first time she has laughed all month."

Nolan took in his sister's face. The worry clouded her eyes. The tension filled her face. He wanted the same for his sister—to hear her laugh again. To see her joy, too. Yet tricking his stepmom hardly felt right. But perhaps if someone found that love story for the ages like Marla wanted, then his deception would be overlooked. He rubbed his chin and considered Annie. "Fine. But you have to go with it, too, then."

Her eyes widened. Her agreement came quickly. "No problem."

Still unsure this was the right course, Nolan set aside his doubts and nodded. He stepped around Annie and walked into the kitchen. "Hey, Marla. I don't think I told you, but Ryan Raskin will be here tomorrow. He's stepped away from his bronc riding temporarily to help me around the ranch, and since his dad is giving an old buddy a hand with his recovery from surgery. Ryan will be with us for the holiday."

"That's wonderful news," Marla said.

"Stop it." Annie's urgent whisper came from behind Nolan. She added a hard yank on his shirt to make her point.

Nolan grinned over his shoulder. "But you just agreed to go with it."

Annie was far from amused.

Nolan twisted and smiled at Marla and Kendall. "Would it be too much to invite Ryan to the party?"

"Of course, Ryan must come to the party." Marla was more than delighted.

Annie's grip on Nolan's shirt lessened. And he swore he heard something close to a growl before his sister moved to his side. He almost felt sorry for her. *Almost.* But he had good intentions for both his sister and his longtime friend.

Ryan and Annie had something. It wasn't history. Like Willow and Nolan, they had never dated. Perhaps it was simply unfinished business and lingering interest. But if Nolan was going to face his unanswered questions about a cowgirl from his past, he wasn't going to do it alone. Annie would have to do the same about a cowboy from her past.

"Ryan was your mother's first crush." Marla's eyes crinkled at the edges. "I believe she was around your age at the time."

"Mom." Kendall's eyes popped wide. "What happened?"

Annie elbowed Nolan in the ribs none too gently, then said, "I don't remember. It was a long time ago."

But the blush staining his sister's cheeks said

differently. Nolan knew he was on the right track. "Ryan thought Annie was too good for him."

"That's not true." Surprise swept across Annie's face. "Ryan has always been way more interested in bucking broncs than romance."

There was an exception. A cowgirl named Annie. Nolan supposed there always was an exception. His was Willow. Although just like Ryan, Nolan had not believed he was good enough for Willow all those years ago. Then Willow's mother, Flora Blackwell, had confirmed it. Flora had unknowingly spurred Nolan's desire into overdrive to be the best. He supposed he owed Flora his gratitude. Yet even after so much time, *thank you* wasn't what he wanted to tell Flora Blackwell.

But this was about Annie and Ryan and their unfinished business. He smiled at his sister. "If you don't believe me, ask Ryan yourself at the party."

Annie narrowed her eyes at him as if silently vowing payback.

Marla pressed her hands against her cheeks as if deflating her gasp.

"What's wrong?" Nolan asked.

"Annie needs a new dress for the party," Marla said, her gaze drifting over her daughter.

"I do not need a dress." Annie crossed her arms over her chest.

"Do you even have a dress, Mom?" Kendall scrunched her nose and considered her mom. "I've never seen you wear one."

"Of course, I have one," Annie said, although her words lacked confidence.

Marla waved away Annie's defense and tapped Kendall's phone screen. "Add dress shopping to our to-do list, Kendall."

Kendall typed on her phone, then pursed her lips at Nolan. "What about Uncle Nolan and his party attire?"

"I have clothes," Nolan blurted.

"You're dating Willow now," Marla countered. Speculation shifted across her face.

"What does that have to do with my clothes?" Nolan crossed his arms over his chest. Same as his sister.

Annie's shoulders shook quietly.

"Willow knows fashion, Uncle Nolan." Kendall lifted both hands. "Willow is sophisticated and trendy and so pretty. She's like the chicest cowgirl around."

Nolan didn't disagree on the prettiest or the sophisticated. Willow Blackwell had always been that. Yet there was more to his cowgirl now that intrigued him. As if somehow time had refined the mystery that had always surrounded her. "So, what are you saying? I need to be a chic cowboy to date Willow."

Annie's laughter burst out. "I'm not sure that's possible."

Marla frowned at her daughter, then studied Nolan. "It wouldn't hurt to try, Nolan. Putting effort into your clothes will show Willow you can put effort into your relationship."

But it was pretend. So pretend his fake girlfriend did not even know about their fake relationship yet. Heck, Willow had not even agreed to fake-date him.

He glanced at his worn plaid shirt, noted the tear at the hem. He supposed a new shirt and pair of jeans couldn't hurt. And he could use his family's help in picking those out. Not to impress Willow or even ensure the longevity of his fake relationship. It was important to Marla. Still, a wardrobe upgrade was not on his Santa wish list. He sighed and nudged his inner grump aside again. "Let me know when you want to shop. I will be there."

Marla grinned, her approval and delight more than obvious.

Annie narrowed her eyes at him.

Nolan shrugged, moved closer to Annie and whispered, "I won't be responsible for dimming her happy."

"I will be there, too, Mom," Annie called out and followed Nolan into the family room. She stopped him with a hand on his arm. "You could have warned me about your plan to get us both fake dates."

"What?" Nolan tugged his sister closer to the massive fireplace and further away from the kitchen. "That was me playing matchmaker."

"No way." Annie swiped her hand through the air between them. Her head shook hard enough to loosen several dark strands of hair from her pony-tail. "You would not do that to me."

Nolan pulled back at the irritation in her words. Annie had what Marla and his dad often referred to as a hard-to-find fuse. But once Annie found her way to riled up, it was always best to take cover.

"We both agreed that love is for fools. And we both know we are not that," Annie rushed on. Her green eyes flared. "I know you would not set me up and play me for a fool, right, big brother?"

Love. Why did everyone insist on leaping straight to love? It was not ever about love. *Ever.* He should have realized Annie would not react well. At eighteen she had been hopelessly *in* love. Then found herself pregnant and alone. Annie had forgiven her daughter's father and herself, but she had yet to forgive love. As for a second chance, love did not deserve one. That was a truth both Annie and Nolan held fast to.

Nolan scrubbed his palm over his face and softened his tone. "I suggested you talk to Ryan at the party. That's all. Nothing more."

"Oh, I'm going to talk to him tomorrow." The frustration in her expression gave way to calculating and clever. "Because our plan is brilliant, really."

Brilliant was not the word he would choose. "What plan is that exactly?"

"The one where we both get to prove to Mom that we have our love lives under control." Satisfaction stretched across Annie's close-lipped smile.

Nolan kept his dating life in control by not having one. That had been working quite well. Until now. He considered his sister and ignored that bad feeling inside him. "You aren't seriously going to ask Ryan to be your fake boyfriend, are you?"

"No." Annie chuckled and shook her head.

False alarm. Nolan exhaled.

Annie added, "I only need Ryan to be my fake party date."

Nolan coughed. His words sounded more like a wheeze. "This is getting out of hand." *Way out of hand.*

"It's for a good cause," Annie argued.

The Marla cause. Nolan squeezed his forehead. "Even so, I feel like this is certain to land us on Santa's naughty list."

"It's not like we haven't been there before." Annie laughed, then just as quickly sobered. "This is about more than cheating at the reindeer games, Nolan. I have to keep my own heart safe. By any means necessary. No one else will."

With that, Annie grabbed her suitcase and headed upstairs.

Nolan agreed with his sister and fully intended to keep his heart safe as well. All while convincing his cowgirl to join his fake relationship team, even though it could very well land her on Santa's naughty list, too. What could possibly go wrong?

CHAPTER SIX

THE NEXT MORNING, Nolan's thoughts continued to circle around a certain cowgirl. Same as they had for most of the night. He stretched his arms over his head, rolled his shoulders and paced around the bedroom to work the kinks from his body. At the French doors, he paused and gaped.

He had the double doors unlocked, flung wide open and was outside on the private balcony within seconds. Only the cold stinging his bare feet and chest chased him inside. He yanked on a pair of jeans and boots and tugged a T-shirt over his chest before rushing back onto the porch. His gaze tracked to the pasture and held. His breath escaped in a long exhale.

His cowgirl.

She was there. Not simply a figment of his morning musings after all.

Willow and her horse Phantom stood in the middle of the pasture. Phantom stretched his stance, extended his right leg and lowered down onto his left knee. Then he tucked his cream-colored head near his bent knee in a perfectly executed bow.

Willow dropped into a formal curtsy, her words lost in the distance. But her smile—brilliant even from Nolan's vantage point—revealed all he needed to know.

Willow adjusted a teal fleece headband around her forehead, covering her ears, and freeing her auburn ponytail. She wore a fitted black one-piece bodysuit and plain running shoes. She put herself and Phantom through a series of warm-ups and stretches before dropping a special saddle Nolan recognized onto her horse.

Nolan's pulse raced. He knew what was coming. He had watched Willow and her sisters perform quite often. Still, he was never quite prepared for the somersault-style flip that took Willow from the dirt to Phantom's back in one fluid motion.

That was only the beginning. Willow was elegance and grace, athleticism and power as she worked through a series of gymnastic and dance moves from a knee stand to a handstand to upside-down splits. All while she was balanced on Phantom's back as the horse circled around the pasture.

Her dark hair billowed behind her. Phantom's pale white tail swished against his muscular cream-colored body. Willow was like the night and Phantom the moon, helping her shine. And shine his cowgirl did, from her broad smile to her flowing choreography. Nolan was nothing short of transfixed.

He could have stood there all morning, watching a cowgirl and a horse in a pasture, and been more than content. That was not a revelation he wanted to examine too closely. After all, content was nothing he aspired to, was it?

Fortunately, the arrival of Kendall and Marla outside spurred him into motion. Willow somersaulted herself off Phantom in an agile move and then walked to the two women at the pasture fence. The trio shared a round of warm hugs. Their laughter lit the early morning air like sunshine.

Too soon, Marla had her arm linked with Willow's and leaned toward Willow as if confiding in his cowgirl. Nolan had to get to them. *Now.* Before his supposed relationship status with Willow was revealed, well, to Willow. And all before he had the chance to explain.

Nolan headed inside and grabbed a plaid flannel shirt on his way out of the bedroom suite. He was still fumbling with the shirt buttons when he reached the kitchen and caught Annie disappearing through the mudroom. At the slam of the back door, Nolan turned to the red-haired cowboy seated on a stool at the kitchen island and said, "Morning, Ryan."

Ryan offered only a slow dip of his chin in acknowledgement. His gaze was fixed on the now-empty mudroom doorway. His expression was perplexed. And his friend's usual ear-to-ear grin was curiously absent.

But Nolan's longtime friend was always—and sometimes regretfully—cheerful from sunup to sundown. Unease dripped through Nolan and had him lingering in the kitchen. "Please tell me that Annie didn't ask you to be her fake date to the party this weekend?"

"That is exactly what she asked me." Ryan swung around and eyed Nolan. His expression was impassive. "In those exact words."

Nolan dropped a coffee pod into the coffee maker, pressed the button for the strongest cup and leaned against the counter. Something told him it was going to be a two-cup kind of morning. "Tell me you told Annie that you would not encourage any of this."

Ryan's smile came slow and spread deep into his ginger-colored, well-groomed, full beard. "I told her I would be happy to be her date."

Nolan's voice sputtered like the coffee maker hissing the last of the hot liquid into his mug. "Why would you do that?"

"Don't you see? This is my opportunity." Ryan lifted his cup of black coffee in a toast toward Nolan. His blue eyes fairly sparkled. "I fully intend to use this opening to show Annie that there is more between us than friendship."

"How do you plan to do that exactly?" Nolan added sugar and vanilla-flavored creamer to his coffee, certain the extra sweetness would offset the sudden sour in his stomach.

"I haven't quite worked out the details." Ryan's fingers tapped an absent beat against his mug. "But I have time."

That was optimistic on his friend's part. The party was in two days. Nolan was feeling slightly more pessimistic. No surprise there. Pessimistic seemed to be his default when it came to things like relationships and love. "What happens if Annie doesn't agree about there being more between you two, what then?"

In the blink of his deep blue eyes, Ryan returned to that good-natured, never-too-serious bronc rider Nolan had known most of his life. Ryan held both his arms out. Amusement twitched through his full beard. "It was all fake anyway, right?"

"That's a bit too much happy-go-lucky, even for you." Nolan frowned.

"I haven't been shy about my interest in Annie. I just haven't been sure how to move out of the friend zone." Ryan rested his elbows on the butcher-block counter. His expression thoughtful, his words resolved. "But Annie came to me. I can't let this chance slip by."

If Nolan was being honest, he wanted a chance with his cowgirl, too. A genuine one. But that required his boots to stick around for more than the holiday. He hadn't been able to do that for his own father. Not to mention his first marriage. The odds weren't in his favor that a cowgirl, no matter how appealing, could change his rambling, restless ways.

Ryan ran a hand through his hair, ruffling the long red strands on the top of his head. "Aren't you doing the same thing with Willow?"

"Willow," Nolan repeated.

Ryan lifted his mug and watched Nolan through

the steam. "Yes. Willow. Your girlfriend. That's what Marla called her when she came in a few minutes ago."

And the word was apparently out. But had it reached his *girlfriend*? Nolan picked his cowboy hat off the chair back where he'd left it last night and slammed it on his head. Time to find out. Time to explain. Once again, his thoughts swirled. Just what exactly was he supposed to say to his cowgirl?

Ryan stood and trailed after Nolan. "Where are we going? We haven't eaten yet and you promised me breakfast."

"You can stay. Make a piece of toast." Nolan stepped outside and scanned the empty pasture. Then caught sight of his cowgirl and Kendall making their way toward the stables and headed for an interception.

Ryan kept pace with him.

Nolan frowned at his friend. "Thought you were hungry."

"I'll eat when my boss eats." Ryan chuckled and lightly tapped his fist against Nolan's shoulder. "In the meantime, I'm here to help, boss."

Nolan shoved at his friend and earned only more laughter from the bronc rider.

"Uncle Nolan. Uncle Nolan, guess what?" Kendall raced toward him, wrapped him in a hug and rolled on, "The Blackwell Belles are getting back together. That's why Willow was practicing just now. How cool is that?"

Nolan slanted his gaze over Kendall's beanie-covered head and looked at Willow. She adjusted her grip on Phantom's reins. Her expression was contained, and her gaze guarded. Much different from the carefree cowgirl beaming moments ago on her beloved horse.

"It's just one performance at the Cowgirl Hall of Fame ceremony," Willow clarified. She brushed a strand of dark hair off her cheek, touched her ear, then her neck. Finally, her arm fell to her side, but her fingers never quite stilled. "I have a video call with my sisters before my afternoon shift at the department store to discuss things."

That was the reason she was restless. Unlike him. He was restless because of her.

"The Blackwell Belles. I remember that name from when Nolan and I first started traveling together on the circuit." Ryan introduced himself to Willow and shook her hand. "How long has it been since you all performed together?"

"More than ten years." Her expression shifted into remote as if she lost herself in her memories and not the pleasant ones.

The Blackwell Belles had broken up several months after Willow's mom had squashed the budding romance between Willow and Nolan. He had been young, hurt, and all too determined not to give Willow a second thought. He had hooked up with Ryan and a group of brash rodeo competitors and doubled down on the bull riding career he chased. He wished he knew more of the details about the Belles. Wished he had paid closer attention back then.

"You know what I think?" Kendall stressed, a plea to her words before continuing, "I think the Belles should practice here. Especially now that my troupe has to practice here."

"You could all practice together." Ryan nodded, then offered all too cheerfully, "Nolan and I could have the arena floor prepped and ready to use by this afternoon."

"That seems like a lot of trouble." Willow's mouth pulled to the side.

"It's no trouble." *But I could be in trouble.* He wanted to tuck Willow into his side and promise… what? That his shoulder would always be there to lean on. Whenever she needed him. For whatever she needed. Those were truths he couldn't give. And the kind of confessions that had no place between them. Nolan started toward the stables. "We have the space. Someone should make use of it."

Kendall cheered. "Now we can practice my flag stance even if it gets dark. I'm still super wobbly."

"That's because you need to tighten your core and keep your gaze fixed between your horse's ears," Willow said gently. "We will work on that this morning while we have all the sunlight we need in the pasture."

Nolan would work on keeping his gaze fixed anywhere but on his cowgirl. And focus on his future. The one he pursued alone like he preferred. His attention trailed back to Willow and held.

"Then it's settled. You can practice here as long as you need." *And if you need me...*

Just then, Annie rounded the corner of the stables. Her gaze swept over the group before returning to Ryan. Suspicion crossed her face. "Ryan. Shouldn't you be out, checking on the cattle and mending fences?"

"Can't leave until my boss is ready and we still haven't had breakfast like he promised." Ryan grinned, seemingly unimpressed with the challenge Annie presented. "Our to-do list has expanded to include the arena. Thanks to the return of the Blackwell Belles."

Annie's eyes popped wide.

"I will explain later." Willow lifted her hand and waved it weakly, then guided Phantom inside the stable barn. "But it is just a phone call. As I keep telling everyone, nothing is official."

Same as nothing was official between Willow and Nolan. Not even their pretend relationship.

"That's where all extraordinary things start." Ryan rubbed his hands together. The corner of his mouth lifted into mischievous. "With a simple conversation."

"And some things stall out in the talking phase." Annie crossed her arms over her chest.

"Not the things that are meant to be," Ryan countered, his expression good-natured.

A smile twitched around the edges of Annie's mouth.

"Well, Ryan was meant to be here so I could

give him his personalized invitation to the party," Kendall exclaimed. "It's in the house. I just need to go grab it."

"Kendall, you need to go greet your friends," Annie said. "Everyone is starting to arrive. The horses need to be unloaded and readied for practice."

"But Mom," Kendall started. "I made a special invitation for Ryan. It has his name on it and everything."

"You can put me on the RSVP list as yes." Ryan's grin lifted into his beard. "There's a conversation I intend to have that night."

Kendall looked between her mom and Ryan and suddenly appeared in no hurry to leave.

"I'll make sure your grandmother gives the invitation to Ryan," Annie assured her daughter. "She's finishing up in the small barn but will be cooking breakfast for everyone. I'm going to head in and get things started for her."

"I can help with that." Ryan stood in the doorway of the stable. "Seems like Kendall's entire team is arriving at once." Peals of laughter and high-pitched greetings rang out in the driveway.

Annie joined him. "This isn't even the full troupe. This is only the ones who have experience riding horses."

Ryan winced at an extra exuberant squeal. "I'll definitely be more useful in the kitchen with Marla."

Annie laughed. "Chicken."

"I'll take it and keep my hearing intact," Ryan said. Kendall squeezed around them and then swung back. "Ryan. Wait. You never told me what your favorite color is?"

Annie's nose wrinkled. "Kendall. Why would you need to know that?"

"I'm just curious." Kendall waved her arms, her movements hasty. "I know everyone's favorite color except Ryan's."

"Sorry about this," Annie said to Ryan.

"No, it's fine." Ryan moved closer to Annie. "I would have said green." He reached out, adjusted Annie's scarf under her chin and added, "But I think my favorite color just might be purple." With that, Ryan tipped his hat at everyone and sauntered toward the house, whistling an upbeat Christmas carol.

Smooth. Nolan had to give it to his friend. Ryan had picked the same color as Annie's scarf.

Annie touched her cheek, caught everyone watching her and blurted, "Kendall, show everyone where the pasture is and start warm-ups."

"Are you coming, Willow?" Kendall asked. "You always lead the stretching."

"I'll be right there." Willow opened a stall door and led her horse inside. "I just need to brush down Phantom."

"Okay. But hurry. I don't want to get it wrong." Kendall sprinted off to join her friends.

"I've got less than a minute before I need to be out there, too." Annie hurried toward Phantom's stall. "So, talk fast, Willow. What is going on?"

Willow shrugged. A weariness settled over her

face. "Flora wants the Belles to perform at the Hall of Fame ceremony."

Annie frowned. "Since when do you do what Flora wants?"

Good question. Nolan leaned against the stable door.

"Since Flora promised me an introduction to Royce Chaney." Willow removed Phantom's special saddle.

Nolan took it from her and set it outside the stall.

"Okay. That's big." Annie whistled, then glanced at Nolan. "Royce Chaney is transforming *Glass Ceilings and Petticoats* into a live theater experience unlike any musical we've seen. I don't know anyone who hasn't binge-watched the entire TV series. Of course, what's not to love about cowgirls running an old Western town with good-looking cowboys, outlaws and loads of drama," Annie said excitedly. "After Royce sees you perform, he'll realize you were made for the lead role."

"Slow down," Willow said, caution in her words and expression. "There's a lot that needs to happen just to get to an introduction. Like my sisters performing."

"They owe you after abandoning you," Annie countered.

"I also walked out." Willow waved her hand when Annie opened her mouth to argue. "We don't have time to debate the past."

Nolan watched Willow. Saw the shadow of hurt cross her face. There and gone. Covered like a fine layer of expertly applied makeup. He opened the stall door and stepped inside, drawing Willow's gaze to his. *Not yet, cowgirl. You can't hide from me just yet.* "So, what's the catch?"

Her deep brown eyes locked on his. "Too many to count."

"Doesn't matter. You have to figure this out, Willow," Annie insisted. "This part in *Glass Ceilings and Petticoats* is tailor-made for you. It's your dream come true."

"Right." Willow watched Nolan for another beat, blinked, then aimed her smile at Annie. "It's everything I always wanted."

Nolan did not believe her. Yet now wasn't the time to press.

"Okay, I have to get out there. But this discussion isn't over." Annie pointed to Willow. "Pack your bags and move in tonight rather than tomorrow. So we can get to talking."

Willow was moving in? Nolan frowned. There was absolutely no merit in that. *None.* Except, his cowgirl under the same roof would give him more chances to discover the woman she had become. Talk about a bad idea. Watching her in the pasture made him feel content. Getting to know her would most likely make him feel even more. And when he walked away, he would only feel even worse.

"I'm not moving in here." Willow worked a round brush in circular motions over Phantom's body.

"Of course, you are." Annie glanced at Nolan.

"The water in Willow's building is being shut off this weekend. She was supposed to stay with us at Sun Meadows."

"I can make other arrangements," Willow said.

"Your horses are here," Annie said. "We are here. It's settled."

Willow shook her head. "It's not settled if I haven't agreed, Annie."

"Reason with her please, Nolan." Annie walked backward out the stable doors. "Don't let Willow leave until she agrees to stay. But make it quick— she's got a team to coach."

"You're a coach now?" Nolan asked, unable to hide his surprise. "Like Flora."

That got his cowgirl's attention. Just as he suspected it would. If he remembered anything from the past, it was that the relationship between Willow and her mother was complicated on the best of days.

"What? No." Willow shook her head and went back to grooming her horse. "I'm just helping Kendall and her friends for the Christmas Eve parade."

She was coaching but didn't want to admit it. Nolan tucked that away for later.

"Just one trick each," Willow explained. "Nothing dangerous. If they can't do the trick safely with me, then they can't do it in the parade. We scheduled practices for every day until Christmas Eve."

"Then it makes sense for you to stay here." Nolan picked up a hard brush from the grooming bucket and swept it over the parts Willow had already rubbed. He knew her meticulous grooming routine well. He used to sneak into her horse's stall at the rodeo to spend more time with her years ago. He asked, "Where else would you stay?"

"I can get a hotel room." Willow tossed the rubber curry comb in the bucket. She returned to Phantom, a soft body brush in hand.

"I'd never hear the end of it from Marla if you did that." Nolan finished a last sweep over Phantom's back, freeing the dirt Willow had already loosened from the horse's coat.

"You won't have to hear anything." Willow chuckled. "I can stay at a hotel."

"Or you can stop being stubborn and stay here." Where he wanted his cowgirl. Now Nolan was sounding slightly unreasonable. Willow wasn't *his* anything. If she was fine at a hotel, he should leave it at that.

"I'm not stubborn, I'm…never mind." Willow dusted her brush across Phantom's face for the last bit of coat care. "I don't want to intrude."

Too late for that, cowgirl. She had intruded on his sleep and his thoughts. "According to Marla you're the second daughter she never had and always wanted." *There.* She was practically like family. That should suspend his interest. But she wasn't family. And his heart wanted her to be his. *Retreat.* Too late for that, too. He was already in too far. He added, "So you pretty much have to stay here."

"Fine," Willow conceded. "For the weekend."

Nolan wasn't certain if that was a win or not.

"Please don't spend too much time on the arena for me." Willow grabbed the hoof pick and checked Phantom's front hoof. "I know you must have other more important things to do while you're here."

Like decide my future. Settle or sell. Retire or ride. Nolan checked Phantom's water bucket. "But the Belles will need a place to practice."

"The Belles haven't been in the same room for over a decade." Willow lifted Phantom's back hoof. "We've barely spoken to each other in the same time. An arena to practice in is the least of my concerns."

It's starting to feel like you could become my concern. Nolan frowned and filled Phantom's feed pan. "Can I ask what happened?"

Willow glanced at him. Surprise worked across her face. "You don't know?"

Nolan shook his head. "Please don't take this wrong. After your mom found me that weekend in Santa Fe and told me that you wanted nothing to do with me, a bull riding wannabe." He paused, then admitted, "Well, I decided I didn't want anything to do with the Belles."

"For the record, I never said that." Finished checking Phantom's hooves, Willow took a comb and untangled his tail. "I went to meet you after our performance finished that night. In our spot. You never showed up."

Their spot had been at the far end of the parking lot behind the horse trailers and temporary stables at the arena. They would slip between the trailers to keep from being seen. Nolan said, "I left after my ride that day." He had been miles down the highway by the time Willow went to find him.

"Then you weren't flirting with a barrel rider in the hospitality tent like I was told," Willow said.

Only cowgirl he had been interested in flirting with back then had been Willow. Nolan shook his head. "That was the farthest thing from my mind."

"One more thing to blame on Flora," Willow said.

"I'm sure she thought she was doing what was best for you," Nolan said.

"I wish I could believe that." Her face scrunched up. The comb stilled in Phantom's tail. "The Blackwell Belles broke up because I shot Maggie with an arrow when we were performing in Houston." She pointed the comb at her upper arm. "Fortunately, it lodged in Maggie's arm, and she recovered. But it could have been so much worse."

Nolan eased the comb from Willow's tight grip. Her fingers flexed and trembled. He finished working the tangles from Phantom's tail and waited for his cowgirl to finish her tale.

"Do you know what Flora thought was *best* for me? To keep me from seeing my injured sister in the hospital." Willow wrapped her arms around the horse's neck and leaned against him. "Flora didn't want me exposed to any further trauma. I never got to apologize."

His cowgirl was hurting still. He could see that much. But he had no idea how to stop it. He wanted to pull her into his arms. Hold her. For as long as it took to bring back her smile. As if he could heal her. There he was, circling back to places he had no business being. He tossed the comb into the bucket and headed out of the stall.

"But that's not all." Willow gave one last hug to Phantom and followed Nolan out. "I overheard Flora tell my dad to convince Maggie that it was all her fault. Flora wanted Maggie to take the blame so that I would keep performing. It was fame above everything else. Never stop reaching for that star. Never."

Nolan stuffed his hands in his pockets to keep from reaching for her. "What did your dad do?"

"I don't know. I didn't stick around long enough to find out," Willow said. "I left when my parents headed back to the hospital. I ran into my barrel racing friend. We loaded Phantom into her trailer and took off. I regrouped at her family's ranch in Cheyenne and that was the start of me making my own way without Flora."

Or her sisters. And all alone. That thought didn't sit well.

"Now you understand why you don't need to make the arena prep a priority," Willow said.

Outside, he stopped and closed the distance between them. "I'm sorry I wasn't there for you. I would have helped you."

"You're doing enough now," she said. "You took in my horses and you're letting me stay, too."

If I asked, would you stay longer? Nolan tried to

sound light and indifferent. "Well, if there is anything else you need, just let me know."

"You're a good one, Nolan Elliot." Her gaze, clear and alert, searched his face. "I always thought that about you."

I thought you could be my world. His gaze connected with her deep brown eyes and awareness spiked inside him. *Maybe I still do.* He cleared his throat, pushed his words into wry. "Even when I was getting bucked off into the arena dirt, getting no scores, and landing at the bottom of the standings weekend after weekend."

"Most especially then." Willow set her palm over his chest. "You always had a big heart, cowboy. And that's more rare than you know."

But he never had her heart. Fortunate that. After all, he had disconnected his on purpose and had no intention of reconnecting it. Ever. "Well, the same could be said about you," he stated. "I saw you this morning with Phantom."

"That was nothing. My transitions weren't fluid. My holds were shaky. It was less than perfect." Willow's fingers flexed on his chest. "If it had been a bull ride, the judges would have given it a no score."

"You can't hide passion," he countered. "I saw that and more in the pasture."

"I haven't been a professional trick rider in years," she said. "That much was obvious. There's a difference between playing around and performing."

"Now you sound like Flora." He frowned.

"That's not…" Her argument faded away.

He arched an eyebrow and waited for her to finish.

"Old habits," she finally said.

"You may have walked away, and you might be out of practice," he said. "But I think your sisters and trick riding still hold a large piece of your heart. Maybe it's past time to tell them that."

"I don't know." Strain was there at the edges of her barely-there smile. Worry, too. In the faintest crease between her eyebrows.

"Just think about it," Nolan urged, then tipped his head toward the pasture. "Now you better get out there, Coach. Your team is waiting for you."

Twisting slightly, she finally noticed the eight girls perched on the pasture fence watching them intently. She snatched her hand away from his chest and chuckled again. "Just how long have they been watching us?"

Long enough he suspected that they were going to have questions for their coach. Nolan scratched his cheek.

"That long," Willow said. "I better get going before they start coming up with one of those relationship names for us. If they haven't already."

"About that," Nolan started.

But Willow turned and set off at a run. She used the top fence post like a vault and flipped herself over it, effectively diverting the girls' attention. She landed with a small hop and full grin and quick bow. Excited cheers filled the air.

Nolan pressed his palm against his chest, over his racing heart, and exhaled. Once again, his cowgirl left him breathless. Not exactly the appropriate reaction for a fake boyfriend.

Nolan turned on his bootheels and headed back to the house. For another cup of coffee. Only this time he would skip the cream and sugar. He already sounded as if he might be too sweet on his cowgirl. Going forward he meant to keep things plain and straightforward.

CHAPTER SEVEN

THE BLACKWELL BELLES were getting back together.

A Christmas miracle. Or a holiday disaster. Too soon to tell.

Willow kept her smile subtle and her poise in place, despite the tightening in her chest. Her words were mellow. "Just to be clear." And she very much needed clarity, if only to banish her sheer surprise. She kept her gaze fixed on her sisters' faces filling her notepad screen. "We are all agreeing to perform together one final time at the Cowgirl Hall of Fame ceremony in ten days."

A nod from Iris.

*Agreed*s from Maggie and Violet.

Then the always practical and frank J.R. "Willow, we told you we would perform at the start of this call. Then again ten minutes into our chat. And now. I'm not sure how much clearer we need to be."

Willow nodded, but that knot in her chest refused to release. "Then all we need to decide is where to practice."

"But first, certain things must be returned to their owners." J.R. arched an eyebrow and kept to the point as was her long-standing habit. "Otherwise, the deal is off."

Willow's other three sisters nodded.

This was it, then. Time for Willow to trust her sisters. Trust that they would return the family heirlooms to each other and perform in order to give Willow what she wanted. And not just take what *they* wanted and leave her. All over again. Still, the days of Willow blindly trusting were long gone.

She tried to seem indifferent when she said, "I'm going to suggest Sky Canyon Ranch for both the exchange of items and practice. It's neutral territory." For the most part.

Even more, her sisters would have to come to her. When they didn't, Willow would finally call their bluff.

"Violet, that includes Ferdinand." Maggie leaned closer to the screen as if to make sure she was seen to be serious.

"I know the deal, Mags," Violet countered and pressed into her screen, seeming to meet her twin eye to eye.

Maggie continued, "You aren't the only one who can take good care of him, Violet."

Clearly Maggie wasn't convinced it would all go off without a hitch either. That fact did nothing to ease Willow.

"I want Ferdinand at Sky Canyon," Maggie added, her words firm. "No excuses, Vi."

Violet lifted her chin and refused to back down. "Ferdinand will be there."

Willow pressed her teeth together lightly. Nolan had offered his property for the Belles to practice at. Now she needed to ask Nolan to board a bull, too. And if Ferdinand was staying at Sky Canyon, Willow should be there to watch over him, shouldn't she? That meant a longer stay in her cowboy's house than the weekend.

Suddenly things seemed to be getting pushed a bit too far into unmanageable territory. And that from the cowgirl who'd once shot burning arrows from the saddle of her moving horse at her sister who had been standing on a cantering bull. If only her sisters would show their true colors. Back out and refuse to perform. Call the whole thing off and walk away. Then Willow would be firmly back on familiar ground. Albeit alone. Again. But that she could manage. She had before.

Willow took a long breath and released it. "We meet at Sky Canyon on Sunday. I will text the address and the time." *And when you don't show up, I won't be disappointed or sad. I will refuse to feel anything.*

Goodbyes and seemingly sincere calls of "see you Sunday" offered, the sisters signed off and Willow's notepad screen went blank.

She flattened her palms on the cherrywood desk in Nolan's office and braced herself. Certain any minute she would hear it. Hear that distinct thunk of the other boot dropping.

It had taken months and months of dedication and practice to make the Blackwell Belles what they were. Less than a day to shatter everything Willow had always believed them to be. Willow doubted one short video chat was enough to repair what had been broken and scattered like so much useless dust.

There were more conversations to be had. Hard, uncomfortable ones, to be sure. There was still time for everyone to walk away again. Willow understood that. Yet she couldn't quite dim that flicker of hope inside her. After all, Nolan had not been wrong in the stables earlier. At the root of everything, Willow missed her sisters with a desperation she struggled more and more to ignore.

She pushed out of the chair, adjusted the belt on the corduroy jumpsuit she'd changed into after her practice session with Kendall's troupe, and headed out. She needed to find her cowboy and convince him a bull would not be an inconvenience. If she talked fast, she could get to her afternoon shift at the department store early and possibly put herself back in her manager's good graces.

She was only steps from the office when that other boot dropped. But it was not the one she had expected.

"Gran Denny. Big E." Willow blinked at the older duo seated on the plush couch, looking relaxed and completely at home in Nolan's family room. She could not quite pull the latest hit of surprise from her words. "What are you doing here?"

"I tagged along, too." Flora strolled in from the kitchen, looking stylishly comfortable in blush-colored velvet flare pants, a white cashmere sweater and ankle boots.

"Mom." Willow stopped in the hallway and tried to make sense of the scene before her.

Flora set what looked to be an artfully arranged charcuterie board on the coffee table with the flourish of a seasoned hostess. Then perched herself on the couch beside Gran Denny.

It was like a Blackwell invasion. Willow had been on her own for the past decade—not even a stray leaf from her family tree had blown in her direction. Now everywhere she turned, she seemingly bumped into a Blackwell family member.

"I called and invited your family to our holiday party." Marla swept in and placed a serving tray bearing two festive teapots and teacups with candy-cane striped handles on the coffee table. "Since you will be staying with us for the holidays, Willow, I thought your family might like to join us."

But the party was that weekend. Her family was unfashionably early. Forty-eight hours, to be exact. Even more, Willow meant to stay for only the weekend, possibly the following week if Ferdinand arrived. But not *through* the upcoming holidays.

Even if the idea of more time with Nolan intrigued her. Her cowboy saw her passion, not her mistakes in the pasture. There was something entirely too compelling about that. So much so she wanted to know what else he saw in her. Now she was seriously off-topic and off-track.

What she needed was her cowboy. To set every-one straight, including herself.

Smiling cheerfully, Gran Denny accepted a mug from Marla. Spreading Cheer was written in tin-sel silver cursive on the side of the cup. "Of course, when we heard about all that Marla and Kendall needed to do to get ready, we offered our assistance."

"I immediately accepted their help." Marla dipped a tea bag into the mug, marked Merry Ev-erything. Her chuckle brimmed with excitement. "I want the evening to be perfect. And I was a bit worried about how Kendall and I were going to pull it off ourselves without some sort of miracle."

"Well, here we are." Big E stacked a slice of cheese onto a cracker, then drizzled honey on top. He gave Marla a satisfied nod. "Consider us your elves, Marla."

"We are ready and more than willing to be put to work." Flora lifted the teacup that said Holly Jolly. Her smile stretched into convincing.

Yet holly and jolly were not suited to Flora Black-well. Willow had to stop this. Whatever this was. She chewed on her bottom lip and considered her op-tions. This wasn't her house. Time to find her cow-boy. Willow pulled her cell phone from her pocket.

"I found the marshmallows." Kendall skipped into the family room and picked up the snowman-shaped teapot. "You have to try the hot chocolate, Willow. I made it myself." Kendall filled a tea-cup, added a handful of marshmallows and a candy cane, then carried it carefully over to Willow. "You get the Peppermint Wishes cup. When you get to the bottom, don't forget to make a wish."

Willow thanked Kendall and was midsip when she heard the heavy bootsteps on the hardwood floor in the kitchen. Soon after, Nolan stepped into the family room. *Wish granted.* Only Nolan looked even more bewildered than Willow. Whether it was from the muffler-dog he held out in front of him like a pair of mud-filled boots or the unexpected gathering in his family room, Willow wasn't certain.

Ryan strolled in behind Nolan yet kept his distance from him and a wary eye on the grumbling dog.

"I'm assuming this was the emergency." Nolan lifted the small, snuffling dog in his grasp, turning it this way and that as he seemed to consider the tiny dog's snowflake print sweater. "Ryan and I found it crying near the back door."

"That's Zinni." Kendall plopped more marshmallows into her hot chocolate and laughed. "She wasn't lost, Uncle Nolan, and she always sounds like that."

Zinni wiggled and licked Nolan's hand as if to reassure him all was well. Nolan's eyebrows drew together. "I got a text about an emergency."

More footsteps sounded in the kitchen. Annie appeared, unbuttoned her coat, but stopped before removing it. Her glance skipped around the room. "Mom texted there was an emergency. What's going on?"

"It's an emergency meeting," Marla corrected and tapped her wrist. "One that you are late for."

Annie paused between Nolan and Ryan, then glanced at Willow. Confusion crossed her face. "What meeting is this?"

Willow shook her head and shrugged.

"It's the first meeting for Operation Get-Your-Holiday-On," Kendall announced from her position in front of the fireplace. Her Gumdrops and Glitter mug seemed to shimmer in the afternoon sunlight.

Zinni snorted. Nolan frowned as irritation seemed to replace his confusion.

"Operation what?" Annie caught sight of the can-tankerous dog, openly gaped and edged closer to Ryan.

"Just come in and sit down." Marla motioned to the couches. "Now that everyone is here, we can get started."

The trio never moved, as if they had collectively and silently agreed to remain standing and within easy reach of the nearest exit. Willow always pre-ferred a clear escape route herself and moved to join them. No one opted to take Zinni from Nolan. Her cowboy gave the dog one more inspection as if looking for her mute button. Yet instead of put-ting Zinni on the floor, he tucked the grumbly dog in the curve of his arm.

"Uncle Nolan, you know how you gave me per-mission to decorate?" Kendall eyed him over the rim of her mug. At Nolan's barely-there nod, Kendall smiled and continued, "Well, Gigi-M and I found decorations out in the storage barn."

"But what we found barely puts a dent in our decoration needs," Marla added.

Kendall lifted her mug high. "So, I'm declaring this the official launch of Operation Get-Your-Holiday-On."

A low groan came from beside Willow. Nolan adjusted Zinni, tucking her closer against him as if in support of her protest.

"With less than two days to spruce this place up…" Marla spread both arms wide and eyed the room. "This is clearly a code Rudolph situation."

Willow heard chewing and slanted her gaze sideways. Zinni gnawed on her holiday attire as if frantic to escape the festivities. Nolan gently worked the sleeve of Zinni's sweater from her mouth and asked, "What more could you possibly need?"

Willow swallowed. Nolan's words were mild, yet he was quite stiff beside her, as if he was bracing himself.

"That is exactly what we are here to discuss." Marla beamed.

Willow worried it was not going to be a short discussion. She had to get to work, but she couldn't very well leave her family unattended.

"Elias and I can handle the fireplace mantel and staircase." Gran Denny tipped her head and considered those spots. "Fresh pine garland. Pinecones, holly, candles. A string of clear lights."

Big E chewed on another stacked cracker and spoke around the bite. "Nothing to it."

"A small, icy-white potted pine would look lovely on the hearth," Flora added, then lifted her teacup at Willow. "I have a talent for bringing the sparkle."

"Mom," Willow chided. "You don't decorate for the holidays. You never have."

"I've been reconsidering that lately," Flora confessed. "With just your father and me, I hardly saw the point."

The point being that no one would see and more importantly appreciate all Flora's hard work. Yet with a crowd expected for the party, it would mean more eyes on Flora Blackwell and that meant more people fawning over her so-called sparkle skills. For her mother that was always a resounding win. But this party was not about her mother.

Looked like Willow was joining the project team and getting her holiday on after all, if only to keep her mother under wraps. Zinni's grumble vibrated into a low rumble. Willow's sentiments exactly. She ground her teeth together.

"Now, what else do we need?" Marla refilled her tea and swirled in extra honey.

"A tree," Kendall declared. She spread her fingers wide and circled her palm toward the wall like an artist describing their vision for a mural. "A really, really tall one for that corner."

"It has to be fresh." Ryan walked over to the coffee table, sorted through the cups and selected the one tagged Jingle and Mingle. He filled it with hot chocolate, seeming more than ready to join the team.

"Ryan isn't wrong," Annie mused.

That earned a big smile of gratitude from Ryan, a deep frown from Nolan and an unimpressed snuffle from Zinni.

"What?" Annie accepted the Jingle and Mingle cup from Ryan and glanced at Nolan. "Tell me that a twenty-foot Blue Ice cypress or Virginia pine wouldn't look spectacular in that corner?"

There was a certain chill to Nolan's stiff silence. Zinni licked the back of his hand.

"We could put those pretty velvet ribbons on it and too many ornaments to count," Kendall mused, warming to her vision. "Crystal snowflakes. And so many twinkling lights."

"Make it all silver, white and ice blue," Marla added.

Flora rose and joined Kendall. "A tree like that would make a statement."

Willow's mother knew a thing or two about making a statement. If Willow called a halt to the meeting, what kind of statement would that make?

"It will be like the stylish ones I always see in the magazines and stores," Kendall gushed. "Can we have more than one tree like that?"

"That's not a bad idea." Marla tapped her chin and turned in a slow circle. "There's more than enough room."

"Why do you need more than one tree?" Nolan

asked quietly. His gravelly voice scratched through the budding excitement.

"More trees mean more places for Santa to leave presents." Ryan plopped several marshmallows into his mouth. His gaze Kris Kringle bright.

Kendall laughed. "He's not wrong."

Big E chuckled. "Certainly, can't argue with that."

Except, Nolan looked as if he wanted to argue. A lot. Willow peered at him. Her cowboy looked as if he wanted to put his boot down and declare an end to the discussion. Even Zinni quieted and cuddled further into the crook of his arm as if not wanting to be included in his holiday freeze-out.

Marla snapped her fingers. "Let's decide on our theme. Then we can determine our need for one or more Christmas trees."

A theme. Willow lifted her eyebrows. She didn't disagree that the house could use some warmth and a hint of holiday spirit. But Nolan was not exactly exuding much cheer. Nor had he offered one small slice of encouragement since his arrival. She highly doubted decorating from the floor to rafters was anywhere on his wish list.

"Mrs. Claus's house." Kendall's eyebrows arched high into her forehead. Delight overtook her expression. "Only the super fancy and sophisticated version of Mrs. Claus's home."

"I like how you think." Flora dropped her arm over Kendall's shoulders and squeezed. "Glamorous glad tidings are what we will bring to every room."

Glamorous glad tidings. Willow sputtered from

the affection Flora freely gave Kendall and her mother's sudden holiday flair. Beside her, Nolan bristled.

"That's lovely." Marla sighed as if enchanted by their vision. "And absolutely perfect."

Gran Denny and Big E added their approval.

Zinni grunted, the sound part croak and part wheeze. Nolan adjusted his hold and rubbed a finger between the dog's trembling ears. Then he said flatly, "Zinni needs to go out."

With that, Nolan turned on his cowboy boots and took off. No one stopped him.

"There's still a lot to do." Marla clapped her hands, drawing everyone's attention back to her. "We need to divide and conquer. There is the foyer, kitchen and family room to decorate."

But what about her cowboy? What about what he wanted? Willow opened her mouth.

"Don't forget the sunroom," Kendall quickly added and pulled out her phone. "I'll start a task list and text it to everyone on the operation team."

Ryan tugged Annie closer to the couches and the others. The discussion picked up. Willow caught the phrases winter wonderland and silver bells. She glanced back toward the kitchen. No sign of Zinni or Nolan. Someone shouted mistletoe and earned a hearty "Hear! Hear!" from the others. Willow stepped back, away from the group.

Then Flora's voice, sharp and polished, rose above the others. "We can't have enough sparkle." Her mother's shrewd gaze collided with Willow's. "It works on Christmas trees and relationships. Remember that."

Flora did not believe that. Her mother had always told her: *Add as much sparkle to your costume as you dare, Willow. It won't ever blind you. But a cowboy, well, he will blind your heart with no more than a wink.*

But her cowboy never once winked. Not back then. Not now. And Willow seemed to be the only one seeing things clearly. The only one not dazzled by the debate over decking the halls or dancing with sugarplums. Although she discovered she had opinions about both.

Willow retreated before she jumped in and released her inner elf.

This was not her house. It wasn't her place. What would her cowboy think of her, then?

Frivolous. Easily distracted. After all, she had more important things to concentrate on. Like keeping her job. Meeting her sisters. Perfecting her performance. Securing that path to her dream role. The one that would lead to a perfect life. When she would finally be truly happy.

None of that happened by hanging hand-knitted stockings on the mantel and stringing up colorful lights. Willow blurted, "I have to go to work."

She turned, hurried through the kitchen and headed outside. But her car wasn't her destination. Rather, she sighted her cowboy and kept moving until she was beside him.

As if he was the only one who mattered. As if he was the start of all her dreams finally coming true.

CHAPTER EIGHT

OUTSIDE, NOLAN CONSIDERED the jarringly acoustic dog he held and turned away from the stables and the pond. The quirky dog would most likely spook the horses, same as it had Nolan. Or snort entirely too much pond water up its nose. He circled around the house and headed for the garden area, which had only ever been home to an array of cacti. But at least it was fenced and private. And given Nolan's prickly mood, the ideal place for him. He set Zinni on the gravel then turned at the sound of footsteps behind him.

"Everything okay out here?" Willow opened the iron gates and stepped through the arching arbor.

"Fine." If he excluded the part about the North Pole getting ready to explode in his living room. His inner grinch stepped fully forward. He didn't bother to check his frown. "Zinni needed air."

Willow followed the paver path that wound through the cactus garden and stopped within poking distance of him. "What was it you used to say to me after I had a fight with my mom or a bad training practice?"

Nolan remained quiet and watched a snuffling Zinni disappear beneath the wispy strands of a feather grass bush.

"I remember," Willow continued, seeming unperturbed by his surly silence. "You would say, 'Okay, cowgirl, I'm not leaving until you spill. Only choice you need to make is whether we'll be sitting or standing.'"

That was exactly what he used to tell her. When her expressive eyes had been filled with unshed tears and her bottom lip had quivered. Her exhales had come out in shaky bursts. And he had wanted nothing more than to steal her pain and make her happy again. His cowgirl's smile was all-encompassing, making him feel like he was standing under the full sun. He had always been drawn to that warmth and her. Quite simply, being around his cowgirl had always made him feel that much better.

But now grief shadowed him. A constant companion he wasn't certain even his cowgirl could outshine. Not that he was asking her to try. Nolan crossed his arms over his chest.

"What's it going to be, cowboy?" Willow set her hands on her hips and eyed him. "Are we sitting or standing?"

Nolan turned and followed Zinni deeper into the cactus garden and farther away from the house. Willow joined them, refusing to leave him alone. Same as he had done with her all those years ago. There would be no shaking her off. Same as she hadn't been able to shake him back then. Finally, he sighed. "I don't belong in there."

"That's your house," she countered.

"That's my dad's house," he corrected, then paused on the paver walkway and faced her. "It should be my dad decorating. My dad chairing the holiday house party brigade. My dad spearheading Christmas. Not me."

"Why not?" she pressed. "Don't you like Christmas?"

I like you. But you shouldn't like me. He was better with bulls than relationships. His ex-wife would verify that much. These days he put more stock in hard work and resilience. After all, love did not conquer all and often fell short. His hasty wedding and seemingly swifter divorce had taught him that much firsthand. *Consider yourself warned, cowgirl.*

Nolan tucked his chin and gathered his thoughts. "My dad *was* Christmas. He adored everything about the holidays. He would have wanted a dozen live Christmas trees, a pair of life-size nutcrackers, and Santa's sleigh with reindeers included."

"Annie has told me stories of your Christmas pasts." Willow's face and words softened, despite the chill in the wind blowing around them. She added, "I wish I had experienced a Christmas with your family."

"The holidays I spent here as a kid were magical. Thanks to my dad, Marla and Annie." But then Nolan had grown up. Distance and time had smudged those childhood memories and dulled that wonder. Now Nolan worried the joy he had once found in the season might be lost in the past.

Willow touched his arm. "Is this all too much?"

"Yes, but not in the way you think." Nolan picked up Zinni and crossed over to a different bunch of feather grass bushes and away from the spines on an overgrown prickly pear cactus that was in her sniffing path.

Willow remained beside him. She reached over and adjusted the collar on Zinni's sweater. Her touch was gentle. Yet her presence was undeniably soothing, making him second-guess his go-it-alone policy. Nolan set the dog down, glanced at Willow and confessed, "I am not my dad. I can't compete with him."

"No one expects you to," Willow said.

"My holiday style is slightly more subdued and far less magical," Nolan admitted. "That is sure to disappoint my family." But if he remained uninvolved in the holiday hubbub that would surely set their expectations and minimize any future letdowns. That was better for everyone, wasn't it? Nolan ground his teeth and swallowed around the sudden sour taste in his mouth.

The wind picked back up. Willow rubbed her hands together. "I think the only sure way to disappoint your family is to not participate at all."

Been there. Done that. He had avoided his family for the better part of the past year. If he was being honest, distance had not lessened his grief or his loneliness. Not at all. Still, he hedged. "I don't know."

"I'm not telling you to put on the Santa outfit and guide the sleigh." Willow tucked her hands underneath her crossed arms and turned her back toward the wind. "You don't have to sing the Christmas carols. You just need to enjoy the music."

What he enjoyed was time with her. But not when she was uncomfortable like she was now. He unsnapped his flannel-lined jacket, removed it and dropped it around her shoulders. He had the copper-colored suede buttoned up under her chin before she could protest. Satisfied, he stepped back. "Look. It's been a long time since I stopped to smell the roasted chestnuts or sip the spiked eggnog." *Or liked a cowgirl.*

"From the face you're making I'm going to guess you don't like eggnog very much," she said.

"Not even a little bit." Nolan scrunched his face even more. "I would rather muck out every horse stall in the county than drink eggnog." That confession drew out her laughter, full and carefree. The inviting sound was more delightful than Santa's hearty ho-ho-ho.

"I'm not an eggnog fan either." Willow slipped her arms into the sleeves of his jacket as if seeking more of his warmth.

That thought drew out his smile. Suddenly, lingering was all he wanted to do. Outside in a cold, overgrown cactus garden with her. He asked, "What is your holiday drink of choice?" *Because you could be my choice.*

"You know, I have absolutely no idea." Her dark eyebrows pinched together. More amusement colored her words. "What are my options?"

There was that laughter again, refreshing and captivating. He found himself hard-pressed to sit inside his own melancholy. Even the weight of his grief seemed impossibly lighter somehow. She had gifted him a reprieve. And selfish cowboy that he was, he wanted to stay right there. Where it was only him. Her. And a surprisingly endearing if not odd little dog. "Well, let's see. There's the tried-and-true hot chocolate. Hot apple cider. Mulled wine."

She lifted one shoulder. "All good and very appropriate seasonal drink selections."

"But I can see that I haven't inspired you." Nolan tapped his finger against his bottom lip and watched her.

Her gaze lowered to his mouth, held, then lifted back to his. Her brown eyes brightened in the early afternoon sunlight. "Not even a little bit."

His same words tossed back at him. He chuckled and dipped his chin in acknowledgment. "Okay. Challenge accepted." He nudged his cowboy hat higher on his forehead and eyed her. "I'll need an hour of your time this weekend."

"What for, exactly?" She studied him.

"To inspire you, of course." One corner of his mouth lifted.

"You've got my attention." There was a tiny, ever so faint, almost breathless catch in her words.

"That's a start." *But I want more than your attention. I want your heart.* Or he would have. If he was the kind of cowboy who could be trusted with things like a cowgirl's heart. And the kind of cowboy who trusted things like love. But he wasn't that kind of cowboy. Not anymore. Nolan frowned and turned toward the arbor gate. "Didn't you mention having to work today?"

"I need to leave soon or I'm going to be late." Willow nodded, but her gaze drifted back to the house. "What about you? Ready to head back inside and get your holiday on?"

Nolan picked up Zinni and tucked the tiny, grumbly dog against his chest. Then he held out his arm to his cowgirl. "I think we will walk you to your car and then decide."

Willow linked her arm around Nolan's free one. Her words were thoughtful. "Maybe it's not about being just like your dad, Nolan. But instead, maybe it's about doing things your own way."

Sounded simple enough on the surface. He had returned to figure things out after all. Yet all he kept running into was his own indecision. *Settle or sell. Retire or ride.* He said, "How about this? I will try not to be too much of a grinch."

"That's a good place to start." She chuckled.

He took in her grin and felt his own smile building. "Besides, it's one more thing that is all for the Marla cause."

Willow walked through the arbor arch. "What's the Marla cause?"

"Annie's term." Nolan closed the waist-high gate to the garden. "This is the happiest Marla has been since before my dad passed away."

Willow peered at him. "What's the other thing for the Marla cause?"

"You." Nolan paused and waited until she turned toward him. "And me."

Her mouth barely parted.

"You don't look all that surprised," he mused.

"Marla made a few references to my boyfriend in the pasture this morning." Willow reached up and secured behind her ear a piece of hair the wind had snatched.

"And you didn't correct her?" Nolan adjusted Zinni to keep from tucking Willow back into his side.

"You should have seen her face," Willow said, her expression earnest and sincere. "Marla was beyond thrilled."

"And you didn't want to ruin that," Nolan added. He knew a little something about that. "Same thing happened to me last night. Annie convinced me it was for the best not to say anything and upset Marla."

"But," Willow pressed.

"But I'm asking you to pretend to be my girlfriend." *While trying to ignore the part of me that wants to ditch the pretend part all together.* Definitely nothing he intended to entertain further. "And now your family is here, too."

"I didn't invite them." She huddled into his over-size jacket. Her mouth slipped into a frown. "But you should know my sisters are coming. Here. On Sunday."

"Okay," he said, noting that she looked anything but thrilled.

"My sisters actually intend to perform," she rushed on. "Can you believe that? Because I still can't. And now I'm going to impose on you even more." She dropped her hand over her face and groaned. "I should change the location. Stop imposing. I just wanted to be someplace where I feel comfortable. Someplace where I know there are people who will have my back. I need that. This is a lot. *A lot* a lot."

It meant a lot to know she was comfortable at his house. Now she needed to know she was not wrong. He reached up and peeled her hand away from her face. "You will meet your sisters here. And if you need me to be there, just say when."

"Thank you. And Nolan," she said, then adjusted her hold until their palms sealed together, and continued, "I'll be more than happy to be your fake girlfriend for as long as you need me."

And if we dropped the fake, would you be happy? Because I'm starting to think I might be. But the risks he took these days were found inside rodeo chutes, not in forgotten cactus gardens. Nolan released her hand and fussed with Zinni's sweater.

"I'm sorry I have to leave you alone with my family." Willow reached into her pocket and pulled out her keys. "You are going to be okay inside there without me, right?"

"Of course." He was usually okay. Yet with Willow he was better. He said, "But I'm not going inside. I'm going with you."

Uncertainty halted her words, turning them into a question. "You want to come with me to work?"

Nolan scratched his fingers through his beard and nodded. "You're my escape clause." It was brilliant really. He would get a bit more time with Willow and get out of the holiday decorating hubbub.

Willow touched her ear as if checking her hearing. Disbelief rang through her words. "You do realize I work in a department store, right?"

"I know where you work." Nolan smoothed his hand over his worn flannel shirt. "As it happens, I'm in need of new clothes. They have men's clothing there, don't they?"

"The entire second floor is dedicated to men's wear," Willow said.

"That's where I'll be, then," Nolan said, warming to the idea more and more.

"I'm working until close." Willow eyed him, her doubt still very much present. "That's nine o'clock."

"I won't be there that long." Nolan barely stopped himself from fumbling his words. "I'll text Annie to come and get me."

Willow pointed at the dog. "What about Zinni?"

"Sorry, little one." Nolan lifted the dog up to eye level. "You'll have to deal with the holiday rush on your own for a while." Zinni licked his nose.

He laughed. "I'll drop her in the mudroom. That's where I found her."

"I'll text Kendall to get Zinni." Willow took out her cell phone.

"Be right back." Nolan jogged up the porch steps, quickly deposited Zinni in the mudroom with a pat and a promise to return. Then he hurried out to the driveway and climbed into Willow's idling car.

"Buckle up, cowboy." Willow chuckled and drove down the driveway. "And get ready to shop 'til you drop."

Funny thing. The shopping didn't scare him. The realization that set him back was that he was ready to be anywhere if it was with his cowgirl.

Thirty minutes later, their debate over the best Christmas movie still unresolved, Willow escorted Nolan to the second floor of Highstreet Treasures. In the men's section, she selected several dress shirts and pants for him to consider. Then she left him in what she claimed were the very capable hands of the debonair-looking sales associate, Arthur Cade. Who quickly proved himself to be that and more when Nolan's escape clause suddenly became a family affair.

One minute Nolan was listening to Arthur detail the value of a well-fitted sports coat and the next Nolan was surrounded by his kin.

Arthur was quick with handshake welcomes for Marla and Annie, then a compliment for Kendall's exquisitely understated holiday attire. Because as

Arthur stated, his salt-and-pepper eyebrows arched slightly, less was often more.

Marla swiftly brought Arthur up to speed on the open house dress code and what Nolan needed. While Annie kindly pointed out that they were there to ensure Nolan made the correct clothing choices.

"Well, then." Arthur sorted through a rack of what he called micro-suede sports coats. He removed a camel-colored one and held it up in front of Nolan. "If we intend to impress Willow, we are going to need to kick this up a notch."

Marla held up a navy pinstriped dress shirt that Arthur shook his head at. Annie lifted a white herringbone dress shirt and earned the sales associate's nod of approval. When Kendall asked how she could help, Arthur sent her on a search for jeans the color of deep denim, which would look both crisp and chic. When Nolan mentioned denim was denim and jeans were jeans, he earned deeply disapproving frowns from the entire group. From then on, he kept his commentary on Silent.

It wasn't much longer before Arthur led Nolan into a dressing room with possibly more clothes to try on than Nolan actually owned. He rubbed his forehead. "You want me to put all of this on?"

"Absolutely." Arthur tugged the cuffs of what Nolan learned was an ocean blue paisley-print dress shirt with double French cuffs. He eyed Nolan. "You want Willow to look at you and know that you are playing for keeps, don't you?"

Nolan wasn't quite sure what he wanted. Other than to perhaps escape his own escape clause. He nodded because it seemed the response Arthur expected. And the older gentleman had been nothing but patient and helpful. Yet Nolan couldn't resist asking, "You're sure my outfit is going to say all that?"

"The right one will." Arthur laughed. "And we won't know the right one until you try every shirt, pant and coat on. Better get started."

It turned out to be less excruciating than Nolan expected. Mostly because everyone had opinions, and no one was shy about sharing them. Two other sales associates and several browsing customers even stopped to offer their own thoughts when Nolan stepped out of the dressing room. He learned all jeans were not the same. Cut and fit mattered. And when it came to dress shirt prints, his preference tended to lean toward the less-is-more style. All in, he cashed out with more than one outfit. And Arthur declared Nolan now had the appropriate attire for a casual date night, an evening of fine dining, and to be the best-dressed guest at a wedding.

The shopping experience transitioned from the men's department to the women's dress section. Where Nolan plopped on the couch outside of the fitting room and offered his opinion on Annie's selections. Arthur even lingered to provide options and give feedback.

Finally, Annie found a dress that made Nolan

wonder if his sister was also playing for keeps, given she chose a color that was curiously the same as the one Ryan had declared his favorite that very morning. Nolan couldn't deny he was starting to look forward to the party Saturday night.

Downstairs, Willow helped Annie pick out the correct shade of tinted lip gloss for her skin tone. Willow glanced at him. "Well, you going to show me what you bought?"

Nolan shook his head. "I just got some new clothes."

"More like an entirely new wardrobe." Annie dabbed lip gloss on her mouth and laughed.

"You must have something special planned if you needed a new wardrobe," Willow said, her words light and casual.

It wasn't something, but rather someone who was special. Yet Nolan was not sure what he planned. And playing for keeps just might require more than he was willing to give. After all, his heart had never been up for grabs. He waited for Willow to finish Annie's purchase, then said, "It's not a big deal. Just time for an upgrade."

"Looks like your time with me is up." Willow tipped her head and grinned. "You two have been spotted."

"So much for giving them the slip," Annie mumbled.

Nolan turned in the makeup chair to see Marla and Kendall making a beeline for them, their expressions determined.

Kendall reached them first. "Our next stop is the arts and crafts store. Flora, Big E and Denny are already there waiting for us."

Just like that, Nolan found his urge to shop fading. He shook his head.

Annie tugged on her ponytail and blurted, "We can't."

Nolan slanted his gaze toward his sister.

Kendall propped her hands on her hips. "But we need to decide on tinsel color. Select the ribbon. Pick out ornaments. Then there's garland for the mantel. Candles."

"We need holiday napkins, utensils and plates." Marla ticked things off on her fingers. "Also, I was thinking holly-print napkins for the guest bathroom and scented soap. Perhaps a homemade potpourri."

Nolan's eyes crossed. He was officially shopped out. A gentle hand landed on his shoulder. Willow said, "Annie, Nolan and I were just discussing shoe options for their new outfits."

His cowgirl's words were music to his ears. Nolan reached up, covered her hand with his and squeezed her fingers. A silent thank-you for the rescue. He said, "I could use new dress boots. There's a place not two stores down." That was a guess on his part, but it sounded reasonable. They were in the shopping district after all.

"I could use new heels. Obviously." Annie jumped in and yanked on Nolan's arm. "So, we're going to head to the shoe department now and let Willow get back to work before she gets in trouble. I see her manager looming."

Nolan caught sight of an impeccably dressed woman watching them with a critical eye. He gathered his packages and smiled. "Good luck at the craft store. We'll see you back at home."

With that, Annie and he made their way to the shoe department. Five minutes later, Annie whispered, "Coast is clear. They are gone."

They returned to Willow's makeup counter and thanked her for the out.

"Aren't you getting shoes?" Willow asked.

"No way. We are getting food." Annie touched her stomach. "I'm starving from all this shopping. Besides, we wear the same size shoe, so I figured you would have a pair I could borrow."

"Of course, you can." Willow chuckled and considered Nolan. "Sorry, cowboy, I don't have anything that would suit you."

She suited him just fine. He leaned on the counter. "I've got the dress boots covered. Now, what can we get you so you have something to eat later when you take your break?"

"Don't go to any trouble for me," Willow said. "I'll be fine."

"I owe you for the double escape clause," Nolan countered. "What's it going to be? Calorie counter or calorie buster?"

Her eyes widened. "You remember that?"

He nodded. *I remember that and so much more.*

"What's a calorie buster?" Annie asked.

Nolan held Willow's gaze. They answered at the same time, "Deep-dish meat lovers with double cheese." His cowgirl's favorite pizza.

"Sounds good." Annie leaned on the counter. "So, what's a calorie counter?"

"Cauliflower thin crust with veggies," Willow answered.

"Which is surprisingly not bad when the veggies are grilled," Nolan said. "And if you finish it off with a slice of pecan pie." Another one of her favorites.

"With double whipped cream and two forks," she added, her smile edged into that shared-secret territory.

"Well, what's it going to be?" Nolan asked.

"Surprise me," Willow said.

"Good choice." Nolan nodded and tipped his hat at Willow. "We'll be back."

Annie and Nolan left in search of pizza for his cowgirl. Only the surprise was on him. Because suddenly, playing for keeps seemed like the only choice he wanted to make.

CHAPTER NINE

IT WAS LUNCHTIME the following day—a mere twenty-four hours later—and Nolan would have sworn he was caught in some sort of time loop. There he was, once again standing on the back porch of his house. Once again holding the ever-vocal Zinni, who was *once again* outfitted in her doggy holiday attire. Only today's fuzzy sweater was snowy white with a snowman's face on the back, complete with charcoal eyes and smile and a bright orange carrot nose. And inside the house, Operation Get-Your-Holiday-On was well under way.

A familiar car pulled in and parked. Nolan detoured from the path leading to the cactus garden and headed for the driveway instead. *Nice timing, cowgirl.* He smiled wider when Willow exited the car, set the strap of a duffel bag on her shoulder and grabbed a hatbox from her back seat. That she was staying for the weekend improved his mood like nothing else could.

Not that he was going to let himself get carried away. Unlike yesterday, he was very clear on what was and what wasn't between him and his cowgirl.

What it *was* was only a polite invitation to a friend to stay at his place temporarily.

What it wasn't was something other than pretend.

Zinni yapped out a greeting and wiggled her body until Nolan set her down. The dog sprinted over to Willow, yearning a cheerful greeting and compliments on her jolly fine sweater.

Nolan tapped his cowboy hat higher on his head, better to take in the glow on Willow's cheeks and her brilliant smile. "I thought you were working today."

"Just came from there." She dropped the hatbox and duffel on her trunk. Her enthusiasm was undeniable in her rapid speech and animated movements. "We did the makeup for the entire dance company from a local performing arts school. Each performer was allowed to bring one family member for a makeover." Willow tugged her cell phone from her purse and rattled on, "Their sold-out matinee performance of *The Nutcracker* will be this afternoon, followed by a fundraiser gala this evening."

"Sounds like it was a busy morning." Nolan moved closer to her, curious if he might catch even a spark of her excitement.

"It was chaotic and loud." Willow laughed and tapped on her phone screen. "Here. Look at Mia. She's only six and the youngest snowflake dancing this year. Mia wanted her mom to sparkle like she was. So, I did that. Her mom and I called it an age-appropriate dazzle. I was really just enhancing the beauty that is already there. Her daughter

was so precious. In fact, the entire cast was, really."
Willow stopped to draw a breath yet continued to
scroll through another dozen pictures of the dance
company. Finally, she paused as if catching herself.
"Anyway, you probably didn't want to see all these.
But that was my morning."

Nolan touched her phone screen and swiped back
two photographs, stopping at the one with Willow
surrounded by half a dozen teenagers and their
moms. The entire group dazzled, each one smiling brighter than the next. Yet the sheer joy in his
cowgirl captivated him. He grinned. "Well, it might
have been chaotic and loud, but it looks like you
enjoyed every minute of it."

"So much." Willow clutched her phone. Her excitement never dimmed. "There's an energy and
vibe working backstage with the actors and per-
formers in theater productions. I can't explain it."

"You're a part of something that you are passionate about," he said.

"Exactly." Willow tucked her phone away. "And
I feel like I make a difference. At least I hope I do.
I hope Mia's mom and all the moms there look in
the mirror today and feel confident and beautiful
from the inside out."

His cowgirl, who was stunning in her own right,
found more joy in helping others find their own
unique brand of beautiful. She was pretty and in-
spiring. And he was slightly in awe of her.

Zinni circled around Willow's knee-high, camel
suede boots and scratched her paws on Willow's

leg. Scooping Zinni up into her arms, Willow laughed and considered Nolan. "This feels remarkably like where we left off yesterday."

"You're not entirely wrong." Only today his cowgirl had on a simple white T-shirt, oversize plaid coat and skinny jeans. She looked fashionably casual and not the least bit cold unlike yesterday. Giving him no reason to fuss over her. He stuck his hands in his jean pockets. "The house party frenzy is happening all over again inside. Ryan and I came back from fixing fences to grab a bite to eat. Only Zinni wanted an escape first."

Willow considered the back door but didn't move toward the porch. "Should I go in?"

"I wouldn't recommend it." Nolan rubbed his chin. "Unless you're prepared to be part of the supercharged Operation Get-Your-Holiday-On."

"What's the plan, then?"

"Make a run for it," Nolan teased. "Come back after the weekend is over?"

"There's no holiday spirit in missing all the festivities." Willow chuckled. "Besides, we would upset Marla if we skipped out entirely, and that's the last thing we want to do."

"Good point." Nolan sighed and started back toward the house. "But I'm warning you. It's over-the-top in there. Like next level. I don't know where it's all going to go. But they assured me it would all come together."

Suddenly Zinni sneezed a sort of growl wheeze. Her tiny body quivered in Willow's arms.

Seconds later, the porch door slammed open, Annie spilled out, followed quickly by Ryan. Annie's shout filled the air before the pair waved and hurried over to them.

Annie greeted Willow with a quick hug, then tossed something at Nolan. "Here. Catch."

Nolan caught his keys midair. "What are these for?"

"You're driving us. You have the largest truck bed." Annie tugged a beanie from her jacket pocket and covered her head. "We need to get a move on or we will be chopping down Christmas trees in the dark."

Zinni grumbled. Nolan curled his fingers around his keys. "What?"

"We've been nominated for tree duty," Ryan explained and rubbed his hands together. Laughter shook his shoulders. "Annie and I escaped when they finally settled on three live trees."

"We were afraid they'd keep adding more." Annie chuckled and shook her head. "It was becoming a bit of a tree rush in there. Flocked or not flocked. Ten feet or twelve feet or taller. Colored lights or clear ones."

Nolan's gaze collided with Willow's. "Told you we should have made a run for it."

"This could be fun." Willow passed him Zinni, opened her passenger door, then set her duffel and hatbox back inside her car. Her strikingly expressive eyes gave away her delight. "I've never cut down a Christmas tree before. We can do this together."

Together. That was the part he most definitely should not be warming up to.

This *was* a fake relationship.

Fake *was not* the beginning of something more.

It *was* strictly for the Marla cause.

After all, his heart *was not* a cause he intended to pick up. Yet he muted his inner grinch, set his hand on Willow's lower back and guided her toward his truck. Then said, "Chopping down three trees is less work than a dozen."

"Wow, that's incredibly positive," Willow said, her eyes sparkling. "You almost managed to sound cheerful about chopping."

"That's me." Nolan snuggled the tiny dog against his neck. "Positively cheerful. Just like Zinni."

"I don't know what is going on with you, brother." Annie circled her finger in front of Nolan. "But I'm not chasing that postage stamp of a dog through the tree farm."

Zinni snorted. Nolan chuckled. "I will drop Zinni back inside, then we can leave."

"You cannot go back in the house." Annie grabbed his arm and tugged him away from the back porch. "If they see you, they will undoubtedly add more to our already too-full task lists."

"We have task lists?" Surprise worked across Willow's face.

"Check your text messages." Ryan took his cell phone from his jacket pocket and waved it at them. "At this rate, we won't be going to sleep until well after midnight tonight."

"What about Zinni?" Nolan asked.

"She's coming with us," Annie stated and frowned at the dog. "But I mean it. I'm not chasing after her."

"I'll text my mom and let her know we are taking Zinni on our tree farm field trip." Willow typed rapidly on her phone, then grinned. "Mom gave my text a thumbs-up. She claims Zinni will have more fun there than at the craft store with them."

Nolan transferred the dog back to Willow. "You're on dog duty while I drive."

"Time to get on the road." Annie spun around and headed for Nolan's truck.

"Willow." Ryan adjusted his cowboy hat as if he wanted to see Willow better. "Did I hear you correctly just now? Have you really not ever had a fresh-cut Christmas tree?"

Willow shook her head.

"As your best friend, I should have known that." Exasperation filled Annie's face. "I would have gotten you one last year or the year before that."

"I wasn't here," Willow reminded Annie, then she glanced at Nolan. "It's not a big deal. We didn't really have Christmas trees growing up. Not live ones or artificial ones."

His cowgirl might as well have admitted she had never sipped hot chocolate.

Annie gasped. Ryan gaped. Even Zinni whined as if in sympathy of all those lost Christmas memories.

Nolan rubbed a hand under his chin and considered her. "You're serious."

Willow fiddled with Zinni's collar and avoided looking at him. Her nod was a mere dip of her chin.

How had he not known that? His inner grinch was grumbling for a whole new reason now.

"You know we traveled and performed a lot growing up, including every holiday season," Willow explained. Her hand fluttered around in front of her. "A tree would have been too much to deal with along with everything else on the road."

Nolan set his hands on his hips, unmoved and unconvinced. She had been just a kid. Surely there was room enough for one of those artificial tabletop trees or a small potted spruce.

"There wasn't a whole lot of extra time between our performances and our practices." Willow chewed the lip gloss off her bottom lip and lifted one shoulder.

Nolan knew that tell. That was his cowgirl trying to nudge that wall up and hide behind it. She was uncomfortable and did not want anyone to know it. Too late. He was on to her.

Willow added, "It was important for our act that we stay focused."

Translation: there was no time for fun. No time for experiencing the joy of the holiday. Nolan's eyebrows hitched into his forehead. Marla and his dad had gone all out during the holiday to ensure Annie and Nolan had more fun than they could imagine. *Thank you, Dad.*

"I should point out that Willow doesn't have a tree at her place now either." Annie snapped her fingers, then tapped her wrist. "But we can change that in less than an hour."

Ryan grinned. "Looks like we have four trees to find."

"There isn't really space at my place," Willow argued. "I live in a studio apartment."

But there was a wish for the space. The tree. The holiday trappings. The fun. Nolan heard that in her wistful words. Saw it in the hope swirling in her deep brown eyes. He wanted to pull his cowgirl into his arms and promise to make every Christmas wish—past and present—come true.

Just like that he was back to those promises he had no business considering. Back to forgetting that his cowgirl was not his. Not his to take care of. Look after. Fuss over. She was simply not *his*.

But if she was… Nolan crushed that thought under his bootheel and hustled toward his truck.

"Don't feel too bad, Willow," Annie said, her frown in place again as she opened the back door. "My own brother hasn't decorated for Christmas in years, either."

"Is that true?" Willow asked.

"No time or space," he said simply, then opened the front passenger door for Willow.

But he was suddenly thinking he could make both the time and the space for a cowgirl like Willow. And not just for the holiday season. And if that wasn't the makings of a Christmas fail, he wasn't sure what was.

CHAPTER TEN

INSIDE NOLAN'S TRUCK, Willow buckled her seat belt, then waited for Zinni to make herself comfortable and the others to get situated. Nolan had the truck started and headed down the driveway when Willow stated, "For the record, I would like to say that my sisters and I did holiday things growing up."

Also, for the record, Willow understood that her relationship with Nolan was fake and orchestrated for Marla's happiness. That Willow had been slightly disappointed after Nolan skipped from wanting to take her on an actual date to instead being her fake boyfriend was a hiccup to be dealt with later. Right now, the idea of picking out a Christmas tree with her cowboy thrilled her. Albeit secretly. After all, she also understood that fake couples did not start holiday traditions together.

"Well, don't leave us all in suspense." Nolan pulled up to a stoplight and glanced at her. His cowboy hat shadowed his gaze. "How did the Blackwell Belles celebrate Christmas?"

The playfulness in his one-sided grin, even hidden mostly inside his beard, distracted her. Taking

CARI LYNN WEBB 161

her right back to those things she did not understand. Like how her cowboy fascinated her and so effortlessly, too. Zinni nudged her wet nose under Willow's palm, keeping Willow from imagining her cowboy without his beard. She petted the dog and said, "Our dad always took us to visit Santa in whatever town we were in. My sisters and I always exchanged presents. And I even ate fruitcake on more than one occasion."

"Why would you do that?" Annie popped her head between the front seats. "Fruitcake is one and done."

"She's not wrong," Nolan added.

"My oldest sister, J.R., convinced me that the only way to prove I wasn't a little girl anymore was if my taste buds were refined. And the only way to tell that was to eat fruitcake," Willow said, unable to keep the amusement from her words. "I wanted to prove I could be every bit as grown up and refined as my older sisters."

Nolan nodded. "So you had a slice of fruitcake."

"Slice." Willow's laughter spilled out unchecked. "I ate the whole fruitcake that year. I refused to let anyone have even a taste." She sobered and shook her head. Yet the joy from the memory lingered. "My mother was horrified, but my sisters were impressed." And for Willow, earning her older sisters' approval and being considered one of them had been the only thing that mattered.

"Wow." Annie patted Willow's shoulder and eased back onto the bench seat. "You just might be the only person I know who actually likes fruit-cake."

"I never said I liked it." She had been desperate. She hadn't wanted to hear she was too little. Even more, she had wanted to hang out with her older sisters. Willow chuckled. "But I did eat it every Christmas after that."

"What about now?" Nolan asked.

"I haven't had a bite in years," Willow said.

"Lost your taste for it," Annie mused. "I'm not surprised."

More like she'd lost her sisters. She would have eaten fruitcake for a year if it might have mended the rift and brought her family back together again. Perhaps it wasn't a bad idea to serve one on Sunday when her sisters arrived. For old times' sake. If she ended up eating it alone, well, she would lean back into her good childhood memories.

Her phone chimed. Then alerts sounded on the other phones in the truck. And Willow was back in the moment.

"That's the Operation Get-Your-Holiday-On group chat," Annie said. "It seems they need you guys to text your theme for the sunroom to the group ASAP."

"Theme?" Willow eased her phone from her purse and tried not to disturb Zinni.

"What about the sunroom?" Nolan kept his focus on the road.

"You and Willow have to decorate the sunroom for the party." Ryan leaned forward and tapped his fist lightly against Nolan's shoulder. "Annie and I got the foyer."

"You can't have winter wonderland. I just claimed it." Annie finished typing on her phone, then glanced up. "Except we're calling it Mrs. Claus's winter wishes."

"Nice." Ryan scratched his cheek, seemingly un-bothered by tree chopping and themed decor. "I think we go for a heavy flock on the tree and call it snow."

"You totally read my mind." Annie's smile blossomed. She lifted her hand to high-five Ryan. "Flocking is totally something Mrs. Claus would do." Soon enough, the backseat duo was absorbed in designing their winter wishes foyer.

"Speaking of things Mrs. Claus would do." Willow hit Send on her text to the group, dropped her phone in the cup holder and slanted her gaze toward Nolan. "You weren't far off the mark yesterday. Marla is literally in the store right now searching for a pair of six-foot-tall nutcrackers for your front porch."

"Marla was always Mrs. Claus to my dad's Mr. Claus," Nolan said, his expression pensive. "They were a perfect match."

We could be a match, cowboy. Yet her handsome, brooding cowboy deserved to have a fairy-tale kind of love story. Though nothing about Willow's life right now was fairy-tale material. It could be when she nailed her performance at the Hall of Fame ceremony. Got the introduction. Got cast in the big new production. Finally proved herself. Definitely too soon to write her fairy tale.

But when she did finally become someone, perhaps then, she would be a perfect match for her cowboy. Perhaps then she would finally be able to follow her heart.

If she wasn't too late.

If her cowboy's heart was even still available to catch.

That sobering thought made her stomach flip.

Yet there was no storybook love without a perfect life. And no perfect life without the perfect career. Those were love's conditions. If she wanted something like lasting love, she had to be something more. Someone more. Someone perfect. Nothing less would do.

Flora and her family had taught her that lesson. Had Willow performed flawlessly that last time in Houston, her family would still be intact. But that wasn't the story. And Willow had work to do.

She swept her hair into a neat ponytail and set herself to rights. *Best face forward, Willow. Never give anyone a reason to think you don't have things perfectly well in hand.* In an upbeat tone, she said, "Unfortunately, my suggestion of a grinchy-themed sunroom was not well-received in the group chat just now."

"That is unfortunate." Nolan's smile was small and quick. "I could have come up with some good ideas."

Zinni stood up on Willow's lap, arched her back,

then jumped on the console. One more hop and she landed on Nolan's leg. Two full turns, Zinni was tucked into a tiny ball on his lap. Nolan didn't shoo the dog away. Rather he fussed over Zinni's silly dog sweater and ensured the grumpy dog's comfort. Lucky pup.

When her cowboy fussed over her, Willow felt special, too. Cared for. That was only her heart getting ahead of herself. After all, love's conditions were far from being met. Willow shut down her heart. It had no place in a fake relationship anyway.

She slipped her lip gloss from her pocket and swiped it half-heartedly across her mouth. To finish off her best face forward. Because some habits seemed impossible to break.

Finally, the sign for Tree Trails Christmas Farm came into view.

Nolan pulled into the parking lot and cut the engine. "Ready to go find some holiday fun?"

With you. "More than ready." Willow tossed her lip gloss into her purse and reached for the door handle.

Annie and Ryan jumped out. The pair promised to meet up later to choose the family room tree, then set off to find an eastern red cedar evergreen for the foyer.

"I'll get the tools." Nolan met Willow at the entrance and transferred the dog back to her. "Feel free to start checking out trees. I shouldn't be long." He headed for the barn, which had a vintage-looking sign that read Tool Shed.

"I won't go far." No sooner had those words come out than Zinni yapped excessively and wiggled herself free from Willow's hold. Zinni's paws hit the dirt and she took off after a squirrel twice her size. Willow gave chase, following the mismatched duo in a zigzag route that took them deeper and deeper into the tree farm.

Ten minutes and what felt like a marathon run later, Willow was out of breath and wedged several feet off the ground inside a plump and exceedingly tall evergreen tree.

Nolan finally caught up to her and called out, "Coming down or going up?"

"Up." Willow scaled another branch and caught sight of a familiar snowman-white sweater. "I can see Zinni."

"Anything I can do?" Nolan asked.

"Find a leash," Willow replied and watched Zinni scratch her way up onto another branch.

"I'll get right on that," Nolan offered, his voice dry.

The tiny dog continued to scale the tree, proving to be nimbler and swifter than most cats. Willow tugged the end of her long plaid jacket off a branch then steadied herself, wishing again she wore gloves. Voices blended into hushed tones below her. Willow tried to see the ground between the thick limbs. "Everything okay down there?"

"A mom needs my help at her tree a couple trails over." There was an urgency to Nolan's words.

"Go ahead." Willow stared up at a panting Zinni perched above her head. "I got this."

"I don't want to leave you," Nolan countered.

"Zinni and I are fine," Willow insisted. Or they would be when they were both safely on the ground.

"But," Nolan said.

"You know where Zinni and I are." Willow stretched her arm out and up, only to connect with a sap-covered branch. She rubbed her palm on her jeans, but that only covered her in more sap. "Help the family, Nolan. We will either be up here or down there."

"I'll be right back," Nolan called out. "Don't fall while I'm gone."

"When have you known me to be clumsy?" Exasperation filled her words as the sap seemed to be spreading like spilled glue all over her skin and clothes. "Get going, Nolan. I need to concentrate."

There was a rustling sound below her. Then Nolan's deep voice tinged with concern. "Just be careful, please. Your boots were made for dancing, not tree climbing."

With that, her cowboy grinch was off spreading his kind of joy. As for Zinni, the dog licked its face one last time, huffed and scrambled onto another branch. Willow blew out a breath and swiftly pulled herself up.

Unfortunately, it was face-first into a massive cobweb. The sticky dense strands tangled in her eyelashes and sealed against her cheeks and nose. Willow immediately swiped at her face. Lost her grip. And tumbled backward. Her squeal sounded curiously like one of Zinni's off-key yaps.

Too soon, her backside thudded against the ground. Yet one quick glance upward revealed her tree climbing feat was less than impressive. From the dent in the branches, she had barely cleared a quarter of the way up. Pathetic showing, really. And to be taken out by a cobweb.

Willow scanned her surroundings. No witnesses to her tree climbing flop. She sprawled backward and laughed.

Bootsteps thudded across the trail. Then came Nolan's low, rumbling voice. "Willow."

She dropped her arm over her face just before he reached her and said, "Okay. I'm ready."

"For what?" came his curt response.

"For you to tell me I told you so," Willow muttered.

"First you need to tell me you are fine," he said. "And that I don't need to chase down a doctor."

"You sound worried." Willow lifted her arm and peered at him.

He stood over her. Hands on his hips. Exasperation on his face. "Of course, I am." He motioned toward her. "Don't think I'm going to let you use falling out of a tree as an excuse to get out of the holiday party." His head shook slowly back and forth. "I am not going alone. Got it?"

What she did not get was that he wasn't criticizing her for being careless. Or unfocused. Or any number of other things.

"I'm waiting," he said, sounding frustrated.

Whatever else he was, he was concerned. About her. And unapologetic about it, too. He would probably carry her out of there if she told him she was hurt. Tempting thought. *Walk it off, Willow. And for goodness' sake, correct your focus.* Right. This was pretend, remember?

Encouraging actual feelings and giving in to those sighs building in her chest went against all the rules of a fake relationship. Willow pushed herself up and brushed her hands together. "I'm fine."

He rubbed his forehead, the motion dislodging his cowboy hat. "Are you sure?"

"Well, my pride took a bit of a hit," she admitted.

"What happened?" He studied the tree.

"Cobweb encounter," she replied.

He glanced down at her. A smile worked across his mouth. "You always hated spiders."

"Still do." Willow plucked a cobweb strand from her hair and wiped it on her sap and dirt-covered jacket sleeve. "Don't let me hold you back. Zinni is still up there, waiting to be rescued."

Nolan widened his stance. "Can't we just call for her?"

"I tried that first," Willow said, her words flat, yet her curiosity slipped out. "You aren't still afraid of spiders, are you?"

"I'm not afraid," he countered. "You and I just share a similar dislike for eight-legged hairy creatures. Did you encounter any live ones up there?"

"I didn't hang around long enough to find out." She kept her expression pleasant and encouraging.

Nolan sighed, slipped off his cowboy hat and handed it to Willow. He tugged a pair of work gloves from the back pocket in his jeans and yanked them on. "Why couldn't Zinni have chosen one of the shorter trees up front? We could have shaken her out by now."

"Where's the challenge in that?" Willow prodded.

Nolan flung his gloved hand toward Zinni's hiding spot. "This tree is easily over thirty feet."

"I'd say it's over forty feet actually." She tilted her head and considered the towering cypress. "I seem to recall you never could resist a challenge."

Nolan eyed her. "I prefer to take those on in the arena these days."

"I find it's good to branch out on occasion." She grinned at him.

"Is that so?" he said mildly.

But his steely gray gaze locked on her as if she could be his next challenge. Willow's pulse picked up. Her cowboy certainly had a way of looking at her. No denying she felt it from her heart to her toes. Not that she would be letting him know that he got to her.

Willow propped his cowboy hat on her head and braced her arms on her raised knees. Grateful her words sounded playful not breathless. "I'll be right here. Just holler if you need anything. Bug spray or whatever."

Nolan made his way toward the wide tree trunk. Minutes later, the bottom branches swayed as he disappeared inside the evergreen. Willow called out, "All good?"

"Fine," came his reply. The next section of branches shimmied, marking his progress.

Her cowboy had some climbing skills. No surprise there. Her cowboy had always been athletic and talented. She hollered, "Watch out for those cobwebs."

"Lucky for me you seem to have cleared those out," he called back.

The branches swayed again. Willow asked, "Can you see Zinni?"

"I think I see a pair of brown eyes," he said.

Seconds later a muffled curse was tossed out. Then the tree listed to the side precariously. And her cowboy popped out into the air as if the evergreen had spit him out. He landed the same as Willow. With a distinct thud. On his backside. Feet away from her. Only he didn't move.

"Nolan." Willow scrambled over to him, ignoring the twinge in her left knee. "You okay, cowboy?" She trailed her hands over his ribs, searching for an injury.

His chest heaved. Then his laughter came out on a deep belly rumble.

Willow poked him between the ribs. "You could've said you were fine."

"I'm fine." He snatched her hand and grinned at her. "I'm also ticklish."

She wasn't supposed to find that charming. Oh, but she did. And now it seemed she was gathering the heart kind of trouble faster than Santa delivered presents. Willow tugged her hand free. "What happened? Spider get you?"

"Squirrel." Nolan stacked his hands behind his head, seeming content to remain stretched out on the trail.

"What?" Willow studied the cypress.

"The squirrel dive-bombed me," Nolan said, his expression bland. But there was amusement in his words. "I can't make that up."

"Zinni made a friend." Willow swiped the hair off her face. "Maybe the squirrel was trying to protect Zinni from you."

"The squirrel is probably confused about what Zinni is," Nolan said.

Willow poked him again and earned another laugh. "That's not nice."

"But it's true," Nolan argued. "I wasn't even sure Zinni was a dog when I first saw her."

"Neither was I." Willow chuckled. "I can't imagine what my mom saw in her the first time."

"I don't know," Nolan mused. "She kind of grows on you, though."

Willow knew a little something about that. Being with her cowboy was growing on her. If she wasn't careful, moments like this one could be something she wanted more of. Her cowboy could be someone she got used to having around. But getting attached led to only one place: a whole bunch of hurt.

Willow steered clear of that these days. She gave him his hat and tucked her hands in her lap. "What now? My mom will want her dog back."

"We could see who comes out of the tree first," Nolan suggested. "Capture it and take that back to your mom."

Willow arched an eyebrow. "I'm sure she would notice if we handed her a squirrel instead of a dog."

"We could chop this tree down and take it home." Nolan rubbed his chin. "They wanted the tree to make a statement. Can't deny this one does exactly that."

"Be serious." Willow stood, noted the protest in her left knee and swiftly adjusted her balance to her right leg before her cowboy noticed. Then she held her arm out.

"I am serious." Nolan gripped her hand and accepted her assistance.

He let Willow pull him right into her personal space as if that was exactly where he wanted to be. Now she was one tug away from a cowboy collision. And there went her pulse again. The beat rapid. Willow held herself still.

His grin came slow as if he read her thoughts. The glint in his steely eyes was persuasive. "Imagine everyone's faces when we brought this tree home. No one would question our Christmas spirit then."

"True," Willow nodded, then promptly shook her head. "No." *I am not beguiled by you, cowboy.* Her words rushed out on her exhale. "We are not cutting down this beautiful tree to prove we have Christmas spirit."

Nolan sighed. "If you're sure."

"I am." *I'm sure my heart is not caught up.* But it was close. Willow released his hand.

"Fine." He tapped the dust and dirt off his boots. "Wait here in case the squirrel spooks Zinni and shakes her loose for us."

"Where are you going?" Not that she couldn't handle things on her own. Willow jammed her hands in the pockets of her knee-length plaid jacket.

"To gather reinforcements. Shouldn't take long." Nolan reached up and skimmed his fingers over her hair. "You look like you're wearing a Christmas tree."

At least she wasn't wearing her heart on her sleeve. Small win there. Willow knocked his hand away lightly. "You look the same."

"But I doubt I look half as charming." That grin flashed before he walked away.

And Willow's sigh was out before she could catch it.

She kept an eye on the cypress. Neither the squirrel nor Zinni made an appearance.

But her cowboy returned. A redheaded boy was propped on his shoulders. An older boy with curly blond hair walked beside him and chatted nonstop. Willow couldn't look away. Her cowboy seemed comfortable and totally at ease. As if he always spent time around little kids.

Willow joined them and introduced herself to the

woman juggling a cherry-cheeked toddler. Claire Maddin had a warm handshake and an even friendlier smile.

"Willow, I'd like you to meet my reinforcements." Nolan lowered the red-haired boy onto the ground, then set his hand on the blond-haired boy's shoulder and added, "This is Aidan and his younger brother, Owen."

Nolan, Aidan and Owen all wore matching grins, equal parts mischievous and lighthearted. And full daredevil.

Willow tried to look stern. "You can't seriously think to send these boys up into that tree after Zinni."

"That's exactly what we intend." Nolan scratched his fingers through his beard. "They are smaller. Less likely to spook the squirrel or Zinni."

Willow shook her head.

"But Ms. Willow, we climb trees all the time," Aidan said, pride lifting his chin a notch higher. "Bigger ones than this one even."

"Besides, we just climbed a tree over there." Owen flung his arm toward the trail.

Their mother chuckled. "That's what we needed Nolan for earlier."

Owen thumped his chest. "I climbed higher than my brother." He paused and his face scrunched. "Then a branch got me stuck. And Mom couldn't get me on account of my baby brother."

"Mom was afraid Charlie would get into something." Aidan rubbed his hand under his nose. "He's always getting into some sort of scrape. Least that's what my mom always says. Right, Mom?"

Claire smiled, but the edges of her smile were strained. "We don't have a big house or big yard and yet my children constantly find things to get into."

"Mostly we used to get into things across the street. We put forts in the super big trees, even though mom said it was too high." Aidan frowned. "But we can't go there no more. The trees are gone so they can build a house."

"But I'm all fixed now." Owen lifted his sweatshirt and twisted to point at his pants. "See. Mr. Nolan cut my belt loops off so no branch can catch me. I'm ready to climb."

Willow hesitated.

"They really want to save your dog." Claire's expression was sympathetic as if she understood Willow's struggle. Yet her words were resigned as if she had long since accepted certain outcomes. "This gives them a chance to put their climbing skills to good use."

"We want to be dog rescuers." Owen puffed out his chest. "Like our dad."

"Except Dad rescues people in his helicopter," Aidan explained.

"Their dad is deployed overseas." Claire ruffled Owen's red hair. "He's an army medevac pilot."

"He's gonna be so proud of us, Ms. Willow," Aidan declared. "Dad always says we gotta look out for our neighbors and friends."

Nolan dipped his chin at Willow. "We can't let their father down."

Unfair, cowboy. Unfair. Willow narrowed her eyes.

"If it makes you feel any better, Zinni isn't even halfway up the tree," Nolan said. "So they won't need to climb all that far."

"We aren't afraid of no squirrels either." Aidan stuffed his hand in his pocket, then pulled it out and lifted his palm toward Willow. "See, I even got nuts for them."

"Can we climb now?" Hope filled Owen's face.

Willow looked at Claire. "It's entirely up to your mom."

The boys glanced at their mom, waited for her nod, then raced to the tree.

Claire transferred the toddler to Willow's arms. "If you can watch Charlie, I can help spot the boys." Claire ran her hands over her leggings. "Believe it or not, I did a lot of rock climbing back in the day, so the boys come by it naturally. Now I keep my feet on the ground. Easier to chase them." She chuckled and hurried after her two sons.

Nolan joined them under the base of the tree. Both Nolan and Claire pointed into the evergreen several times. There were pauses while they waited for the boys to nod. Then Nolan guided first Aidan, then Owen up inside and they were off on their dog rescue.

Nolan swung up onto a lower branch and appeared to be keeping a close eye on the happenings above him. Claire circled the other side of the tree.

Charlie yawned and rested his head on Willow's shoulder. Willow wished she could be as unconcerned and content as the adorable child. She rubbed Charlie's back and tried to work the kink out of her knee.

It wasn't long before Nolan hopped down. Soon after, he guided Owen to the ground. Then Aidan jumped down, excitement crowding his face.

Owen kept his arms wrapped around his stomach and made his way carefully to Willow. Owen's giggles reached her first. Then she noticed the front of his hoodie seemed to be squirming. Owen's shoulders shook. Then Zinni's head popped out of the top of his sweatshirt, and she licked the boy's chin. His laughter peeled out. "I think she likes me, Ms. Willow."

Aidan cooed to the tiny dog, then said, "Ms. Willow, we're gonna get back on Santa's good list now. Right?"

"I'll tell Santa myself," Willow said.

"Speaking of Santa, we need to get our Christmas trees so Santa has a place to put all those presents." Nolan motioned toward the trail. "Everyone ready?"

"We'll show you where the tree we picked out is, Mr. Nolan." Aidan grabbed Nolan's hand. "It's this way."

Owen curved his arms around Zinni again and joined his brother and Nolan.

Willow kept Charlie, offering Claire's arms a reprieve, or so she told the patient mom. The truth was slightly more selfish. Carrying the sleeping toddler allowed Willow to keep her pace slow and the twinge in her knee to a minimum.

Forty-five minutes later, the trees were netted. Willow transferred Charlie to his car seat in the family's SUV and took Zinni back. After quick hugs for her dog rescuers, Willow turned to Claire.

But Claire was staring at Nolan, surprise spread across her face. "I can't believe it. I finally figured out why I know your name." Excitement rushed her words. "You're the bull rider, Nolan Elliot. Two-time national champion. You have more than twenty event wins. And you're a likely future hall of famer."

Aidan gaped at Nolan. "I told Mom you were somebody."

Nolan eyed the boy. "Everyone is somebody. Don't ever forget that."

Willow softened at the sincerity in Nolan's expression and the earnestness in the little boy's face. She wanted to believe it. Wanted the somebody she was right now to be enough.

"But you are *the* current national champion," Claire stated. "A back-to-back champion, which doesn't happen often."

"I am," Nolan conceded. "I'm also a rancher with a herd of longhorn cattle, horses, and land for two young cowboys to roam and not get in too much trouble."

"And you're famous," Aidan added.

"I wouldn't go that far. I just worked hard at my job, and it paid off," Nolan said. "But the offer stands. If the boys want to come out to the ranch, just let me know."

Owen jammed his finger into his chest. "Do you mean us?"

Nolan nodded and gave his phone number to Claire. She entered the number into her cell and laughed. "Would it be too much to ask for a picture? My husband is going to be really jealous. He follows the rodeo. He's the reason I know your name."

Willow adjusted Nolan's cowboy hat on his head and said, "Don't forget to smile, cowboy." Then she snapped the picture of the family with Nolan.

An enthusiastic Claire announced who Nolan was to the parking lot attendant and soon word spread about the local celebrity. Nolan was gracious, shaking hands with several fans and even offering rodeo advice to the two delivery workers in charge of dropping off the statement tree at Nolan's ranch that evening.

Soon after, Annie and Ryan arrived and loaded their flocked tree into Nolan's truck. Ryan proved to be as patient as Nolan as he listened to Owen and Aidan's colorful retelling of Zinni's rescue. The bronc rider turned ranch hand even told the boys he looked forward to seeing them at Sky Canyon.

Inside the truck, Willow waited for Zinni to settle on her lap. "That was really nice. What you did for Claire and her boys."

"It's not a big deal." Nolan started the engine and pulled out of the parking lot.

But it was a big deal to Claire, a mom of three super rambunctious boys and in need of a break.

And it was a big deal to Willow. She had seen another side to her cowboy. Discovered he really wasn't so very different from his father after all. Good with children, kind and endearing. Even more of a cowboy prince deserving his own fairy-tale story. If only she was a cowgirl princess.

CHAPTER ELEVEN

CONTENT. NOLAN HAD gone full circle, and he was back to being content. *Again*.

And it was all thanks to the cowgirl seated beside him.

He ground his teeth together and kept his focus fixed on the private road leading to Sky Canyon Cattle Ranch. As if he hadn't driven the two miles of windy curves his entire life. As if he didn't already know the smoothest sections and precisely where to avoid the dips in the shoulder.

There was nothing inherently wrong with contentment. But there was everything wrong with Nolan *feeling* content. After all, contentment had him spending an afternoon at a Christmas tree farm and enjoying himself. Worse, it had him offering up his time and his ranch to an adorable family as if he was going to be living there full-time. Even more, it had him rethinking his entire nonparticipation approach to the holiday season. An approach he might add had been serving him quite well for years.

Sure, maybe he was not entirely happy. But he

certainly had not been anywhere near miserable. That counted for something.

Because if he continued on this reckless road of contentment, he would no doubt start to feel other things like a connection to his cowgirl and tugs on his heartstrings. Things that would surely leave him feeling worse than miserable when it all ended. If there was anything he knew, it was that this would end. Because when Nolan's heart got involved, things always went awry.

Best to keep his feelings in check and step back into those fake relationship parameters. Nolan stopped his truck in the driveway near the front door and cut the engine. His gaze tracked to his cowgirl. And those possibilities of what they could be together skated through him.

"Get a move on, you two." Annie shoved Nolan in the shoulder and climbed out of the back seat. "Ryan and I aren't hauling these trees inside by ourselves."

Willow gathered Zinni in her arms, then touched her leg. Just a skim of her fingers over her left knee. Nothing alarming. But that wasn't the first time Nolan had caught her. He opened his door and said, "I'm sure Zinni could use a bathroom break. I can handle the Christmas tree if you can keep Zinni out of the backyard trees."

"Don't have another tree climbing session in you?" Willow teased.

"Not without my reinforcements," he said.

Willow climbed out and met Nolan at the tailgate. She lifted the dog up to eye level. "You stay out of trees from now on, little one. All four paws on the ground. At all times. No exceptions."

"Good luck with that." Ryan eased the flocked Christmas tree out of the truck bed.

"Maybe you should give Zinni to Flora." Annie grabbed a section of the flocked tree netting and tipped her head toward the open front door. "I'd give anything to see Flora Blackwell scramble up a tree after her dog."

Nolan would, too. He chuckled and watched Flora glide down the front porch stairs like cowgirl royalty. He turned around, slid their sunroom Christmas tree out and propped it against the tailgate. He was about to lift it when Flora reached them.

"Willow, you look no better than Zinni. You're both completely covered in dirt." Flora tsked and pulled up as if fearing the dirt would rub off on her. Then her face darkened. "And I saw you limping after you got out of the truck."

Gotcha. His cowgirl was hurt. Nolan braced the netted Christmas tree against the tailgate with one arm, then set his other hand on Willow's lower back, drawing her gaze to his.

"I'm fine," she whispered. "You don't need to worry about me."

That was where she was wrong. He was already worried about her. And she was not fine. He tucked her into his side. *That's right, cowgirl, I'm not going anywhere. Until I'm sure you are, in fact, fine.*

Willow turned back to her mother. "I tweaked my knee at the tree farm. It's nothing."

He might have been convinced if Willow hadn't sagged against him ever so slightly. He anchored her more firmly against his side, keeping his arm around her back and his hand on her waist.

"Honestly, Willow." Flora fluttered her fingers as if shooing away her daughter's explanation. Disappointment creased into the lines on her forehead. "You know what this upcoming performance means. You must be more diligent. Certainly, I don't need to tell you that nothing other than your best will matter."

Nolan stiffened, his earlier contentment giving way to irritation. He clamped his teeth around his retort.

Willow squeezed his fingers resting at her waist, then stepped forward and thrust Zinni into Flora's arms. Her words crackled like so many crushed winter leaves. "I wouldn't have tweaked my knee if I hadn't been climbing a tree to save your dog, Mother."

Flora gathered Zinni closer as if protecting the dog from them and frowned at Nolan. Her expression hardened. "Just where were you when my daughter was putting herself in danger?"

Nolan opened his mouth.

"Where do you think he was, Mother?" Willow struck first. Her expression every bit as brittle as Flora's, Willow charged on, "Nolan was cheering me on, Mother. Encouraging me to climb even higher. To do my best. Like you used to do." She paused and chuckled, yet the sound was false and harsh. "Only Nolan was there for me when I fell."

"I was there, too, Willow. I always made sure you got back up. Made sure you didn't give up," Flora retorted. Her diamond stud earrings glinted in the fading sunlight. "You will thank me one day."

"I'm fine by the way." Willow released another abrasive laugh. "So is Zinni. And Nolan. Not that you asked."

"I can see that for myself," Flora stated. "Now I need to get Zinni cleaned up and into a new sweater." Flora walked away, cooing to Zinni, and promising the dog an abundance of extra pampering.

Willow twisted around and lifted her arm, palm out. "Please. Don't say anything."

Nolan wiped his hand over his mouth.

Willow exhaled, long and slow. Then she made her way over to the tree and curled her fingers in the netting. "Let's get this inside."

"Willow," Nolan set his hand over hers.

"No, I won't allow it, Nolan." Willow's fingers clenched underneath his. "I will not allow Flora Blackwell to ruin this." Her fingers released. Her gaze collided with his. "I'm having fun. Real fun, Nolan. For the first time in I can't remember. She will not ruin this for me. Please, Nolan."

He leaned forward, kept his gaze on hers and slowly curved his arms around the tree. He had the tree lifted and propped on his shoulder before she could protest. "We will keep having fun as long as it doesn't hurt you or your knee. That's the only deal I'm making."

"Deal." Her smile came quick and blinding.

There she was. His cowgirl. Nolan adjusted his hold on the tree and headed for the front porch. "Let's figure out where we want this."

Fully opened, the tree filled an entire corner of the sunroom. Its bare branches brushed against the windows and the tip was inches away from the sloped ceiling. But it was standing straight, thanks to the stand Marla had kindly left for them.

Outside in the family room, opinions and voices collided as the others debated the lights and specific decorations for the statement tree that had been delivered minutes after Nolan had carried the sunroom tree inside. The debate, good-natured yet unrestrained, gained traction. The opinions became more lively and the noise level lifted.

Suddenly Zinni in her new fuzzy, gumdrop-bedecked green sweater trotted in. She gave Nolan's boots a grumbly snuffle then launched herself onto the small sofa where she burrowed behind two throw pillows. Nolan grinned. "Looks like Zinni found a good place to hide out from the decorating frenzy."

"That's it." Willow grabbed Nolan's arm.

"What?" he asked. "You want to close the doors and hide away with Zinni?" The idea had merit. He was starting to prefer it when it was only him, his cowgirl and the little, vocally unique dog.

"No. That's our theme." Willow set another pillow in front of Zinni to completely conceal the dog. "The sunroom can be the Clauses' secret hideaway."

Or it could be our secret hideout. Where they reconsidered the value of fake. And drew outside those friendship lines. *Never mind.* He was never good at art and not much better when it came to dating. Nolan turned back to the barren tree. "I like it. Now, what do we do with our tree?"

"I have no idea." Willow touched a branch. "This is basically my first real live Christmas tree. You've done this before, so you tell me."

Tell you what? That I think I like you. That I know it's a bad idea. But a part of me—mostly my heart—doesn't seem to care. Nolan crossed his arms over his chest. "I haven't had a Christmas tree since I've been living on my own."

"What about when you were married." Willow picked up the spray bottle Marla had left for them and spritzed the branches, following Marla's instructions. "You must have celebrated with your wife."

"We spent Christmas at my in-laws' house on the East Coast," he explained. "My ex's parents always provided the tree and the holiday cheer."

Willow gestured at him. "I'm guessing it was not the same as the Christmases you spent with your dad and Marla."

"Not even close." Nolan took the bottle from Willow and sprayed the top of the tree. "Yet it wasn't my in-laws' fault. My ex and I swept in precisely two days before Christmas. We attended the required gatherings, lifted our glasses for every toast and recited the appropriate seasonal small talk at all the right times. The day after Christmas, we left."

"You could have celebrated at your home." Willow watched him. "Had a couple's holiday for just the two of you."

"We were away more often than we were ever home together. I was on the circuit, and she was working on her news correspondent career." Nolan set the bottle on the table. "Those few days with her family were the only time we took our focus off our career goals. Even then, I don't think we were ever all in during the holidays." The truth was they had never really been *all in* as a couple. Not exactly a resounding endorsement for his relationship know-how.

Willow searched his face.

He waited for her to pry into his failed marriage. He saw the questions in her perceptive brown eyes. *Go ahead and ask me, cowgirl.* Then she would know for certain he was a bad boyfriend bet. A burst of laughter ricocheted from the family room. Nolan waited, silent and ready.

Finally, she said, "Well, then, tell me about your Christmas trees growing up."

Nolan released the breath he was holding. Unsure if the topic change was a relief to him or not. He said, "Our Christmas trees were mostly homemade."

Her gaze drifted over their tree. Her expression was thoughtful. "Like with popcorn garland and candy canes on the branches."

"Just like that. Dad called it our free-rein Christmas tree." His dad had always told them to do what made them happiest. Nolan gladly stepped into the welcome memory. "There was no theme. No color coordination. One year it was bursting with bulb ornaments of every shape, size and color. The following year we added paper snowflakes and every shape of bell we could find. Every year we added the ornaments we made at school."

"My dad drove us around the towns where we were performing to check out the Christmas lights and front yard displays," Willow said, her words soft and wistful. "Whenever I saw a Christmas tree in a front window, I always imagined it looked like the one you just described."

"Then that's the Christmas tree we are going to create now," Nolan said. "For our secret hideaway."

"Don't you mean the Clauses' secret hideaway?" Willow arched an eyebrow.

"Who says we can't be like the Kringles?" He held out his arm to her. "We chopped down our own Christmas tree. Now we're going to make our own garland and ornaments. I'd say we are well on our way to being just like them."

"You're serious?" She wrapped her arm around his. "What happened to your inner grinch?"

"I sent him away for the evening. We're supposed to be having fun, remember?" He drew her closer.

"Now come on, we need to get our Christmas craft on. This tree won't decorate itself."

Thanks to a quick internet search, they found a salt dough ornament recipe. The oven preheating, they were well into rolling out the dough when Kendall walked in to investigate and decided to join in. Within minutes, there was a crowd around the island as everyone selected a cookie cutter. Three replays of the salt dough how-to video and they had the dough rolled to the correct thickness and the cookie sheets filled with cutout ornaments. Cookie sheets in the oven, they continued their crafting spree.

Kendall expertly manned the popcorn machine, allowing Nolan and Marla to move seamlessly into stringing thick strands of popcorn garland. Flora fashioned cranberry garland. Annie and Ryan worked on paper snowflakes. While Big E, Gran Denny, and Willow constructed everything from popsicle-stick sleds to cinnamon stick tree ornaments.

Nolan finished wrapping his popcorn garland around the tree, checked on Zinni, still snuggled behind the pillows, and admired his handiwork. Laughter and muted conversations from the family room swirled into the sunroom. That familiar contentment filled him again. Yet this time, he was hard-pressed to chase it away.

Funny, he hadn't wanted to be inside his house. Then along came a cowgirl. Now his house was full and soon to be brimming with even more that weekend. And Nolan couldn't think of anywhere else he would rather be.

"Uncle Nolan." Kendall peeked into the sunroom. "Willow says the ornaments are cool now. It's okay to start painting them."

It was time to get back to his cowgirl.

Tomorrow he would welcome back his inner grinch, remember he preferred to be alone, and realize that content was not a good long-term strategy for restless cowboys like him.

WILLOW ADDED THE final touches to her reindeer ornament and hummed along to the Christmas carol playing in the background. Beside her, Kendall and Nolan tied braided green yarn scarves around their snowmen ornaments. She was surrounded by family and friends and couldn't have been happier.

Even Flora was being helpful, not critical for once. And Willow had to admit that her mother's draping of the glittery, wide silver-and-red ribbon on the tall Christmas tree looked more professional than the artfully done Christmas trees at the department store. All in all, the evening was shaping up to be everything she had always wanted her holiday to be.

"Mom, look. Willow painted extra-long eyelashes on her reindeer ornament. It's so cute." Kendall leaned into Willow's side at the kitchen island. "And Willow's Mrs. Claus's face looks almost real."

Willow held up her ornaments. "Mrs. Claus and Vixen are ready for a night out on the town."

Nolan slid a Santa ornament over to Willow. "Maybe you can touch up Santa so he can go out on the town with them."

"I'd be delighted." Willow picked up a fine-tip brush and dipped it in the palette of paint colors she had mixed on a paper plate. "It's all in the small details."

"I can see that." Nolan leaned back on his stool, stacked his arms behind his head and watched Willow paint. The corners of his mouth were tipped up ever so slightly. An inviting warmth was there in his slate gray eyes.

She would not have guessed Christmas crafts would relax her cowboy. Then again, she had been learning new things about him all day. And the more she discovered, the more she wanted to know. As a friend, of course.

Kendall spread purple paint on a stocking ornament. "Willow, could you help with my makeup and hair tomorrow for the party?"

"Mine, too." Annie raised her hand.

"I'd like to be included as well." Marla tossed dried, bloodred orange slices and cinnamon sticks into a large plastic bag along with pine cones.

"Happy to help." Willow blew on Santa's newly painted rosy cheeks.

"Willow is so talented." Kendall outlined her stocking with yellow paint. "She's an artist, but with makeup and faces."

"You should see the work she's done at the community theater downtown," Annie said. "I got to go backstage with her last fall for *The Wizard of Oz* production. It was amazing how her makeup brought the characters to life."

"And her customers at the department store rave about her." Marla added several drops of scented oil to her potpourri bag. Affection softened the lines around her mouth. "I've read all the reviews online."

"Putting your skills to good use." Gran Denny sat at the kitchen table and cut strips of candy-cane-striped string to use to hang the ornaments on the tree. "Nothing wrong with that."

"That's hardly the future we imagined." Flora fluffed a sparkly bow she'd tied onto a wreath she'd declared needed extra pizzazz. At the silence, Flora glanced up from her chair at the end of the kitchen table and shrugged delicately. "Well, it isn't. Willow isn't meant to remain backstage."

Willow should have known the unspoken truce between herself and Flora wouldn't last. "What is wrong with being backstage?"

"That would be like Nolan breeding bulls or Ryan breeding broncs. They were meant to be in the arena. Center stage." Flora worked on another bow. "Look what they've accomplished. And it wasn't out in the back pastures."

"I don't know." Ryan scooped a handful of buttered popcorn from the snack bowl Kendall had prepared. "It's funny how quickly I'm becoming partial to Sky Canyon's back pastures."

Flora pursed her lips. "Moving cattle hardly seems as exciting as winning in a sold-out arena."

Ryan tossed several popped kernel pieces into his mouth, his expression pensive. "We've got half a dozen heifers preparing to calve in the next week or so."

"They calve in the woods believe it or not," Nolan explained, his words gentle as if they were standing in the forest, not sitting around the kitchen island. "The pregnant heifer goes into the woods alone and comes out with her newborn." Nolan reached for the popcorn bowl, then stilled. "I have to say there's something pretty special about that."

That confession surprised her cowboy. Willow caught the flash in his gaze. One more thing she wanted to ask him about. Nolan rarely spoke of the ranch, but when he did, she saw his passion. Same as he had seen hers. Willow said, "I'd like to see that one day."

"I can take you out there any time you want," Nolan offered. "Just say when."

When I remember that getting to know you isn't part of our fake dating deal. Or good for my heart. Yet she couldn't deny a day spent riding with Nolan appealed to her. Way too much.

"Willow will be too busy training soon." Flora snipped off a section of glittery ribbon from the roll. Her words held the same sharp edge as the scissors she used. "She won't have time for lei-surely rides out in the back pastures."

Big E scoffed and threaded the string—that Gran

Denny cut—through a hole on a snowflake ornament. "It can't be all work, no play. There's no joy in that."

Willow aimed a grateful smile at her great-uncle. When her mother looked ready to argue, Willow decided on a conversation detour. "Ryan," she said swiftly, "it sounded like you might be considering getting off the circuit or did I misread that?"

"Retiring, you mean." The edges of Ryan's eyes creased, proving the easygoing cowboy was hard to rattle. "It's been crossing my mind more and more recently." His gaze slanted toward Annie. "I've been thinking that perhaps it's time to look outside the arena for a change."

"What about being number one?" Flora huffed, in her usual defense of all things number one. "Surely that matters."

To her mother, it was all that mattered.

"Who says I can't be successful outside the arena?" Ryan challenged, his expression never shifting from good-natured. "I'm relatively healthy. At least enough to chase down some new dreams that don't involve getting thrown from a bronc on the regular."

New dreams. Willow had been chasing the same dream for so long. She feared if she failed, she would be too afraid to chase any new ones.

"Smartest thing a cowboy can do is recognize when his passion and love for the ride isn't what it once was," Big E mused. "Because if you get on that bull or that bronc without that fire in you, well, you're only setting yourself up for disappointment or, worse, injury."

Willow still had passion, didn't she? Her cowboy thought so. Surely it only mattered that the fire in her still burned, not how bright.

"What about you, Nolan?" Ryan munched on more popcorn, his words casual. "Any thoughts on retirement?"

Nolan removed his hat and scrubbed his hand through his wavy, wheat-colored hair, as if shuffling through his possible responses.

"Nolan can't retire," Flora declared, disrupting the silence. "He fought his way to get to number one. Now he needs to fight to stay there. It's the only way to prove himself."

Prove himself worthy was what her mother did not say. But it was what Flora meant. Number one was not simply a goal, it was a lifestyle. And only the worthy were chosen to live it. *Listen to me, Willow, and I promise your star won't burn out.* It wasn't her star that had concerned Willow. It was the people she burned along the way. Her gaze flickered back to her cowboy.

"Flora isn't wrong." Nolan dropped his hat on his head. His neutral expression gave nothing away. He touched the watch on his wrist. "What time are we heading out to those back pastures tomorrow, Ryan?"

Her cowboy never answered the question about retiring. And Willow wasn't the only one who noticed. Both Annie and Marla were watching him closely.

Ryan rolled easily with the topic shift as if he knew his friend well enough not to press, and said, "If we're out there really early we might have the herd moved before lunch."

Nolan nodded. "We're moving our pregnant heifers closer to another section of the forest."

"If you're moving cattle, Nolan, then you might consider opening your east pasture," Big E said. "I walked it today. It looks best suited for a bull."

"A bull." Ryan frowned at Nolan. "When did you pick up another bull?"

"It's not Nolan's." Big E chuckled. "It's Willow's."

"It's Maggie's bull, but Violet has been caring for him," Willow corrected. "So, not my bull." Yet still a conversation she should have had with Nolan. But she had been too busy having fun with her cowboy at a tree farm instead.

"Well, that's all being sorted out among the sisters." Big E waved his hand. "What matters is that there's a bull coming, and he needs a pasture."

Willow gave her great-uncle a small headshake.

Big E stroked his white beard. One eyebrow lifted. "You didn't tell Nolan yet, did you?" Disapproval coated his words.

Willow shook her head more forcefully and avoided meeting Nolan's gaze. Nolan and she had been caught up in Christmas trees earlier. Quite literally. She hadn't wanted to talk about her sisters or performing or her fears.

"That's not surprising." Flora rose and held up her wreath to inspect. "I had to text Violet to find out about their video call yesterday." Flora frowned at Willow. "Leaving people in the dark is a poor strategy, dear."

Willow squeezed her paintbrush. "It's not relevant if my sisters don't show up on Sunday."

"Of course, they will be here," Flora stated and eyed Willow over the top of her wreath. "Willow, I'm beginning to question your commitment."

"I called my sisters. I arranged to meet them here." Willow flattened her palm on the butcher-block counter and searched for a calm she wasn't feeling. "I'm committed, Mother."

"Then you best prepare for a bull." Flora swept by the island. "And Ferdinand is not coming on Sunday. They are arriving tomorrow."

"I'm sorry," Willow said. "What did you just say, Mother?"

"Your sisters will be here tomorrow." Flora kept walking away and never bothered to look back to see how that news landed.

Tomorrow. Willow sputtered, "Why would my sisters come here tomorrow?"

"Because we invited them to the party." Gran Denny stacked the extra craft supplies into a large plastic bin Marla hauled out from the loft in the storage barn.

"We thought it would be a nice gesture." Marla patted Willow's shoulder and crossed to the table to help Gran Denny clean up.

No one had discussed it with Willow. Or Nolan. She wasn't quite ready to face her sisters. She needed more time to prepare.

"It's getting late." Big E finished cleaning off the table, then stood. "I think I'll be calling it a night."

Late? Willow blinked and read the time on the oven clock. It was much later than she realized. And her family was still there. *Wait*. Willow's breath caught. Her family was still there *and* appearing not to be in any real hurry to get on the road. Willow touched her stomach. She had what her Aunty Dandy had often referred to as that seed of a bad feeling.

"That sounds like a very good idea." Gran Denny rose and leaned against her cane. "Lots to do tomorrow. We'll need an early start ourselves to get it all done."

"Denny, we still have time to work with my gelding pair tomorrow, don't we?" Annie asked.

"Absolutely. I'm looking forward to it. Best way to start a day is with a pair of spirited horses. It's a much-needed energy boost for these old bones." Gran Denny chuckled. "I'll meet you at the stables after breakfast."

Pleasure spread across Annie's face.

The bad seed feeling took root inside Willow.

"I'd like to ride with Ryan and Nolan, if that's okay." Big E fairly bounced in his boots. "Always enjoyed seeing the calves, especially longhorns."

"We welcome the company," Ryan said. "We can ride after breakfast."

What was going on? Her family was easing into the entire ranch, not just the decorating committee. This was what happened when Willow had fun. Her family caused mayhem. She should stop them, but where to start?

Marla hugged Gran Denny and asked, "Are you sure you don't want to sleep inside the house tonight?"

Inside the house. That bad feeling blossomed like an out-of-control wildflower field in spring.

"RV suits us just fine." Big E made his way toward the mudroom.

RV. Willow jumped off her stool, quickly shifting her weight to balance on her good knee.

"I'm coming, too." Flora returned from the family room, her long sweater belted around her waist and a sleepy Zinni cradled in her arms.

Willow rushed after her family, pushing past the twinge in her knee. "You can't stay there."

"It's all right, dear. I've gotten used to the RV the past few months. Believe it or not," Flora remarked. "Besides, you'll need the guest rooms in the house for your sisters."

Willow had invited her sisters to practice at Sky Canyon. Not stay here. One crisis at a time. Willow blurted, "How long are you staying?"

"At least through the weekend," Flora stated.

Willow asked, "What about Dad?"

"He'll be here tomorrow for the party." Flora touched her cheek. "He had scheduled the farrier for today and wanted to be there. You know how particular he is about proper shoeing for the horses."

Willow shook her head, refusing to get distracted. "You promised not to interfere, Mother."

"And I won't. I'll observe," Flora stressed, then added, "Marla assured us it would be fine if we stayed here."

"But this is Nolan's house." Willow speared her arms out to the sides.

"We're your family," Flora countered. "Of course, Nolan wants his girlfriend's family here."

Now her mother chose to recognize Willow's relationship status. Most likely because it suited Flora's needs. Willow wanted to pull her hair out.

"Night, dear." Flora waved and helped Gran Denny into the RV, Big E leading the way.

The lights turned on inside the motor home. A generator hummed into the quiet night. They had plugged in already like it was a campground, not Nolan's ranch. Willow squeezed the back of her neck and stepped away from the window. She had to find Nolan and apologize. She spun around. Too swiftly. Her knee buckled slightly, and she swayed forward.

Strong hands framed her waist, steadying her. That deep voice that always seemed to soothe her like no other surrounded her. "Willow. It's okay," Nolan said.

"I'm sorry about all this. My family just infiltrated your house and your life." Willow dropped her forehead on Nolan's chest, then muttered, "You need to kick them all out, Nolan. Now. Right this instant."

His hands smoothed up to her shoulders. "Does that include you?"

"Yes. No." Willow lifted her head and met his impossibly patient gaze. "Do you want me to stay?"

He framed her cheek with his hand. His touch was warm. His expression tender. "I want you to be happy."

No. Don't be thoughtful. Understanding. Supportive. Like a partner. Then she might believe they were more than pretend. That they could face anything if it was together.

But he couldn't want her. Not like she was. Her own family had turned their backs on her for good reason. She had injured her sister badly. Who could trust her? Surely not her cowboy. She searched his face, struggling not to lean into his steady touch even more. "You cannot be happy about all this."

He opened his mouth.

Kendall's shout for *Uncle Nolan* disrupted his response. Footsteps sounded on the hardwood.

"I think this conversation is to be continued," he said.

What was there to say? I'm not the cowgirl you should want.

"There you guys are." Kendall rounded the corner, her words urgent. "Come on. We're playing cards at the dining room table and we've already dealt you both in."

Nolan's gaze drifted over Willow's face. "What are the stakes?"

Heartbreak high, cowboy. Far too much to leave to chance.

"Losing team is on dish duty all weekend," Kendall announced gleefully.

"I thought you were on dish duty," Nolan countered.

"That was before. When it was only us," Kendall replied. "Now with the Belles coming, we need a cleanup crew of two." The teenager did not sound the least bit put out by the change. She sounded even more elated.

"Then Willow and I are partners," Nolan said. He too sounded more intrigued than irritated.

Partners. There was that word again. But not for life, only for a card game. *Don't get confused, Willow.*

"Obviously, you're a team," Kendall huffed, spun and skipped away. "Hurry up or you lose by default."

Strange. Willow already felt like she'd lost something.

"Well, we can't have that." Nolan reached down and took Willow's hand. "Think you can handle a little bit more fun with me?"

Willow asked. "What if we lose?"

"Then I guess I'll have to find a way to make dishwashing entertaining." His eyes gleamed. "Would it surprise you to know I already have a few ideas?"

Willow shook her head, unable to stop her chuckle

from escaping. She welcomed the lightness and humor. And stepped back into the festive and fun.

Just for tonight.

Tomorrow was the start of getting what she wanted.

Still, there was time left in the evening to pretend her cowboy was all that she needed.

CHAPTER TWELVE

READY OR NOT. It was time to face her past and all that water under the bridge—deep enough to sink in really, if she wasn't careful.

Willow stepped out onto the front porch with Nolan and Flora. The air was cool and crisp. The sun hardly strong enough to cast a shadow let alone warm the winter morning. Willow tucked her chin inside the collar of her faux-fur-lined vest and stuffed her chilled hands into her pockets.

Five minutes ago, she had been swirling her favorite honey into her first cup of tea. Laughing with Marla and Kendall over their lively late-night card game that had ended in a draw, after each team had won a round. Marla had called it a night, declaring that the battle was not over, and card play would resume sometime today.

As for today, Ryan's text to the group chat had arrived earlier, letting them know he was stuck behind a caravan on the private road leading to the ranch. Enough trucks that it apparently looked like the rodeo was coming to Sky Canyon. No sooner had Willow read the text than Flora strolled into the kitchen, released Zinni, and announced that the Belles were here.

Willow's phone vibrated in the hidden pocket inside her vest. She slipped it out and checked the caller ID, then glanced at Nolan and Flora. "I have to take this."

"Your sisters are coming up the drive, Willow." Flora smoothed the fringe on the front of her tan suede jacket. "You should be here to greet them. If they see you on the phone, they're going to think you have more important things to concentrate on than them."

Translation: *they will question your commitment.* Same as Flora. Willow said, "It will just take a minute." She pressed Accept on her phone screen.

Her manager at Highstreet Treasures skipped the seasonal pleasantries and got straight to the reason for her call. "We need you at work today."

Willow switched her phone to her other ear, stepped off the front porch and edged around the corner of the house. She said, "I'm not on the schedule."

"You are now." Her manager's words were clipped. "I had three sick call-ins already this morning and we are still a few hours from opening. It is less than two weeks from Christmas. I don't need to remind you that the holiday shopping rush is in full swing."

Willow glanced at the driveway. Heard the rumble of the trucks drawing closer. Also in full swing was the reunion with her sisters. Ten years in the making. Willow widened her stance as if preparing to wade into those deep waters.

"I don't need to remind you, Willow, that you owe me," her manager said, firmly. "Or that you promised to fill in whenever I needed. That you assured me you would make up all the hours off that I've given you."

Willow winced. That had been part of her plea whenever she had asked to leave early for a last-minute audition or an emergency call for a makeup artist at the community theater. Her words took on an urgency. "I know and I will."

Her manager's sigh scratched across the speaker.

Willow clenched her phone. That engine rumble grew louder. It was precisely because of all that water under the bridge that Willow had to be here. She had arranged their meeting, given her word to uphold her end of their bargain. She had to be there to make sure her sisters followed through on their end. She couldn't leave before anything had been settled. Everything she always wanted was riding on today.

She had no choice. It was time to trust. Trust that her sisters would not let her down. That this was not all for nothing. Choice made, Willow exhaled and said, "It's just that today is a really bad day. I have family obligations and I can't come in to work."

"And I have a responsibility to the company that employs me," her manager stated, her voice flat.

Willow's breath caught. She recognized her manager had been more than fair and perhaps too lenient at times. And maybe Willow had taken advantage. Besides, Willow couldn't deny her manager had warned Willow that she'd used up her excuses the day of the fire.

"You are excellent at customer service and cosmetics, Willow. But you are not committed to this job. And I must have staff that I can depend on."

It seemed everyone around her was questioning her commitment. Willow asked, "Am I being fired?"

"Yes. I wish you all the best," her manager said brusquely. "You can pick up your final paycheck this week. Human Resources will contact you when it is ready."

The line went silent. Willow stared at the blank screen on her phone. She should feel something other than slightly numb, shouldn't she?

"Everything okay?"

Willow looked up to see Nolan not a foot away from her. She zipped her phone into her inner pocket and straightened her shoulders. "I was just fired."

Nolan's eyes widened. His eyebrows disappeared underneath the brim of his black cowboy hat.

"But I'd prefer it if we could keep it between us," Willow rushed on. No need for her mother and family to learn about another check mark in the fail column, after all.

"Are you okay?" Nolan eyed her.

"It's good. This is good." She nodded sharply as if that would prove she meant it.

Now she had no excuse not to be all in for the performance. In fact, she *had* to be all in. She had no fallback plan now. She squashed the panic pinching inside her chest, worked her mouth into a sturdy smile. "I needed to concentrate on our training and practices this week, anyway. Now I can do that."

All in. That was what it would take to get everything she wanted. That started now.

Nolan wiped his palm over his mouth as if catching his first response. Then he said, "Well, if you're good, we should go greet everyone."

"Right." Willow walked forward slowly. Good. She was good. No problems here. A tremor skimmed through her. No time to second-guess now.

Buckle up your grit, Willow. The show is about to go on.

The tremor built. Willow jammed her hands into her vest pockets to stop herself from reaching for Nolan. She would handle her nerves on her own. Like always. After all, she was going all in to get what she wanted. But that did not include her cowboy.

Nolan stayed beside her as they went back around the house to the driveway. He whistled low. "Ryan wasn't kidding. The troops are here."

Willow gaped. There were more than half a dozen trucks and trailers, including one carrying a blond-colored bull. Two vintage RVs were pulling in tandem beside Big E's motor home on the far side of the stable. Vehicle doors opened as if on cue. Cowboys, cowgirls, kids and dogs spilled onto the gravel.

"When the Blackwells show up, they certainly do it in style," Nolan drawled.

"This is nothing." Big E stepped forward and laughed. "Just wait until the Eagle Springs and Falcon Creek Blackwells join this crew. That'll sure be a sight."

Willow was struggling to take in the sight before her. Flora, the fringe swaying on her suede jacket and coordinating tan boots, was weaving her way through the vehicles, calling out greetings and handing out hugs like candy canes, as if she were Mrs. Claus dressed as a cowgirl.

Marla guided Gran Denny down the porch stairs and into the fray. Handshakes, hugs and introductions continued. Willow spotted her sisters. Maggie in a rich red and navy flannel held the hand of a friendly-looking cowboy and greeted J.R. and the cowboy with his arm anchored securely around J.R.'s waist. Iris carried a curly-haired little girl in sequins and white boots while the tall cowboy beside her corralled two young boys. Violet laughed at something the cowboy beside her whispered in her ear. Her sister's cheeks turned the same shade as the bold pink plaid scarf wrapped around her neck. It was hard to tell which of her sisters looked the happiest.

Willow shifted her weight. A hand landed on her lower back. That steady strength was becoming familiar and almost too welcome. She should move away. Stand on her own. Instead, she glanced at Nolan.

He leaned toward her and whispered, "We can make our getaway right now. Disappear among the trailers like we used to."

Willow found her first real smile and searched his face. "You would, wouldn't you? Disappear with me."

"Say the word," he said, assurance in his slate-colored gaze.

"I can't," she said, but her pulse picked up. She could lose herself in his incredibly gentle yet exceedingly perceptive eyes. "I have to join them." *Go all in. There are things I want. Things that could make me a cowgirl you might deserve.*

"Then lead the way." He gestured toward the vehicles. "I'll be right beside you."

"And if I need to get away?" The question was out before she could catch herself.

One side of his grin tipped into his cheek, shifting his beard. "Just say grinch."

Willow's laughter slipped out. She let it fill her and push away the nerves. "Come on. It's time to meet the Blackwell Belles again."

Willow took Nolan to meet Violet first. Most often the peacemaker in the family, Violet didn't allow any awkwardness between her and Willow. Violet's hug was all-encompassing and sincere. If Willow clung to her sister a beat longer, Violet didn't complain. Neither did J.R. or Iris. Iris's fiancé, Shane Holloway and J.R.'s boyfriend, Hunter Robbins also greeted Willow with warmth and kind embraces. And Nolan, with hearty handshakes and appreciation for hosting everyone.

Soon enough, Willow found herself face-to-face with Maggie. The sister she would have tapped as her favorite once upon a time. And the one Willow had injured and lost. Perhaps for good. Her throat was tight, so many unsaid words jammed there. Willow managed, "Hey, Mags."

"Hey, Willow." Maggie was polite.

Yet there was a distance in her sister's gaze that Willow doubted she could cross. That water under the bridge threatened to take her under. Sink her right there. Willow introduced Nolan, then found herself lifted off her feet and wrapped in Clem Coogan's warm hug.

Maggie's fiancé whispered, "She misses you. You miss her. Don't give up." Clem set Willow back on the ground and held his hand out to Nolan. A wide grin appeared instantly on his face. "Saw you ride in Amarillo at the Stagecoach Pro Buckle Series over the summer. Impressive handling of Storm Maker."

"Still not sure how I stayed on him. He was unwieldy from the minute I approached the chute." Nolan chuckled. "Stubborn bull for sure."

"I think you pick those bulls on purpose." Maggie's teasing seemed to relax her, and she gave Nolan a quick hug. "Keeps the fans and the rodeo hands like me well entertained."

"One bull that won't be bucking but will follow you around like a puppy is Ferdinand." Garrett McCoy, Violet's fiancé, joined them.

"But it looks like Nolan has plenty of room for Ferdinand to roam." Violet scanned the pastures, then glanced at Willow. "Did you get my text about

Ferdinand's hay and supplement blend? His diet is very refined, and he likes it that way."

Before Willow could respond, Ryan stepped up and introduced himself to the group. Ryan said, "Nolan and I have taken care of Ferdinand's feed and pasture. He'll be pampered here at Sky Canyon the same way we pamper our entire longhorn herd."

"We're heading out to see Nolan's cattle now." Big E strolled up and smashed his hat on his head. "Gotta check on the pregnant heifers and see how they are faring."

"Mind if I ride along?" Garrett rubbed his chin. "Wouldn't mind seeing how you do things around here."

"Wouldn't mind a ride myself." Clem stretched his arms over his head. "Could use some fresh air. The roads from Oklahoma to here got nothing on a horse and a saddle."

"As long as you don't mind helping," Nolan said. "We're moving the herd."

"Cattle drive." Clem nodded, his smile wide. "Count me in."

"Me too." That came from Hunter, J.R.'s boyfriend.

Just like that, the cowboys found common ground and an easy rhythm. Willow wanted the same for her and her sisters. She cast her gaze toward Maggie, noted that distance was still there in her gaze.

A young boy tugged on Nolan's arm. Hope swirled in his bright eyes. "Mr. Nolan, can I go on the cattle drive?"

Shane stepped up and set his hand on his nephew's shoulders. "I'll be happy to ride with Eric."

Shane was clearly protective of his ten-year-old nephew. Not surprising. Willow had learned from Gran Denny that Iris's fiancé had adopted his two young nephews and his niece after the unexpected death of the children's parents.

Eric wrinkled his nose and tugged on his uncle's arm. Shane bent down and Eric whispered something into his ear. Surprise flashed across Shane's face before he quickly recovered. Then Shane said, "Well, you'll have to ask him yourself."

Eric worried his bottom lip, then turned to face Nolan. His thin shoulders pushed back. "Mr. Nolan, could I ride with you?"

Nolan crouched down to be level with Eric and considered him. His expression was serious. "How good are your eyes? I need a cowboy with really good eyesight."

"I got that," Eric boasted. "I once saw Uncle Shane kiss Aunty Iris outside the stables. I was hiding in the loft. They never saw me."

A round of coughs circled the group as the onlookers covered their laughter. Nolan never flinched. Simply held out his hand to Eric. "Sounds like you're the cowboy I need for a very special job."

"What's that?" Eric asked, delight and pride on his face.

"I need a cowboy to count the calves," Nolan said. "I need to know if any baby calves snuck into the herd while we weren't watching. Can you do that?"

"Oh, yeah," Eric said. "I catch my brother and sister sneaking cookies from the secret jar all the time."

With that, the pair started plotting their baby calf spotting strategy and headed for the stable.

Iris gave Shane a one-armed hug. "You aren't upset about being passed over for a champion bull rider, are you?"

"I'm thrilled the kid's branching out." Shane laughed and gave Iris a quick kiss. "Now I gotta go. I'm not missing the cattle drive."

Just like that the cowboys cleared out, laughing and talking as if they had been working the same ranch for years. Who knew a cattle drive could be an icebreaker? Willow turned back to her sisters. Too much time and silence between the sisters had given them all a guarded reserve. Willow wasn't sure how to break through that, or even if she could. It was all that water rushing under that bridge, she supposed.

"Well, I have hot cinnamon rolls in the kitchen and pancakes if anyone wants them," Marla announced. "Gran Denny and Ms. Annie are already inside, getting the skillet heated up."

Eric's little brother Miles patted his stomach and arched his eyebrows. "I really like cinnamon rolls and pancakes a lot."

"Her name is Gigi-M," Ruby Rose, the younger sister of Eric and Miles, declared. The six-year old rocked back and forth in her white cowboy boots and tipped her head to the side. "Ms. Flora, do you got a name?"

Tessa, J.R.'s ten-year old daughter, brushed her long blond hair off her shoulder and smiled. "I call her Glamma."

"Glamma Gran." Ruby Rose's eyes lit up. "Or we could call her Glam Gran."

"Well, now I feel extra special." Flora preened and held her hands out to Tessa and Ruby Rose. "I'm quite honored. To have multiple special names is truly something. I believe I will answer to all of them."

Tessa shared a fist bump with a delighted Ruby Rose, then the girls each took one of Flora's hands.

"Can you teach me how to do a handstand, Glam Gran?" Ruby Rose asked, clearly testing out the new name. "Like the way you used to teach Aunty Iris?"

"We can work on that right after breakfast," Flora said.

"I could show you how to do a backbend," Kendall offered and hurried onto the back porch with the others. "And a kickover."

"I gotta see that," Tessa exclaimed and disappeared inside the house.

And so, for the first time in over a decade, it was just the five Blackwell Belles. What now? Willow was suddenly desperate for that icebreaker. Anything to keep her nerves in check.

"Did they leave us without a backward glance

for cinnamon rolls?" Iris stuck her hands in the pockets of her fleece-lined denim jacket and considered the empty driveway.

"Don't forget the cattle drive," Maggie offered, her voice unimpressed. "We got left behind for longhorn cattle and quite quickly, I might add."

Violet adjusted her scarf. "And I believe backflip lessons as well."

"So, the reunion of the Blackwell Belles is less interesting than cattle and baked goods." J.R. crossed her arms over her chunky brown sweater. Her lips twitched.

"Appears that way," Willow said slowly. Her giggle slipped out before she could catch it in her palm. "To be fair, Marla makes an incredible cinnamon roll. And Nolan's longhorns are supposedly very easygoing."

"Still, we are less interesting than Glam Gran or Flora Gram or whatever Flora's name is now." Iris shook her head. Her amusement ruined her disgruntled expression. "Why am I surprised by this? I should not be surprised."

"Flora Gram." Maggie tugged at Iris's sleeve. "Did you just call our mother Flora Gram?"

Willow wasn't certain who laughed first. But soon enough, their laughter rang out, filling the air like so many chiming jingle bells. That ice splintered and the water under that bridge seemed a little more shallow.

"Well, ladies, I would like to point out that one male hasn't abandoned us. We still have Ferdinand," Violet offered and linked one arm around Willow's and the other around Maggie's.

J.R. wrapped her arm around Willow's and said, "I say we get Ferdinand settled into his new digs."

"I can't think of a better idea." Iris took Maggie's free arm.

Who knew it would take a good-natured bull to finally bring the five sisters back to working as a team?

That teamwork continued through lunch and afterward when the sisters gathered in the sunroom aka the Clauses' hideaway. Where Aunt Dandy's heirloom items were all presented as per the sisters' deal. J.R. held the cowboy hat with gentle reverence. Violet smoothed her hands over the saddle, admiration in her expression. And Iris delicately touched each charm on the silver bracelet resting in her palm as if recounting special times with Aunt Dandy.

Willow had known the items were important to her sisters. Now she understood the true emotional connection that linked each sister to their aunt. She believed her sisters meant to hold up their end of the bargain and perform.

Minutes later, Marla shimmied into the sunroom and twirled. Her face lit up. "Ladies, I'm interrupting and I'm not sorry. We have a party to get ready for."

Willow glanced at the clock on the side table, surprised so much of the afternoon had already slipped by. "We still have a lot to discuss."

"Not tonight. Tonight is about celebrating with friends and family." Marla wrapped her arm around Willow's waist. "But first you have faces waiting for your expert makeup skills."

"Wait." Violet jumped up. "Willow is doing your makeup. Can I come?"

"She certainly is. And you certainly can join us." Marla's voice was bubbly bright. "If we hurry, we can all fit in the primary bathroom for our makeovers and shoo Nolan to the guest bathroom when he gets home."

Not half an hour later, the primary bathroom in Nolan's suite bustled with girl talk, merriment and shimmery eye shadows in every shade. Maggie and Iris worked Ruby Rose's curls into an updo. Violet painted Tessa's nails a sparkly green. J.R. and Marla discussed lip gloss. While Kendall and Annie followed Willow's instructions on the correct sweep of the blush brush. Even Flora got into the mix, weaving through the room, offering her own tips on how to sparkle.

Joy spread through Willow. The sisters had gathered in dressing rooms over the years just like this. Only now, there were no nerves. None of the pressure to look impeccable and perform even better. Now it was all for fun. A refreshing and very welcome change, to be sure. Willow couldn't wait for the evening to get started.

The celebration turned out to include Claire Maddin and her sons, to whom Flora had given a personal invitation. Flora wanted to thank and recognize Zinni's dog rescuers from the Christmas tree farm. Owen and Aidan became instant friends with Miles and Eric.

Willow and Violet stood under a heat lamp on the back porch and watched Nolan escort Claire's boys over to Ferdinand's pasture for a close-up view of the friendly bull. Maggie and Clem were already at the pasture fence with Miles and Eric. It seemed the four boys declared Ferdinand deserved a holiday treat like all the other party guests. And they wouldn't give up until the adults relented.

"Good with kids." Violet sipped her mulled wine and bumped her shoulder against Willow's, speculation in her words. "That's a box you should definitely check."

"On what?" Willow swirled the mulled wine in her glass, reluctantly admitting it was not much to her liking.

"The box on your cowboy checklist." Violet eyed Willow over the rim of her glass.

"My what?" The memory came at her swiftly and all too vividly. Willow put her palm to her forehead and half groaned, half laughed. "I completely forgot about that."

"Good thing I haven't," Violet said with entirely too much glee. She tapped her nail against her chin, her expression thoughtful. "Now, what else was on your cowboy checklist? Had to be cute. Charming. Or was it chivalrous?"

"Chivalrous." Willow lowered her hand and

peered at her sister. "I was reading that time travel series where the heroine fell for a knight."

"That's right," Violet said, looking all too thrilled. "Then there was funny. Kind and not just to his horse. I personally liked that one."

"Don't forget he had to be taller than me. Be a good hugger. And he had to smell nice," Willow added, because if they were going to go there, the sisters might as well go all the way into the memory. Back when she was a naive but headstrong teenager about Kendall's age and fancying herself an expert on how to pick the perfect cowboy.

"Well, don't leave me hanging." Violet sipped her drink. "How's your cowboy doing with that checklist?"

Her cowboy checked every box. Every single one Willow had written down all those years ago, and ones Willow hadn't known she should have put down. Like attentive, a keen listener, and patient. But a checklist was not a guarantee that a relationship would last. And Willow couldn't risk her heart for anything less.

Garrett slipped his hand into Violet's and twirled her into his arms. He said, "Stop picking on your sister, Vi."

Willow smiled wide. "Thank you very much, Garrett."

"It's my pleasure." Garrett spun Violet again and grinned at Willow. "You don't mind if I take your sister off your hands for a bit, do you? They are playing our song."

"We don't have a song." Violet laughed and made no move to leave her cowboy's embrace.

"You should do something about that," Willow suggested and took Violet's wineglass from her sister's grip. Then she lifted her eyebrows. "Now you can hold onto your cowboy tighter."

"I couldn't agree more." Violet curved her arms around Garrett's neck and the pair found the rhythm of the slow dance among the other couples swaying together on the back porch.

Violet and Garrett were a perfect match. If Willow was counting, she would say her other sisters had found their ideal matches too. She was thrilled for her sisters, if not a little envious. Her sisters had carved out their own paths and discovered true happiness. Willow would be lying if she said she didn't want that.

She walked into the kitchen and set the wineglasses in the sink. She caught Nolan's reflection in the dark panes of the wide window over the sink, smiled and turned around. Her breath caught.

Her cowboy wore a charcoal sports coat that matched his eyes and could have been tailored for him. His jeans were a deep denim shade. His boots were polished. His black cowboy hat lint-free. His crisp white button-down and neatly trimmed beard elevated him into debonair and, dare she say, dashing.

But what made her breath hitch, and her pulse race, was the way her cowboy looked at her. The way he had looked at her the moment she had stepped into the family room earlier. As if she was all he saw and all he ever wanted to see.

"You are stunning, Willow Blackwell." His gaze traveled over her, drifting from her hair down to her heels and back. "Ryan told me that Annie took his breath away when he first saw her in her purple dress. I started to tease him, then you walked into the room. And I was breathless and speechless all at once. Still am, every time I look at you."

She knew the feeling. It was one more thing to add to her checklist: sets those butterflies inside her to flying.

He ran a finger over his bottom lip and considered her. "If I said grinch right now, what would you do?"

Her smile came gradually, but it was unstoppable. "I'd take your hand and sneak away with you."

"Just like that," he said, appreciation in his tone.

Willow nodded. *Just like that, cowboy. Before my heart caught up.*

He approached her, his eyes, piercingly clear, never leaving hers. Then he moved right into her space. Closer than some of the couples slow-dancing on the back porch.

Those butterflies inside her took flight. And there was nowhere else Willow wanted to be.

He was silent for a beat. Then another as if memorizing her face. Finally, he leaned in. His lips brushed against her ear, his breath warmed her skin, and he whispered, "Grinch."

CHAPTER THIRTEEN

As soon as Willow put her hand in his, he swept her into the mudroom, letting go only long enough to drop his sherpa-lined jacket over her shoulders and wrap a fuzzy scarf around her neck. Satisfied that she wouldn't be cold, he guided her outside, away from the back porch, where Annie rested her head on Ryan's shoulder and swayed to the beat of a slow country love song. Away from the grassy area between the stables and house where the boys played a rowdy game of flashlight tag. Away from the main house where Marla and Flora hosted what was sure to become the new standard for holiday parties.

Nolan tucked Willow into his side and did exactly what he intended. He snuck his cowgirl away.

"But this is the cactus garden," Willow said, pausing to wait for Nolan to open the gates.

"Or it could be our secret garden," Nolan said.

"I like that," she said and followed him under the arbor arch.

Inside, he heard her small gasp.

"You did all this?" She stepped around him and

moved to warm her hands over the glowing rocks of the gas firepit set in the center of a round table. There were twinkle lights, decorations everywhere, and a sprig of mistletoe at the top of a cactus.

"I had some help." Nolan motioned to the small two-seater outdoor sofa on the other side of the table. "I asked you for an hour to inspire you and that time starts now."

"It's wonderful." Willow sank onto the plush-cushioned sofa.

Nolan dropped a thick plaid blanket over her legs. "Now for the fun part."

Willow laughed. "There's more?"

"Well, I noticed you barely drank your mulled wine." Nolan grinned as surprise lifted her eyebrows. *That's right, cowgirl. I noticed.* He added, "And you skipped the spiked eggnog, which is legendary in these parts according to my neighbors."

She chuckled. "Saw that, did you?"

He saw that and more. But that was for later. Nolan picked up a tray of cocktail glasses he had set aside before he went to find her.

"What is all that?" Willow asked, interest and curiosity in her words.

"Hopefully one of these is your holiday drink of choice," he said.

"You made all these?"

"To be fair, I asked what people's favorite holiday drink was on the cattle drive today," Nolan explained. "Then I came back, researched the recipes and selected the ones I thought you might prefer."

She leaned over and studied the tray. "How do you know what I might prefer?"

"This is a hot toddy, only with black tea and spices." He picked up the highball glass and handed it to her. "I know you like honey. I heard you telling Marla that Sweet House of Bees in the Panhandle is your favorite brand. And you drink tea every morning, so I thought a hot drink might suit you."

Willow took a deep sip and sighed. "Very nice."

Not as nice as being alone with her for the first time all day. He said, "But you're not quite ready to declare it your favorite."

"I would hate to waste all the other samples that you took the time to mix for me." She set the tumbler down and considered her other options.

"Then let's get to it." He picked up a stemless wineglass. "Marla made her apple cider sangria, which she is only serving upon special request. It's her favorite, so she insisted I include it as a sample."

"Hmm, I can't disappoint Marla and not try it." Willow chuckled and took the glass.

Nolan leaned back into the sofa. "How was it with your sisters? Were there any surprises today?"

"The entire day was a surprise," she confessed and set the sangria back on the tray. "I think I like my wine and fruit enjoyed separately."

"Fair enough. We won't tell Marla," Nolan said then asked, "What surprised you the least?"

"That Iris is such a good mother. Iris could always handle whatever came at her with such poise and strength." Willow picked up a cheese straw and took a bite. "Now she is helping to care for three kids, and she doesn't look the least bit stressed. She seems to be thriving."

"As do all your sisters." At least from what Nolan had seen and heard from the sisters' partners during their ride in the pastures. They couldn't have talked about their cowgirls more and the lives they were building together. And that had gotten Nolan to thinking. He picked up the pomegranate spritzer. "Big E claimed his wife enjoys this when she's sitting on their porch swing."

"That's a lovely image of my great-uncle and aunt." Her smile was wistful and distracting.

"What was your biggest surprise?" he asked. That he now very much wanted a porch swing surprised him.

"That it wasn't awkward for long." She tasted the spritzer and wrinkled her nose. "That everyone seems to be genuinely glad to be together."

"I get that." He eased the spritzer glass from her and took a tentative sip. His nose wrinkled, too. He returned the spritzer to the back of the tray. "Too much mint."

Willow nodded. "You were saying."

"When I saw my ex-wife at a rodeo in New Mexico six months after our divorce was finalized, I thought it was going to be bad. Messy and uncomfortable."

She studied him. "It wasn't?"

"Not at all," he said. "In fact, we went to dinner

and had the most honest conversation we'd probably ever shared."

"It gave you closure."

"That closure I think healed the hurt," he admitted. "I would say we are better friends now than when we were married."

"Can I ask what happened?" Willow picked up the cranberry margarita and knocked the salt off the rim.

"We were focused on our careers. One day I turned around to look at my marriage and realized we didn't have one." He lifted a shoulder. "Turned out love wasn't enough. Victoria agreed."

"I'm sorry."

"The divorce was seamless. Straightforward and swift." Like a business transaction. They hadn't mingled their finances or lifestyles as a typical couple building something together should. Lesson learned. Nolan scratched his cheek and set the past back where it belonged. "Enough about me and my relationship mishaps. What about you? Have any dating fails you care to share?"

"I have a series of first dates gone wrong." She set the margarita on the tray untouched. "The last guy I dated broke up with me when he got the lead role in a rom-com movie turned musical show. He decided he should be with the lead actress instead. Better publicity."

"That's…" Nolan paused and gathered his words. "That is harsh."

"That's the business." She picked up the hot

toddy—his personal favorite—and wrapped her fingers around the glass.

"Doesn't make it right." He frowned.

Willow shrugged and sipped her drink. "At least he only bruised my heart and didn't break it."

Nolan arched an eyebrow at her. "Should that make me not like him any less?"

She chuckled and toasted him. "Suits me just fine because he did hurt me."

I don't want to hurt you either. But he wasn't certain he could give her what she wanted. And the last thing he wanted was his cowgirl to be unhappy.

"After that, I stopped dating," she confessed. "Concentrated on me and my goals and learning to be happy alone."

"Are you happy alone?"

"For the most part. It's better to be alone than to be with the wrong person and still be lonely." She studied him. "What about you?"

I thought I was happy alone. Until you. He picked up the peppermint martini and said, "After my divorce I decided I was better off alone."

"Do you ever think about trying again?"

"Trying what?" He swapped glasses with her. "Marriage and all that?"

"Or just dating and all that," she said.

"I haven't had time to give it much thought. I know that I don't want to fail twice."

Willow nodded and tasted the peppermint martini. Her smile stretched wide. "This I like."

He liked his cowgirl. Too much. But he feared

heartbreak over her just might be the kind he wouldn't come back from. And if his love wasn't enough again… Some things were simply better off avoided. Nolan straightened and set the glasses on the tray. "We have a clear winner."

"It's a tie between the hot toddy and this." Willow took another sip of the martini. "Definitely."

"We have to arrange a tiebreak another time." He stood and picked up the tray. "I hear the bells ringing. Marla's signal for the big toast."

"Don't forget the cookie swap." Willow rose, folded the blanket and draped it over the back of the couch. "I set aside ginger snaps for you."

If I set aside my heart for you… Nolan shook his head. "That's not necessary."

"But those are your favorites." She walked beside him as they left the garden. "You used to have them whenever you competed."

"Those were my dad's favorite. I liked them by default." And those cookies made him feel somehow closer to home when he was on the road.

"Good to know." She closed the gate behind them.

"Why is that?" He took the shorter route and cut through the yard to the back porch.

"I just might need to inspire you next time." Willow laughed and waved to her sisters motioning for her on the back porch. "Thanks for that. I needed it."

He nodded, stopped himself from saying, *Anytime.* "Better see what they want. I got this."

She squeezed his arm, then hurried up the stairs. Nolan headed to the kitchen, set the tray on the counter and went into the family room to join the party.

Flora intercepted him and handed him a flute of champagne punch. "You wouldn't want to be without a glass to raise to your family and friends."

Nolan accepted the drink and eyed Flora. Her cheeks flush, her smile sincere. Yet there was a calculating glint just beneath the sparkle in her gaze. He said, "You've been quite busy tonight. Spreading the news that the Belles are back together." More than one guest had commented about it to him.

"It's important for people to know." Flora swirled the champagne in her flute and touched her earring. "That's how awareness is built. And after that, a fan base. After that, national recognition."

Nolan stopped himself from frowning. "But it's only one performance. That's all they've agreed to."

"It only takes one whisper to start real buzz," Flora remarked.

"Maybe they don't want buzz," he countered.

"I don't expect you to understand." Flora slanted her gaze toward him. "I knew it was too much to hope that Willow would not get distracted being around you."

Nolan never flinched. Simply lifted his glass in a mock toast to his neighbors sitting on the couch and kept his expression serene. Willow passed into his line of sight and drifted under the mistletoe someone had thoughtfully hung between the family room and sunroom. Too bad he hadn't noticed that before. He would have stood there and possibly missed his Flora encounter altogether.

"Promise me this," Flora said, her voice low. Her face was holiday bright, her words anything but. "When it's truly time for my daughter to chase her dream, promise you will let her go."

"Only if you promise to do the very same." Nolan lifted his champagne glass and held it toward Flora. "Can you make that promise, Flora? To let your daughter chase her dream."

"Absolutely." Flora clinked her glass against his, lifted it to her lips and paused to eye him over the rim. "We are agreed, then?"

Nolan nodded and barely tasted the champagne punch. It might have been the first time he'd ever agreed with Flora Blackwell about anything.

He would let Willow go. When the time came.

He should step back. Tonight. Or even tomorrow.

But right or wrong, Nolan wanted as much of his cowgirl's time as she would give him.

Because he had forgotten it was supposed to be pretend for his stepmom's happiness.

Yet he was happy. More than he had been in a long while.

Because of a cowgirl.

And right or wrong, he was not ready for all of it to end.

CHAPTER FOURTEEN

THE NEXT MORNING, Willow was awake before the sun. Too restless to stay in bed, she dressed and headed to the kitchen. She went to make a pot of tea and glanced out the window. Realizing she wasn't the only early riser that day, Willow set the teapot down and made coffee instead. She filled a travel tumbler, shoved several apples into her coat pockets and headed out to the pasture. For that hard conversation. One that was a decade past due.

"Funny." Willow stepped up beside her older sister, her insides all twisted up. "I made you coffee and realized I don't even know if you drink it. Let alone how you take it. I added cream and a little sugar." A dash of sweetness couldn't hurt, right?

Maggie accepted the travel mug. "Thanks."

"I used to know everything about you, Mags." Willow braced her forearms on the fence and gave Ferdinand an apple. "You liked milkshakes with double whipped cream and two cherries, double dares, and you could make me laugh until my stomach hurt."

Maggie was silent beside Willow.

Willow fished out a second apple from her other pocket and offered it to the bull. "And now, I recognize you—I see the sister I wanted to be just like—but I don't know you. And I hate that." Willow turned to face Maggie. "I hate myself for that."

Maggie pushed off the fence, started to speak.

"I have to say this." Willow held up her hand and rolled on, "It's years overdue." *Please don't let it be too late.* "I'm so sorry, Mags. I never meant to shoot you or ruin our family."

Maggie crossed her arms over her chest and frowned. "Flora ruined the Belles long before your arrow ever landed in my arm."

There was much to lay at Flora Blackwell's feet, but not this. Willow shook her head. "I shot that arrow with a hurt shoulder. It was my fault."

"You were hurt?" Maggie's eyebrows slammed together. "Why didn't I know you were injured? Did anyone know?"

That would have meant Willow revealing a weakness. Flora never accepted those on performance nights. Or any other for that matter. "That doesn't matter now. It was my fault." Willow touched Maggie's arm. "I came to the hospital. They wouldn't let me in without Mom or Dad there."

"You came to see me?" Maggie's arms loosened.

"Of course." How else was she supposed to apologize? Willow knocked her hair off her face, wanting nothing to blur her confession. "But Mom thought seeing you would traumatize me more. I can only imagine what Flora told the hospital staff." Not that it mattered then or now.

"Mom wanted you to keep performing," Maggie said.

"How was I supposed to do that?" Willow wrung her hands together. "Without you and the others. We were the Belles plural. Not Belle."

"It wasn't all your fault." Maggie swept off her cowboy hat and ran her hand over her head. "I wasn't focused that night. I lost my balance. Didn't correct in time."

"We all lost our focus and balance from time to time and didn't end up with an arrow stuck in our bodies," Willow countered.

"But I had been losing focus on the daily, Willow." Maggie adjusted her hat and held Willow's stare. "What I once loved, I was starting to despise."

"You never said anything." Surely, she would have noticed a change in Maggie, whom she'd always looked up to. "You spent all your time joking around and making us laugh. You seemed so happy."

"You never mentioned your bum shoulder." Maggie arched an eyebrow. "Why not?"

"The show had to go on," Willow said, repeating their mother's overused words. And if she hadn't performed, the Belles might have stopped.

"Right." Maggie's smile was tight-lipped. "It was always the show before all else. So none of us said anything."

"But if you were miserable, why do it?" Willow asked.

"For our little sister." J.R. joined them and lifted her arm toward the sky. "So her star could shine the brightest."

For me? Willow twisted and took in her other sisters. Iris and Violet had their arms linked. The truth was there on their solemn faces. In the unspoken silence. They had all rallied around Willow. Kept performing so that she could have the spotlight. Willow hadn't known. Had never wanted her star to shine at the cost of her sisters'.

"And we're willing to do it one last time for you." Iris took Willow's hand.

"Annie filled us in on the *Glass Ceilings and Petticoats* production and your chance at the lead role," Violet explained.

Mags whistled. "Mom certainly is an expert at getting what she wants."

During their video chat, Willow had told her sisters simply that Flora had something that Willow wanted. Now her sisters wanted to step up again. For her. Willow was floored. Overwhelmed.

"And Nolan filled us in on your job situation." J.R. rubbed Willow's shoulder.

"That was supposed to stay between us," Willow grumbled.

"He was trying to help." Violet smiled softly.

Iris nodded and squeezed Willow's fingers. "He wanted us to know how much this meant to you."

"You gave up your job for this?" Maggie asked.

"For us, really." Willow smiled.

"We need to make sure Willow shines," Violet said, resolve in her words. "So that Royce Chaney casts her in his newest and best production."

Willow wasn't entirely sure what to say. A decade on her own and now this. Her sisters were in her corner once again. Ready to help her get what she always wanted. How would she ever repay them? *Make your dreams come true, Willow, and you can have anything your heart desires.* She would find a way.

Violet added, "We need to figure out exactly how we're going to do that for our little sister, given we haven't performed in a hot minute."

"I would first like to reassure everyone that I'm on board." J.R. put her hands on her hips. "However, I must point out some of us have had a child and our bodies are not the same."

"Your body is better now than it ever was," Willow assured her oldest sister.

"I have curves that I didn't have as a teenager." J.R. twisted one way and then the other.

"You also had pimples as a teenager," Willow countered. The teasing drew out her sister's grin. "Trust me, you were pretty then. You are hot now, J.R. And if you don't believe me, ask Hunter. He couldn't seem to keep his eyes off you last night at the party."

Her other sisters laughed and agreed.

"Actually, you all are beautiful. And so happy and that only makes you glow even more." Willow flung her arms out. "And I can't tell you how much I've missed you."

Suddenly Willow was surrounded in a Blackwell Belle group hug. The same kind they used to share before their performances. Only now there was forgiveness and the promise of a fresh start.

J.R. shifted and glanced over Willow's shoulder. "I would like to point out that we have an audience."

The sisters tightened their group huddle.

"It's Flora Gram, isn't it?" Iris asked, drawing out more giggles as if they were kids again, plotting a way to skip out on practice and go ice-skating instead.

Willow wasn't certain her happiness well could get any fuller. She wanted to hang on to her sisters. Stay right in this moment. Where it felt like her dreams had already come true.

"You know the rules, little sister." Maggie wiped at Willow's damp cheeks. "There's no tears on center stage."

"But backstage wail all you want." Violet waggled her eyebrows. "Just don't let Flora Gram hear you."

"Violet," Iris said, disbelief on her face. "You never wailed or cursed or had one tantrum."

"Not that you heard." Violet grinned proudly.

More chuckles. Willow eyed J.R. "She's coming this way, isn't she?"

"Not exactly." J.R. adjusted her stance. Her mouth twitched. "But they are sending in a spy."

They? Before Willow could ask, a tiny body was wedged between herself and Maggie, then popped into the center of the circle.

Ruby Rose hopped up and down, smiling wide.

"Hey, Ruby Rose," Willow said. "Watcha doing?"

Ruby Rose giggled. "They said they couldn't see your faces. I told 'em, I could. And see, I can."

Iris was smiling just as wide. "What do *they* want to know?"

"If you're sad." Ruby Rose touched Iris's cheek, then Willow's. "Are you sad? Cause Mr. Nolan said he'd be upset if it was true. And Uncle Shane said he was leaving then. And Mr. Clem won't tolerate nothing like that."

"Happy tears." Willow set her head on Maggie's shoulder.

Maggie squeezed Willow's waist. "These are happy tears."

"How come they look sad?" Ruby Rose pouted.

Everyone's laughter swelled and finally burst free. The sisters were surrounded as their cowboys swooped in with the rest of the family.

Assured their cowgirls were, in fact, fine, the cowboys headed back out for another cattle drive. Or so they claimed. Willow considered Nolan and asked, "What are you really doing?"

"Important cattle things," Nolan said, his face impassive.

Willow folded her arms.

"We might be checking on the newborn calves," he admitted and tried to slip an arm around her shoulders but she stepped away. "Seeing if any new ones are making their way into the herd as we speak."

"I still want that ride," Willow said. "In those back pastures."

"Say the word, cowgirl." He tipped his hat to her.

Nolan walked off, whistling a Christmas tune. Her father was on one side, Ryan on the other. Willow's dad wanted to ride Phantom to make sure the retired gelding knew he was still special, since Willow would be practicing for her performance on Stardust. Willow shook her head and turned back to her sisters. "I guess we should get practicing."

J.R. agreed. "We need to decide what we can still do safely and what has to be scratched from the act."

Iris leaned forward and touched her toes. "That's a good sign. Haven't lost all my flexibility yet."

Violet appeared less than convinced. "I'm thinking we should keep it simple and basic."

"That's what mom calls my riding lessons. Simple and basic." Tessa wrapped her arms around J.R.'s waist. "Mom, after you practice, could Ruby Rose and me go for a ride?"

"Please, don't say no, Aunty Iris," Ruby Rose begged.

Iris glanced at J.R. who then looked at Willow. "Tessa and Ruby Rose are both just learning."

"I planned to work with Kendall later today," Willow explained. "I've been teaching Kendall and her troupe tricks for the Christmas Eve parade. I'd be happy to give Tessa and Ruby Rose a riding lesson afterward."

"Can I, Mom?" Tessa asked. Her excitement clear. "Please. Can Aunty Willow teach me?"

"And me too, Aunty Willow." Ruby Rose shimmied in her boots.

Aunty Willow. That made Willow excited to hear. She even stood up a little bit taller. Yes, she liked the sound of that a lot.

"You have to do exactly what Aunty Willow says." J.R. eyed her daughter.

Iris considered Ruby Rose. "You have to listen with your best ears."

Ruby Rose stilled and tapped her ears. "Got it."

J.R. turned her serious, don't-mess-with-me face on Willow. "And Aunty Willow needs to stick to basic riding. Absolutely, no tricks."

"I promise to do everything Aunty Willow tells me." Tessa hugged her mom tight, then joined Kendall and Ruby Rose.

"Come on." Kendall grabbed each of the girls' hands. "Let's go practice those backbends."

"If we practice really hard, we might be as good as the Belles one day," Ruby Rose declared with all the confident authority she had gained in her six years.

"You'll be better!" Willow called out and smiled at J.R. Her oldest sister raised her eyebrows. Willow held both arms out. "I promise. No tricks. They will stay in the saddle at all times."

"Don't forget." J.R pointed at Willow. "I know

what you were doing on a horse at Tessa's age and Ruby Rose's for that matter."

"Yes, I was trying to keep up with my sisters." Willow put a hand to J.R.'s back. "Especially my oldest sister, who set the example for me to follow."

J.R.'s shoulders shook with silent laughter. "I cannot believe what we did at their age."

"It is hard to believe, for sure," Willow mused. "Do we thank Flora or blame her?"

"The jury is still out on that one," Maggie added.

Willow caught sight of Flora standing on the back porch, holding Zinni. "Mom is waiting." Or rather pacing. That was odd. Willow had never seen her mother seem unsure or hold back. Even more peculiar, her mother's obvious indecision made her slightly more approachable. Almost relatable.

Maggie sighed. "What are we going to do about Mom?"

"She won't stay away from our practices," J.R. said. "We know that."

"Then let's get her involved," Willow suggested.

"You want Flora involved," Violet said, then stressed the word again as if perhaps she might have mishcard Willow. *"Involved."*

"Yes." Willow watched her mother strut to the porch railing, stop, then repeat her steps. "If she's with us, we can keep an eye on her."

"Little sister, that is a very good point." Maggie grinned. "We will know what she's up to."

"Exactly," Willow said. "And we aren't kids that need to be managed anymore."

"So it's settled." J.R. waved to Flora. "We will manage Flora Gram as a team."

Team. One more thing Willow liked the sound of. She was back with her sisters. Preparing to perform again. She was definitely on the right path. On her way to securing that introduction and that coveted lead role. Launching her star. Capturing that elusive success to live a perfect life and be perfectly happy, at last.

"That is quite a sight." Violet shielded the sunshine from her eyes. A wide grin on her face.

"Sure is." Maggie tapped her cowboy hat higher on her head. A smile on her face, too.

Willow turned around and caught sight of eight cowboys and the two younger ones in training, all mounted on an impressive display of horses. They trotted across the wide pasture, framed by sunshine, saddles and strength. Willow spotted her cowboy. There in the center, leading the group. Looking every bit in command and right where he should be. Right at home.

Home. Willow's sigh was soft and out before she thought to stop it.

Still, she managed to catch her heart before it fell and confused a cowboy for home.

CHAPTER FIFTEEN

"You haven't stopped smiling since the party." Nolan eyed his friend walking beside him in the woods bordering the southern pasture. If anything, Ryan's smile had gained wattage the past two days.

"It's the season for joy and merriment." Ryan picked up three large pine cones and started juggling. His smile was broad and unapologetic. "This is me being merry. You should try it more."

Merry suited his friend. Ryan had a definite extra spring in his step, despite the predawn hour and cooler-than-normal temperatures. Nolan stepped over a fallen tree trunk. "So, this jolly new you is just related to the holidays. It has nothing to do with a certain cowgirl?"

Ryan's smile leveled up, straight into high voltage. He continued tossing the pine cones like a skilled performer and chuckled. "It has everything to do with Annie."

Nolan was glad for his longtime friend and his stepsister. "How did you get out of the friend zone?"

"I had that conversation." Ryan caught the pine cones, balanced them in one hand, then patted his other palm on his chest. "I told her all the things that were in here."

Ryan had opened up. Put it all out there for Annie to take or leave. Admirable, for sure. But a gamble, nonetheless. Nolan kept his hands in his coat pockets and folded his elbows against his sides. "And you didn't scare her off?"

"You know full well Annie is made of stronger stuff than that." Ryan launched the pine cones at Nolan's shoulder like snowballs. "Besides, it turns out some of those things I'm feeling, Annie happens to be feeling, too."

Ryan made it all sound so simple. Just a conversation. Share what was on his mind. Discover that he and his cowgirl were on the same page and find a new spring in his step. Or he could land flat on his face. Nolan jumped over a stretch of mud, easily missing the muck. His spring was clearly fine. Perhaps it was best to keep those thoughts to himself after all.

"Look at that." Ryan held out his hand and stopped Nolan. "I would say we missed that little one's arrival by less than five minutes."

In the middle of the copse of trees was Opal, the herd's all-white heifer, cleaning her newborn. The newborn calf was white with brown ears and a splash of brown spots across its back and trailing down its side like spilled sprinkles. The calf shook its head and blinked as if adjusting to its new surroundings.

Ryan and Nolan crept forward. The first-time

mom lifted her massive horned head and edged closer to her baby. All the while she watched the men diligently. Nolan paused and whispered, "Opal is telling us that we are close enough."

Ryan stilled.

Nolan called out praise for Opal's job well done. Ryan added his congratulations.

Opal released a low bellow and returned to caring for her newborn. Nolan and Ryan watched in silence. Sunlight stretched gradually across the sky. The morning was sluggish to arrive as if in no hurry to rush the two cowboys along to their tasks. The baby calf wobbled onto its spindly legs. It swayed and toppled as Opal continued her patient nuzzles. Still, Nolan and Ryan waited, offering hushed encouragement to the tiny calf to try again. It wasn't long until the calf was on all fours, rickety but upright. Eventually, the little one worked its way over to suckle from its mom. And like that, one became two.

Nolan exhaled. "They both look healthy."

Ryan nodded, then whispered, "Can't hurt to observe a few more minutes before we head out."

Nolan agreed. "Something special."

"Sure is," Ryan murmured. "And now I'm not sorry we skipped breakfast."

Nolan wasn't either. More and more he was beginning to understand what had drawn his father to the land. He couldn't deny he was feeling a similar pull since he had been home. This morning—this moment with Opal and her newborn—was no exception. And he was starting to like the idea of planting his boots right where they were. Growing what his father had begun. Making it his own. It was starting to feel more than right. And something inside him was whispering louder and with more insistence that he just might be over his restlessness, after all.

Of course, there were those conversations to be had. Things to be shared. Nolan turned and started heading back to where they'd left their horses to graze. He glanced at his longtime friend and figured the bronc rider turned ranch hand was a good place to start. Nolan said, "Zach Evans is married to Big E's granddaughter, Georgie."

Ryan chuckled. "Why are you telling me this?"

"Because Zach is a saddle bronc rider like yourself. Well, a retired one," Nolan corrected. "And Zach happens to be breeding rodeo broncs now. Big E mentioned Zach would be more than willing to show us his setup in Falcon Creek."

Ryan hopped over a log, his boots crunching in the dried brush. "Are you suggesting I breed broncs?"

"I'm simply suggesting that I've got the land, if you want to consider it," Nolan said, easing into that conversation. Testing his comfort for sharing. He added, "As it happens, I just might have an open ranch manager position in the new year."

Surprise twitched across Ryan's face. Yet interest lit his gaze. "Are you offering me a job?"

"I'm offering an idea," Nolan hedged, still checking that ground underneath his feet. His boots were nothing but steady on the dew-coated grass. "It's a possibility, if you will."

Ryan ran the back of his hand under his chin. "And does this idea come with the possibility of you working this land on the daily? With me."

"That would be the idea." Nolan reached his horse and swung up into his saddle. "Like I said, it's just a thought. Something to consider."

Ryan adjusted his seat and tipped his cowboy hat up. "Anyone else know what we are considering?"

Nolan shook his head. "Just you, me and the herd."

"Can't imagine the cattle will be spreading any rumors." Ryan grinned. "Neither will I."

"Appreciate it." Nolan turned his horse and scanned the fence line. "Suppose we could get to it and see if my idea of us working together has merit."

"I'll follow your lead, boss." Ryan shrugged at Nolan's frown. "You have to admit it has a catchy ring to it. Boss." In an amused tone, Ryan stretched the word out into several syllables.

Nolan shook his head and nudged his horse into a trot, unwilling to admit anything other than he was having thoughts. Thoughts about his future at Sky Canyon and his cowgirl.

As it turned out, thoughts about his cowgirl were all the day awarded him. When Nolan and Ryan returned to the house for a quick lunch, Willow was working with Kendall and her troupe on their parade tricks. They passed each other later in the stables when Nolan was heading out to finish fence repairs and Willow was preparing Stardust to practice with the Belles. Then the collapsed section of fence at the stream required reconfiguring and a complete rebuild, taking him and Ryan longer than expected.

Their boots waterlogged and their jeans soaked, the pair finally returned to the stables. Horses rubbed down and fed, Nolan walked outside and stretched his arms over his head. "Not a bad way to spend the day."

"Not at all." Ryan removed his hat and knocked the dried mud off. "I could use a shower and food, though."

"We've both inside the house," Nolan offered.

"I'll take you up on that offer." Ryan grinned, but his gaze was fixed on Annie's truck parked in the driveway. And his friend's boots were already taking him toward the back porch.

Laughter and good-natured shouts spilled from the front of the house. Nolan smiled and went to investigate. He had barely turned the corner when Shane's young nephew Miles raced toward him. "Mr. Nolan. Mr. Nolan. Look what we did."

Nolan froze. It was Santa's team in his front yard, but not. Nolan shook his head, yet his gaze kept on the first reindeer figurine. The red nose and thick red scarf at odds with the mop of shaggy blond hair on its head and twinkling starlights in its antlers.

Miles hopped around in front of Nolan like a

grasshopper. His tiny frame unable to contain his sheer exuberance. "We made Rudolph look like Ferdinand." The little boy clutched his stomach and released a long belly laugh. "It's a red-nosed bull. Or a bull reindeer. No. It's a bull-deer."

Well, that explained that. Nolan skipped his gaze from what he now knew was the lead reindeer or rather bull-deer, to the rest of the life-size 3D reindeer standing in his yard. One wore ballet slippers. Another one had impossibly long eyelashes, red lips and eyeshadow. Another was adorned in hearts and a bow-and-arrow set. The creatively attired team of eight were attached not to a sleigh, but instead to one of Nolan's UTVs. Only the two-seater was decked out in an extraordinary amount of garland and lights and two cowboy hats. The small bed of the UTV contained a half dozen or more burlap wrapped metal gifts that Nolan could only assume would light up in the dark.

"I gotta go tell everyone about the bull-deer." Miles dashed off to join the other kids, who were putting what looked like the final touches on the front porch. More garland. More lights. More Christmas everywhere.

Just then, Willow appeared around the other side of the house, carrying a box. "This is the last of it from the storage barn," she called out.

Kendall hurried down the steps, took the box from Willow and brought it to the porch.

Willow caught sight of Nolan. Her smile went from sweet to radiant and had his pulse racing in seconds. She walked across the lawn and didn't stop until she was in his arms, hugging him tight.

"What do you think? It's yard art. Belles' style. The kids decided the outside and inside of the house didn't match. I agreed." She squeezed him and rushed on, "Don't you love it? I do."

I think I might love… Nolan checked that thought and set Willow back down. "Yeah. I kind of do. Love it."

Willow cheered. "I knew it."

"Knew what?" *That I love you?* He supposed that was good. It would make those conversations easier, right?

"I knew that your grinch is all for show." Willow laughed.

The sunny sound was what brought joy to his world.

She added, "I think you might actually love Christmas more than your dad."

Or I just might love a cowgirl the most. But that was just a possibility. An idea he was considering. Nothing to be concerned about. And more than he cared to share.

"Come on and meet your personal reindeer team." Willow grabbed his arm. "We'll see if you can tell us which Blackwell Belle designed which reindeer."

"Let me guess, Maggie came up with Ferdinand as Rudolph," Nolan said.

"No." Willow chuckled, her cheeks flushed. "That was all Ruby Rose."

The kids surrounded them. And soon, the rest of the Blackwell family. Everyone it seemed had a hand in embellishing his reindeer team. The debate over the best-dressed reindeer continued through dinner and a lively round of charades. The only thing Nolan realized he was missing was his cowgirl's hand in his.

Later that evening, the house was quiet. The fire in the fireplace crackled. The younger kids had been put to bed. The adults watched a Christmas movie. And Nolan searched for his cowgirl. He found Kendall and Ruby Rose in the kitchen. Kendall was mixing butter into a bowl of fresh popcorn.

Ruby Rose sipped on a glass of milk she claimed would put her right back to sleep. But from the little girl's wide eyes, Nolan wasn't certain Ruby Rose wanted to sleep just yet.

He scooped out a handful of popcorn and asked, "Has anyone seen Willow?"

Kendall shook her head.

But Ruby Rose chewed on her bottom lip and studied her milk as if she'd lost her favorite ring in the bottom of the glass. Nolan dropped into the chair beside the adorable little girl who seemed to have the information he wanted.

Minutes later, Nolan was outside and heading for the storage barn and his cowgirl. Though he was convinced Ruby Rose may have confused some of her details. But it was nothing he wouldn't sort out with his cowgirl when he found her.

The storage barn looked more like a two-story

modern carriage house than a typical shed, with its high-peaked, slate-shingle roof and dormers. Nolan had teased Marla and his dad that they had the nicest storage barn in the county. Marla had always laughed, claimed she had big plans for her private barn. Yet after his father passed, Marla had left the storage barn untouched and unopened. And Nolan hadn't ventured much past the main house, and that left the storage barn undisturbed.

Now the windows glowed a soft yellow. At the single door, he heard the low hum of music. Ruby Rose had not led him astray. He opened the door and decided he would not doubt Ruby Rose again.

His cowgirl was inside. Just as the little girl had told him she would be.

And Willow was dancing. Just like Ruby Rose had whispered to him.

Once again, clad in dark leggings and a fitted, long-sleeve shirt, Willow moved across the hardwood floor as if the emotional pop song spoke to her, and her body answered.

She was lost in the music. In her movements. Nolan was lost in her. And utterly spellbound.

Willow's back was to him. Her left leg swung straight out. Her upper body bent backward. In a blink, her body was floating in the air. Then twisting and flowing toward the floor in a smooth slide. She tucked, splayed her long legs in a fanning motion and then rolled back up all the way to her tiptoes. Her long hair billowed out around her. Her eyes were closed.

The song came to a crescendo. His cowgirl followed. Another effortless twist. An impossibly long stretch of her limbs. Weightless jumps. And graceful turns. Until she wrapped her arms around her center, as if holding onto the last notes of the song. She swayed to the last beats, an exaggerated yet elegant wave of her whole body.

The opening bars of a new song filled the barn. Willow extended her right leg in an open sort of jump. But she caught sight of him standing in the doorway. She adjusted her move and spun herself over to him. Barely out of breath, she said, "Hey, there, cowboy. What brings you out to my barn?"

A sheen covered her face. A stillness surrounded her. And a calm mellowed her dark brown eyes. She was captivating. He reached up, smoothed a piece of hair off her cheek. "You snuck away without me."

"And yet you found me." She leaned into his touch.

"I have inside sources," he confessed and tucked her hair behind her ear, let his fingers linger on her neck just above her pulse. "Ruby Rose apparently caught you holding your dance shoes in the mudroom."

Her eyes flashed. Her shoulders shook. "I bribed her with candy canes not to tell anyone where I was going."

The sound of her amusement vibrated through him. He wanted to hold on to the feeling. And her. He said, "I bribed Ruby Rose with a trip to see

Santa for any last-minute wish list requests. Santa, it seems, trumps everything."

"I'll have to remember that for next time." She chuckled.

Next time. He liked the idea of finding her dancing in the barn again. When it came to his cowgirl, he liked a lot of things. Too many things. And that conversation hovered. He lowered his arm, stepped around her and glanced at the open space. "What are you doing out here?"

"I didn't realize this was more than a storage barn until I came out here with Marla for decorations," Willow explained. "Marla told me she had planned to use the first floor for her painting."

That explained the windows on three of the walls. Natural light would fill the room. And the workbench tucked under the second-story loft was meant for paint and an artist's supplies. Nolan made a slow circle around the perimeter. "But you aren't painting."

"Not my talent," she said. "But this open space is a decent dance floor."

He agreed. He would never see the storage barn and not envision his cowgirl fairly floating across the hardwood.

"I came out here to clear my head." Willow gathered her hair into a ponytail. "Take a moment for myself."

"Should I leave?" he asked, hoping she'd say no.

"No." She held out her arm and flexed her fingers, motioning him to her. Her brown eyes glinted. Her grin challenged. "You should dance with me."

He scratched his cheek. "That's probably not the best idea."

"Why not?" She lowered her arm.

"You know how people have two left feet on the dance floor." He pointed to his boots.

She chewed on the corner of her bottom lip as if stalling her smile.

"Well, I don't even have those," he confessed.

She tipped her head and considered him. "Or perhaps you just didn't have the right partner."

Could you be my partner, cowgirl? Not just here in this storage barn either. Nolan watched her.

"You aren't scared, are you, cowboy? You sit on two-thousand-pound bucking bulls for a living." She twirled in a series of circles that brought her closer, just out of his reach. "I'm just a cowgirl asking you to dance."

She wasn't just any cowgirl. And she was more dangerous to his heart than anyone he had ever known. Still, he couldn't resist her. Try as he might. He held out his arms, silently waiting for her to step into his embrace.

Her eyebrows hitched slightly. Delight and triumph flared across her face. She moved over to her phone on the workbench. Soon enough, a country love song streamed across the portable speaker connected to her phone. She returned to him, set his arms on her waist, then wound hers up and around his neck.

He pulled back to look in her face. "This is more like swaying than dancing."

"Nothing wrong with taking it slow to start with." Her fingers twisted around the hair at the base of his neck. "Unless you are eager to move straight to a waltz or perhaps a Texas two-step."

"This is exactly my speed. There's no need to get ahead of ourselves." Like with those conversations where he shared more than he should.

He pulled her against him. She rested her cheek on his chest. He tucked his chin near the top of her head and let the music fill the silence. One song became two. Their sway stayed slow and in sync. He could have stayed in that storage barn until sunrise, swaying with her in his arms.

But the song ended. An upbeat country one about fireflies, midnight stars and dancing in the moonlight came on.

Willow straightened away from him. Her grin was crooked and playful. "Ready to try more?"

"I want to remind you that I warned you, for later, when you must put ice on your toes." Same as he kept warning his heart to stand down. But he seemed unable to resist his cowgirl on all fronts.

"Just the two-step." She chuckled and set his right arm where she wanted it on her shoulder and took his left hand in hers. "We're walking. Two quick steps followed by two slow ones. Start with your left foot."

She counted out the steps to the rhythm she wanted. Her eyes fixed on his and her toes pointed away from his boots. Together they circled the room. She added a gentle correction or positioned him where she wanted occasionally. Patient and encouraging with each pass around the barn. Almost a dozen songs in, she lifted their joined arms, spun around and declared, "You, my bull riding cowboy, are a fine dancer. With exactly the right feet."

"I wouldn't go that far." His fingers twitched at his side to tuck her hair behind her ear again. Or pull her back into his arms. "But I enjoyed it." Really, the joy was in watching her. Holding her. Being alone with her.

"We should probably call it a night." She turned off the music, dropped the speaker into a tote bag along with her dance shoes. She slid her feet into a pair of fur-lined boots and tugged an oversize sweatshirt over her head, then adjusted the tote bag straps on her shoulder. "I have to get up early for practice with the Belles and Kendall's group."

He held the door open for her, waiting while she shut off the lights. "How is practice going?"

"It's okay." She buried her hands in her sweatshirt pocket.

"Just okay?" He slanted his gaze at her, but the night shadowed her face. "You don't sound satisfied." Unlike him. He had never enjoyed a cold storage shed turned dance studio more.

"My sisters are doing terrific." She brushed her hair off her shoulder.

"But…" he argued.

"But this performance needs to be special." On

the back porch, she turned to face him under the low porch light. "It has to be memorable."

Special and memorable. He would use those same words to describe his time with her. Not just tonight. But every moment since she'd raced toward a burning stable. He searched her face. Understanding came in the silence. In the determined set of her chin. "You want to do more in the act."

"I want to try." She hesitated, then nodded as if coming to a decision. She met his gaze. "I need to try."

She wanted to risk more. He wanted to protect her. Yet he had to trust she knew what she was doing. How far she could push herself. But he was worried. He massaged the back of his neck. "What about your knee?"

"It's holding up fine. I'm being careful."

"Then why do you need to do more?" She was already enough. Surely anyone could see that, including the famed producer she so wanted to impress.

"There's a lot riding on this," she said, a gritty resolve in her words. "The performance has to be perfect."

But you already are perfect. To me. Yet what she wanted waited far beyond Sky Canyon property lines. A fact he would do well to remember. Perhaps it was that ticking clock, the one counting down their time together, that made him reckless. He said, "From what I've heard and seen, the Belles look pretty impressive, especially since it's been years since you all performed together."

"That is kind." Her smile was faint. "And to be training with my sisters again is a gift."

"Then why not enjoy it?" he said. "Why push everyone out of their comfort zones?"

"Only me." She twisted the string of her hood around her fingers. "I have to show them I'm not wasting this opportunity. They're sacrificing so much for me."

"But what about you?" he pressed. Her sisters surely wouldn't want her putting herself at risk. Neither did he. Now he knew how his parents must have felt each time he climbed onto a bull. Yet they had never stopped him. Only supported his goals. He ground his teeth together.

Willow set her palm on his chest. "Please don't look at me like that."

"Like what?" he asked, heard the hoarse snag in his voice.

"Like you're worried about me," she said. "Like you care about…"

"I am." He covered her hand with his. "Worried about you."

Her fingers pressed into his chest.

"And I do." He closed the distance between them. "Care about you." *Too much to stand in your way.*

"I have to do this. I'm not…" Her face flinched. She shook her head as if discarding her thoughts, then said, "I can't let them down. Not again."

He wanted to argue, yet only nodded instead. "I don't have to tell you to be careful. But I'm going to anyway."

"I don't deserve your worry," she said.

She deserved that and so much more than he could give her.

"I know you don't understand why I need to do this." Her eyebrows drew together. "And I can't seem to explain it well, either. Other than I know I'll regret not trying."

He couldn't seem to explain what he thought of her, and as for what he felt , he was still searching for the right words. And regrets? He knew there would be many.

So he did the only thing that came to mind. He wrapped his arms around her and kissed her. Under the stars, moonlight and mistletoe.

Her reaction was instant. Her arms curved around his neck. And she kissed him back. Unrestrained and so very giving, as if she had only one goal. To sweep him off his boots.

And his cowgirl did exactly that.

She slowed the kiss and finally pulled away. "That was way too real to be fake."

One side of his mouth lifted. "Glad you noticed."

"Why did you do that?" Her words were still breathless.

He could ask the same of her. Instead, he pointed over her head. "Just following the rules."

She lifted her gaze and whispered, "Mistletoe. When did that get there?"

He had no idea, but he would be forever grateful. And he would do it again. Kiss her under every sprig of mistletoe hanging in his house if he could.

Show her just how far away from pretend he had strayed.

But his cowgirl was stepping back. Reaching for the door behind her, not him.

And he wasn't about to stop her.

After all, this was preparing him. Preparing him for when he had to let her go.

Her fingers connected with the door handle at her back. She stammered, "I should…"

He nodded.

"Night." She opened the door and stepped inside.

"Willow." He stopped her, waited for her to glance over her shoulder. "You might want to watch where you stand. Some enterprising elves hung mistletoe all over the place."

"And if I get caught under it?" she asked, her voice mild, as if she didn't care one way or the other.

"I just might have to kiss you again." He tapped the side of his nose as if channeling his inner Kris Kringle. "It's bad luck not to follow the mistletoe tradition, you know."

"I wasn't aware you started following holiday traditions," she countered.

"Only this one," he said. "And it seems only with you."

He heard her soft inhale before she said, "You should probably watch where you stand, as well, cowboy. Otherwise, I might have to kiss you breathless. You know, for tradition's sake."

He wanted to dare her. To test her bravado. But

he already knew what kissing his cowgirl felt like. Exhilarating. Enchanting. Undeniably unforgettable. Instead, he tucked those sharing conversations away where they belonged and touched the brim of his hat. "Sweet dreams, Willow."

"Where are you going?" she asked.

"Last check of the stables." Last test of his resolve. He started for the porch stairs, refusing to look back.

After all, Flora wasn't wrong. His cowgirl deserved to fly and live her dreams.

And if she kissed him again, Nolan might find it impossible not to fly with her.

CHAPTER SIXTEEN

"UNCLE NOLAN!" Kendall's shout, panicked and desperate, rang through the kitchen the next morning. The back door slammed like an omen. Kendall's urgent cry came again. "Uncle Nolan!"

Nolan's heart pounded. He raced from the sunroom.

His niece, her face pale, launched herself at him when he reached her. "It's Willow." Kendall scrambled for his arm and yanked hard. "Uncle, it's bad."

Nolan was instantly in motion, sprinting through the mudroom, his niece hot on his bootheels. Outside, he said, "Where?"

"The arena," Kendall huffed.

Behind them, the back door slammed again. Boots pounded. Voices collided in the crisp morning air. Nolan paid no mind to the others. He ran.

Be okay. Be okay. Be okay.

He charged into the arena. Noted Stardust, saddled, but no rider. Maggie held the horse's reins, her back to him. Where was she? He swallowed his shout and scanned the area.

There. Nolan's feet barely touched the dirt. He was running again. His boots kicked up dust. His heart slammed inside his chest.

Willow was sprawled not far from Maggie and Stardust. Her head was propped in Violet's lap. Her sister's long hair blocked his cowgirl's face. *Be okay. Be okay. Be okay.*

Violet jerked her head up. Saw him. Relief and fear washed over her face.

Nolan saw his cowgirl's face. Stained with blood and dirt. Too much blood. He almost fell right there. But his cowgirl needed him. Nolan skidded to Willow's side. He ripped his flannel off and set it against her hairline, where the blood seemed to be flowing the worst. His fingers shook. He wanted to scream yet managed to whisper a gentle but gruff "Willow."

Her eyes fluttered open. Anguish tinted her brown gaze. Her lips barely parted. "I'm sorry."

"Tell me where it hurts," Nolan said, his words soft yet insistent.

"All over," she mumbled.

"The most," Nolan pressed. He had to know if he could lift her. Had to know if he had to call an ambulance. He had to get her help. Now. The sight of her suffering was undoing him.

"Knee." She winced as she attempted to move her leg.

Nolan slid his gaze over Willow's black bodysuit. Torn in places. Her left knee was already swelling.

Violet touched his arm, drawing Nolan's attention to her. Violet mouthed the words: "No ambulance."

Nolan blinked. His cowgirl needed help. *Now*.

"Stand." Willow peeled her eyes open. "I need to stand."

There was no walking this off. Surely his cowgirl knew that. "You need an…"

"No." Willow clutched his hand, her nails digging into his skin. Her skin paled even more. "No… ambulance."

Violet soothed Willow's sudden agitation and sent a warning look at Nolan. It was clear Violet would not tolerate him distressing her little sister any further.

Nolan scrubbed his hand over his face and tried to stay calm. "Willow, we have to get you to the hospital."

She barely nodded. "You." She panted. "Take. Me." One more pant as if each catch of her breath managed the pain. "Please."

How was he going to move her without hurting her? He refused to cause her more discomfort. Nolan opened his mouth.

Her gaze connected with his. "Please."

Undone by the torment in her brown eyes, Nolan caved and nodded. Willow's eyes fluttered shut. He glanced at Violet. "Hold my shirt to her head. We need to lift her." A firm hand landed on his shoulder. Nolan glanced up to see Clem behind him,

Garrett beside the rodeo cowboy. The rest of the Blackwells waited at the metal fence. Worry and tension stretched between them.

Clem's words were steady. "I'll take her right side. You take her left side." Clem looked at Maggie. "Get someone to pull Nolan's truck up as close to the door as possible."

"Not sure if Stardust is spooked or injured." Maggie handed Stardust's reins to Garrett, then glanced at Nolan. "Keys?"

"Mudroom. Hook just inside the door." His directions were barely out, and Maggie was gone.

Nolan concentrated on his cowgirl. "Willow, we are going to sit you up." Clem moved to Willow's right side. Violet kept the pressure on Willow's temple. Nolan met Clem's gaze. Together they slid their hands underneath Willow and paused. Then Nolan counted to three and they lifted her slowly upwards.

Willow gasped. Her head rolled awkwardly forward, then she sagged against Nolan's chest. Limp and trembling.

Urgency slammed through Nolan. "Willow."

"Good," she muttered.

Not even close, cowgirl. Nolan wanted to give her time, but he could not wait. She needed a doctor's care. He adjusted his hold and wedged his arm around her left thigh, flinching at the jarring he caused to her injured knee. Clem braced Willow's right side in a similar hold. And slowly and silently the two cowboys stood.

Violet kept up a play-by-play for Willow. Her quiet voice and detailed instructions served to reassure all of them.

Ten more feet to the gate. Breathe, Willow.

Nolan inhaled.

Almost to the door. Breathe, Willow.

Nolan exhaled.

The truck is close. Breathe, Willow.

Nolan reined in his panic.

We're outside. Hang on, Willow. We got you.

Nolan firmed his hold on his cowgirl.

At the truck, Shane waited in the back. Clem transferred Willow completely into Nolan's embrace. Nolan eased Willow inside the truck and Shane guided her across the bench. Finally, his cowgirl was stretched across the rear seat. Iris draped a blanket over Willow, while Nolan jumped behind the wheel.

Gran Denny ordered Shane to help her into the back. Together, Shane and Denny propped Willow's head on Denny's lap. Denny pressed a clean towel against Willow's injured head and glanced out at her family gathered next to the truck. "You all take care of each other. Elias and me and Nolan will see to Willow."

Big E climbed into the front passenger seat and gave a firm chin dip to Nolan.

Nolan shifted to check on Willow, then met Gran Denny's composed gaze.

Gran Denny said, "I expect you will step on it and keep it smooth." At Nolan's acknowledgment,

Gran Denny added, "We don't need to be jarring her and causing her to suffer more."

No. Nolan definitely did not want his cowgirl to suffer. The drive to the hospital was silent. Tense. And not without worry. At every bump, Nolan glanced in the rearview mirror to check his cowgirl's reaction. Willow remained still. Too still under the blanket. Her eyes never opened.

Hang on, cowgirl. I got you.

At last, the hospital came into view. Nolan parked in the roundabout outside the ER. A team was already waiting. A nurse in light blue scrubs informed Nolan they had received a call from a family member about Willow and her accident. Willow was loaded onto a gurney. A doctor rattled off orders as the medics guided the gurney inside.

Only then did Nolan fully exhale. He folded forward and braced his palms on his thighs. He wasn't certain his pulse would ever return to normal.

A hand smoothed over his back. Gran Denny said, "You did real good."

Good would have been protecting her. Good would have meant being there before the accident happened. Nolan scrubbed a hand over his face and straightened. "I'll park and meet you in the waiting area."

Big E helped Gran Denny onto the sidewalk and called back to Nolan, "You couldn't have stopped her. Her mind was set. And once a Blackwell sets their mind like that, there's no changing it."

Nolan climbed into his truck. His mind was set, too. He had to let her go.

His cowgirl wanted more than what he could offer. She wanted it so much she was willing to put herself in harm's way to get it. He had done the same every time he climbed on a bull. And his father had never tried to stop Nolan or talk him out of it. His father had supported Nolan's dreams, even when they hadn't included his dad.

Now Nolan had to do the same for his cowgirl. He wouldn't hold her back. If that meant he had to love her from afar, so be it.

The first hour in the waiting room, they learned Willow was undergoing testing. The second hour, they were told the laceration on her head was being treated by a plastic surgeon. The third hour, Nolan finally stopped pacing and lowered into a chair between Big E and Gran Denny.

Gran Denny patted his knee. "Waiting is the worst part."

Even worse when he knew what was coming. A goodbye and not the kind that ended with the promise of seeing her in the morning. Nolan leaned back in the chair and crossed his arms over his chest. The glass doors at the ER entrance slid open and a familiar group of cowgirls spilled inside.

Clem entered behind them. He took his cowboy hat off and ran a hand through his hair, an apologetic look on his face. "They refused to stay at the ranch any longer."

Nolan skipped his gaze over Willow's four determined and concerned sisters. Flora and Barlow walked inside next. Flora's arm was firmly tucked around her husband's as if she required the support to hold herself together.

Barlow shook Nolan's hand and never lost his grip on Flora. Barlow said, "Any more updates?"

Nolan shook his head. "Still waiting."

Flora wilted and dropped into the chair Nolan had vacated between Big E and Denny. The Blackwell clan closed in around the trio. Nolan edged off to the side and propped his shoulder against the wall. He kept his gaze fixed on the doors marked No Admittance, his patience unraveling like a worn Christmas stocking. He was letting her go, but first he had to know she was okay. That she would be okay.

The doctor who had met them on their arrival stepped through the double doors, spotted the Blackwells and headed for them. Nolan straightened away from the wall. The doctor's report was succinct, kind, and lowered their collective worry.

Willow had torn her ACL in her left knee. Received extensive suturing at her temple. Suffered two bruised ribs, no breaks. And was currently under concussion monitoring for the next twenty-four hours and waiting to be transported to a room. All told, the doctor believed Willow was fortunate not to have suffered more severe injuries. The doctor attributed that to Willow's training on emergency releases from her saddle and her awareness of how to land to minimize damage. Visitors would be allowed as soon as she was moved to her room. The doctor patiently answered questions, then disappeared behind those doors again.

Let me back there. Just for a moment. I need to see her. He needed to tell her that he… Nolan crushed that thought. How he felt wasn't relevant. She had to focus on her recovery and get back to those dreams she was chasing. Nolan sighed and shifted his attention to the Blackwells.

J.R. crossed her arms over her chest and frowned at the group. "I should stay with Willow tonight. I'm a mom and the oldest."

"I'm parenting three adorable kids." Iris set her hands on her hips. "So, J.R.'s reasoning doesn't fly."

"I looked after Ferdinand for years. Quite brilliantly, too, I might add." Violet skipped her gaze from one to the other as if challenging them to deny her claims.

"I'm Willow's favorite sister." Maggie tapped her finger against her chest. "Me. Being the favorite is the most important factor. I should stay with her."

The other sisters grumbled at Maggie's self-nomination for Willow's favorite sibling.

Gran Denny stood, leaned on her cane, then waved her other hand. "Don't let me interrupt. I just need to stretch my legs."

The sisters parted to allow their grandmother to exit but then went back to their debate. Gran Denny circled the waiting room and came to stand beside Nolan. Gran Denny shook her head. "Too bad an accident had to happen to get them fighting for each other again."

Nolan watched the siblings, saw the love and compassion. They would look after Willow. Take care of her. That should relieve him, not make him want to grumble with frustration.

The double doors parted again. A nurse stepped into the waiting room and scanned the anxious crowd of worried friends and family waiting on news about their loved ones. Her gaze connected with his and she headed his way.

Nolan eased around Gran Denny and met the nurse. She was brisk and friendly. "Are you Nolan Elliot?"

"I am," he said.

"Willow has asked to see you." Her smile was small and polite. "I can take you back there now."

Nolan glanced at the Blackwells, who were still immersed in their debate.

Gran Denny moved closer to Nolan and said, "You won't leave my granddaughter tonight."

"No, ma'am," Nolan said and felt his shoulders relax. "I'll be right beside her." *As long as she wants me there.*

"Elias and I will handle the family," Gran Denny assured him. "You watch over my granddaughter."

Nolan joined the nurse.

Gran Denny touched his arm. "I don't need to

tell you that I expect a personal update. Not a text either."

Nolan grinned. "You have my word I'll call you first."

Satisfied, Gran Denny shooed him away and turned back to her noisy clan.

And Nolan walked through those double doors. At last.

Two long hallways and many patient rooms later, the nurse opened a door and motioned him inside. "We should have a room for her upstairs soon." With that, the nurse was gone, off to check on her other patients.

Nolan turned toward Willow and took in his cowgirl. A bandage stretched from her left temple into her hairline. Her left eye was swollen, already an angry black color. An IV line extended from her left arm and her left leg was raised in a sling of sorts. He hurt for her.

"I look worse than I feel," she said, her voice raspy.

"Everyone says that. I've said that before." He moved to her right side and picked up the chair to set it closer to her bedside. He sat down and added, "And you know what I know. Everyone is usually lying when they say it." *And I'm going to lie to you, just not yet*.

She reached out, waited for him to take her good hand. "I'm sorry if I scared you."

I'm the one who's sorry. I should go, but I won't. I've made a promise. He squeezed her fingers.

"There are a lot of people in the waiting area that are anxious to see you."

She squeezed her eyes closed. "I can't. Not right now."

His cowgirl was afraid. The tremble in her voice gave her away. He was instantly alert. Instantly wanting to protect her. "Willow."

Her gaze, a mixture of sadness and dread, met his. "I disappointed all of them and you."

"No. They are worried about you," he said. A tear slipped out of her uninjured eye. He caught it with his thumb. Her tears wrecked him. He cleared his throat and said, "Whatever you want. I can talk to them. Just rest. You need to rest."

"Don't leave, please. I need…" she started, linked their fingers together and said, "…this. It's all I need."

Nolan scooted the chair closer and raised their joined hands. He put his lips to her fingers. "I'll be right here." *Until you remember I'm not your dream.*

Then he would let her go.

But for tonight, he would hold her for as long as she let him.

CHAPTER SEVENTEEN

WILLOW TUMBLED. In slow motion. A freefall. Head over heels. The ground was up. Then down. She lost track. Lost her spot. Lost her horse. It was all wrong. Her vision blurred. Suddenly, the dirt was coming for her. Fast. Hard. Angry.

Willow gasped and popped her eyes open. The room was dim. Quiet. A machine beeped softly. A dull ache throbbed in her ribs. Every bit of her body was sore. She inhaled gently and oriented herself.

The hospital. She was in a hospital room. She lifted her arm, noted the IV hooked there.

One more breath, slightly deeper. Her ribs protested. She went to touch her side, yet her right arm was anchored to a strong, warm hand. That touch she knew. That touch she could rely on for more than one night. For something like forever. *Careful, cowgirl.*

Willow tried to focus on him. Her cowboy was there. Sprawled in the chair beside her bed. His long jean-clad legs stretched out, boots still on, his ankles stacked one on top of the other. His cowboy hat was tipped over his face. His fingers were wrapped securely yet tenderly around hers as if she was precious.

That was all wrong. She had turned his world upside down, pulling him into a house and memories he wanted to avoid, tossing him into Christmas and the chaos of her family. Now this.

He had spent the night. In an old, worn recliner. To look after her. He was gentle, kind, big-hearted. She did not deserve him. She was… Willow swallowed. She was a broken and bruised cowgirl. One who let down those she loved. Worse, she hurt those she loved. A shiver skimmed over her.

His fingers tightened around hers. His body shifted.

Willow jerked her gaze to his face.

He was watching her. His slate-colored eyes intensely alert and overwhelmingly clear as if he knew even the truths she hid from herself. She dampened her lips and said, "I can't believe you stayed."

"Of course, I would." He turned his body toward her. His hand never left hers.

"Sure goes above and beyond those fake relationship boundaries," she said, her words wry.

"I thought we were already past those," he countered, his tender tone bordering on affectionate.

No. Don't care about me, cowboy. She had a bad track record. And hurting him would break her heart beyond repair. She eased her hand out of his. Immediately felt the sting of the cold air. The loss. *Stay strong, cowgirl.* This was better. Or it would be. She touched the bandage on her temple. "I don't imagine anyone mentioned when I could get back in the saddle."

His eyebrows twitched upward, opening his eyes for a beat. He pushed out of the chair. "I'm sure you can ask the doctor when he comes in this morning."

"I know you've seen bull riders ride in worse shape than me," she stated. "Heck, I imagine you were one of them, getting back on the bull despite being banged up."

"Is that what you want?" He stood at the foot of the bed and considered her. "To be back in the saddle, risking it all?"

I want to be someone you deserve. But look at her—broken and bruised. More flops than triumphs. Besides, love was not a risk she could take. Not until… "You and I both know there are risks in what we do."

He ran his hand over his bearded cheek, his palm covering his mouth.

She plucked at the thin blanket covering her. She was cold, but a heap of blankets wouldn't warm her. *This is for your own good, cowboy.* She said, "You ride bulls for a living. You don't back away. You don't change your mind. You get on the bull. Every time. I must do the same."

"Not anymore," he stated simply, yet there was a finality to his words.

Willow searched his face, but he was closed-off and guarded. Only feet away and yet unreachable. She whispered, "What?"

"I'm not getting back on the bull." He shoved his hands into his jean pockets and tucked his arms against his sides. His stance stiff. Inflexible. "I've decided to retire."

"And do what?" Willow blurted, chastising herself for feeling even slightly betrayed. He owed her nothing. Not an explanation. Or an invitation to join him. His life decisions were his own. Not her concern. Same as her decisions belonged to her. Not his concern.

"I thought I might experience life outside the arena." There was irony in his weak smile. "You know, run a cattle ranch. Get married. Raise a family."

Her heart leaped. She rolled her lips together, catching it just in time, and said, "Married?"

"I scare you." His smile cracked into his cheek. "Don't deny it. It's written all over your face."

Not so fast, cowboy. She blocked his volley and stopped him from turning the tables on her. "That was exactly what you wanted to see. Your words were a test, knowing I would flinch and prove you right."

"Prove what exactly?" he asked, his voice mild.

Her cowboy was already on the run. She should be relieved. Cheering him on. Celebrating. She couldn't hurt him that way. His heart was never hers to catch. Never hers to worry about. And that ache building in her chest? That was only the aftereffects of her accident. Not her own heart breaking. *Silly, Willow.* He already knew not to trust her with his heart. "Don't worry, cowboy. You're not in any danger around me."

He yanked off his cowboy hat and tugged at his hair. "What about you, cowgirl?"

There was nothing endearing in how he drawled *cowgirl*. She lifted her chin, wanting to welcome the distance between them. He was giving her what she wanted. Those tears shimmering below the surface, those were happy ones. "What about me?"

"You push everyone away because you don't believe you deserve love." The glint in his gaze was sharp.

And that table spun neatly around, stopping right in front of her.

"But, news flash," he charged on, not waiting for her to catch her balance. "You made a mistake, Willow. We all do it. Yours meant you hurt your sister, all your sisters. But it was an accident. You aren't perfect. And none of that means you are excluded from love."

"Love," she sneered. "This was never about love." This was about quitting her feelings once and for all. Quitting her cowboy before she hurt him like she had her own sisters. Why couldn't he see she was no good at love?

"Right." He tapped his hat against his leg in a restless, off-key beat. "This is about putting yourself in harm's way for a dream that isn't even yours."

Willow sucked in a breath and stopped her wince, refusing to let him witness any weakness. "What are you talking about? Of course, this is my dream."

"No. I don't think it is. If it was really your dream, you would be doing it your own way. Not the way you were told."

"Don't pretend to know me," she shot back. That table spun, making her dizzy. She scrambled to gain the advantage. "I know what I want. And I won't stop until I get it."

His hat stilled against his leg. "Well, I hope it's worth it."

"Do you?" she challenged.

"Believe it or not, I do want you to succeed beyond your wildest dreams." His shoulders lowered. His stoic indifference faltered. That glint in his gaze thawed. "Because I do love you, Willow."

"Keep your lies to yourself, Nolan." She trembled from pain. So much hurt. She wanted him gone. She wanted him to stay. Love her beyond her wildest dreams. Now she was lying to herself. "If you loved me, then you would be supporting me and my dreams." *Sticking by me.*

But her kind of love wasn't worth sticking around for. *Pay attention, Willow. Even your family abandoned you.*

"I do love you," he insisted. "But I can't protect you and I won't stop you. I won't hold you back."

He wasn't even bothering to put up a fight. To convince her to love him back. He just dumped his love on her like so much unwanted baggage. She frowned. "Looks like you were right all along. Love really is not enough."

He smashed his hat on his head and eyed her. "Then I guess there's nothing left to say."

"Only goodbye," she said, keeping her bottom lip stiff.

He considered her. One beat. Then another. Finally, he walked to the door but turned back. "Love might not be enough." He paused, waiting until her gaze clashed with his. "But I can tell you this. You are enough, Willow Blackwell. Just as you are. And maybe, just maybe, one day, you will believe that, before it's too late."

The door clicked shut behind him.

And maybe one day she would believe she was better off without her cowboy.

One day, when she was fine again. If she was ever fine again.

But love should not be able to hurt now. After all, she never really had it.

Willow yanked the blankets over her face and wept. Hot, burning tears that only made her core that much colder. The pain was unlike any she had ever felt. Gut-wrenching. All-encompassing. Dream-shattering.

And she knew, with a certainty that chilled her, the hardest thing she had ever done—and would ever do—was quit her cowboy.

CHAPTER EIGHTEEN

TOO MANY TEARS and one very damp pillow later, a knock sounded on her door. *Her cowboy.* He'd come back. Willow dried her cheeks off with a corner of her blanket and held her breath.

But an aide in scrubs, not a cowboy, breezed into her room.

The aide carried two blankets and gave Willow a warm greeting, then said, "A gentleman in a cowboy hat said you were cold in here. He wanted me to bring you several of the blankets we had in the warmer."

And still her cowboy looked after her, even after what she'd said. Willow blinked back more tears. Welcomed the heat from the blankets the aide fluffed over her. After a check of her monitors and IV bag, the aide told Willow to press the call button if she needed anything else and left.

Willow had no chance to huddle back under the covers and finish crying her eyes out. In truth, she was beginning to think that might be an impossible feat. Her doctor came in for his morning rounds, telling her he was going to get straight to those health details that mattered most to her.

"The referral to Dr. Grant Sloan should be sent within the next few hours. He's one of the best orthopedic surgeons around," Dr. Avner said. "If anyone can get you back in the saddle quickly it will be Grant."

"That would be good," Willow said. "I'm teaching my nieces to ride." She'd miss coaching the troupe for the Christmas Eve parade too.

And there was dancing, her stress relief. Her private passion, until her cowboy discovered her. And she'd realized the appeal of the right partner. Though late-night storage barn dances weren't part of her future. Willow pressed her lips together, pushed back those tears.

"We tried to entice Dr. Sloan to set up here after he completed his fellowship, but he chose to build his practice near family. Can't see as I blame him." Dr. Avner pumped hand sanitizer into his palm and chatted amiably. "I have always believed in the value of a good support system."

Support system. Willow had taken care of herself for a while now. Then her cowboy had stepped in, steady and strong. He had supported her all the way through last night. But he was not hers to lean on now. As for her other support system, it was still fragile and new. She would lean gently and figure out how to stand on her own again quickly.

Dr. Avner took out a penlight and told her to follow it without moving her head. "I suspect you should be receiving a call from Dr. Sloan's office soon."

"That's fast." Willow tracked the penlight as it dipped toward her chin.

Dr. Avner chuckled. "That's the power of a personal connection."

"Well, thank you," she said.

"Don't thank me." Dr. Avner clicked the light off and dropped the penlight in the pocket of his white lab coat. "My nurses are submitting the proper referral paperwork. But it was your boyfriend who called Grant Sloan himself."

"Nolan?" Willow curled her fingers into the blanket as if she was holding on to her cowboy.

"Your boyfriend was on the phone with Dr. Sloan out in the hallway when he flagged me down. Grant and I had a quick chat. That was less than a half hour ago." Dr. Avner finished his notes on the computer attached to the wall and grinned at her. "Okay. Discharge orders are in. We'll remove that IV from your arm and get you back to your family and your holiday celebrations."

Dr. Avner departed. The next two hours proved to be the distraction Willow needed. Breakfast was delivered. IV lines taken out. Her stitches checked, and bandages replaced. Her left knee was wrapped. Physical therapy appointments were scheduled. Pain management instructions were given.

Phone calls filled in the time between the various hospital staff's appearances. Willow arranged her ride home via texts with her sisters. Too afraid to speak to any one of her siblings lest she might start crying all over again. She worried she might not stop.

Her parents called and unknowingly solved her temporary housing situation, offering to have her move in with them. Her studio apartment was on the fifth floor and there was no elevator. Returning to Nolan's house was a no-go. Looked like she was going home. Nothing she'd ever imagined she would do. Heartbreak certainly opened up a new rock bottom.

But wallowing was not her style. *Chin up, cowgirl. You've been knocked down before.*

Her phone vibrated in her lap. She accepted the call and greeted the cheery office assistant for Dr. Sloan's medical practice. Ten minutes later, she had an appointment booked and a path forward for her physical recovery.

As for her heart, it would just have to fall in line.

Maggie arrived to take her home. Just not the place where her heart wanted to be. The ache in her chest expanded. Willow grabbed her ice water bottle the nurse had refilled and took a deep sip, trying to wash away the lump in her throat.

Maggie gave her a careful hug, then fussed with Willow's blankets.

Willow had been afraid to see her siblings last night. Afraid to see their disappointment. But Maggie only showed compassion and concern. Perhaps Willow's support system wasn't so fragile after all.

Her tears swelled again. Still, she wouldn't burden her sisters with her heartbreak.

"I raided Nolan's closet." Maggie dug into a cloth bag and pulled out a pair of men's flannel navy-and-gray plaid pants. "You'll have to cinch up the waist quite a bit, but there's a drawstring inside the waistband. These should fit over your knee wrap and not be too constricting."

Not like that lump in Willow's throat. She removed the lid on the water bottle and shook the crushed ice into her mouth. Surely the cold would freeze her tears and that unshakable ache.

"I swiped one of Nolan's hoodies while I was at it." Maggie grinned and tugged a dark gray sweat-shirt from the bag. "It was too warm-looking to pass up. I didn't think Nolan would mind since it was for you." Maggie waggled her eyebrows. "Be-sides, if you are going to be in pain, you might as well be comfy, right?"

Willow accepted the clothes and managed a weak "I suppose."

Except the oversize sweatshirt smelled like her cowboy's spicy cologne. And the soft gray color of the pants reminded Willow of Nolan's muted, gentle gaze right before he'd kissed her the other night. On the porch. Under the mistletoe. When she'd kissed him for all she was worth. As if she had already known it would be her first and only kiss with her cowboy.

Now she was going to leave the hospital wrapped up in her cowboy's clothes. But not his embrace.

Yet when he had held her, it had felt like she was…
Willow squeezed the sweatshirt and willed her
tears back.

Maggie watched her, an expectant look on her
face. "Do I help you get dressed?"

Willow blinked and edged away from her heartache. "I just need to call the aide." She pressed her
call button. "Hospital rules."

"Well, I can brush and braid your hair while we
wait." Maggie waved a brush at Willow. "I promise
to steer clear of the stitches." Her sister set about
untangling Willow's hair.

Willow set about finding a distraction. "Do you
know Grant Sloan? He's an orthopedic doc."

"Not personally. But I know competitors from
all over the country travel to the Panhandle to see
him." The brush stilled in Willow's hair and Maggie leaned over Willow's shoulder to peer at her.
"Word on the circuit is if you're injured, you want
Dr. Sloan."

That seemed to be the consensus at the hospital.

"Dr. Sloan did surgery on one of the Done
Roamin' pickup riders and Emmet said his shoulder had never felt better. I swear Dr. Sloan had him
back in the saddle the next week." Maggie shifted
and resumed braiding Willow's hair. "Why do you
want to know about Dr. Sloan?"

"He's going to see me after Christmas."

"That's impressive," Maggie said. "It took
Emmet over a month to get an appointment."

That was her cowboy. A tear leaked down Willow's cheek and landed on her arm.

"Don't cry, Willow." Maggie pressed a tissue into Willow's hand. "I know it's overwhelming. There's surgery and all that to deal with. We'll get through it together." Maggie put her arm around Willow's shoulders. "Actually, there are a lot of people ready to help you through this."

Except for one. Willow dabbed the tissue against her eye. "Even though I ruined everything."

"You didn't ruin anything." Maggie's words sounded disgruntled. "Who told you that? Nolan?"

No. Her cowboy told her that he loved her. Willow sighed. "No. Never mind. It's nothing. My mind is scattered." Just like the pieces of her heart.

Maggie finished Willow's braids just as the aide arrived to help Willow change out of her hospital gown and into Nolan's clothes. Minutes later, another aide rolled a wheelchair into the room, helped Willow into it and escorted them down to the patient drop-off and pickup area. She was loaded into her dad's SUV without too much jarring to her injured knee and bruised ribs. Soon enough, they were on their way. Violet at the wheel and Maggie in the front passenger seat.

Maggie lowered the volume on the radio, cutting into an upbeat Christmas tune. "Explain to me again why we are going to Mom and Dad's house?"

"Their house is a ranch. Single story," Willow said, repeating what she had typed in her texts to her sisters earlier. "There are no stairs to navigate." And no cowboy to fear running into.

"But Nolan would have made adjustments for you at his house." Violet adjusted the rearview mirror. "You were already staying in one of his first-floor guest rooms."

Willow flipped up the hood of the sweatshirt to hide any tears that escaped. "Mom wants to host Christmas this year. She made a big deal about it on the phone earlier. So I gave in."

"But Nolan could have driven you over on Christmas Day," Maggie argued.

Nolan wasn't driving her anywhere. Not anymore. She was on her own. Again. She inhaled to stall those tears. "This is easier. Better." Except when she breathed and caught her cowboy's cologne again.

"Don't be so sure," Violet said, her words dipped in doubt.

"When was the last time you lived with Mom?" Maggie asked. "Trust me. This is not going to be better than what you had at Nolan's place."

"What I had was fake," Willow wailed. "Fake! All of it."

"Finally." A satisfied expression splashed across Maggie's face. "Now we are getting somewhere."

Violet lifted her arm and fist-bumped Maggie. "Told you making her wear Nolan's clothes would get her talking."

It was a setup. Willow sucked in a breath and lowered the hood to gape at her siblings.

"Time to tell us what's really going on, little sister," Maggie said, understanding in her gaze.

"Because we all know there is no way you would willingly go to Mom and Dad's house to recover. Especially not with Flora rehearsing her speech over and over for the Hall of Fame ceremony in two days," Violet added and frowned. "In fact, Zinni would've happily stayed at Nolan's with you. I think Zinni loves Nolan more than she loves Mom."

But not as much as Willow could've loved her cowboy. Willow jammed her hands into the sweatshirt pocket and opened her mouth.

"Don't even try to sell us on you and Mom having turned over a new leaf. You've barely spoken to each other," Maggie continued.

That had been her argument. Weak as it might have been. Because her cowboy was not up for discussion. Willow rubbed her forehead.

"Also, I talked to your cowboy in the hospital lobby," Maggie confessed.

Looked like her two sisters hadn't picked up on her wanting to avoid the topic. Willow lifted her head and eyed her sister. "What did Nolan tell you?"

"Nothing," Maggie said. "He didn't have to. He looked worse than you. And you were flipped face-first off your horse, who, I might add, was sprinting at top speed around an arena."

Her cowboy was miserable, too. Same as her. That should suit her, but there was nothing fair about that. At the idea of her cowboy hurting, well, she hurt more. Willow sniffled. "I just told you. It was fake between Nolan and me."

Violet dug around in her purse, then tossed a packet of tissues at Willow. "Didn't look that way to us."

Didn't feel that way, either. But what else was she supposed to tell her sisters? They couldn't take away her pain. It was going to be bone-deep and lasting. And for her alone to get through. "It was pretend. It's over now. There's nothing more to say."

Except that her sister did find more to say. Violet asked, "Are you sure this isn't like a fake breakup?"

Her heartache sure felt real. Nothing pretend about it. Willow dropped her head on the headrest. "I'm positive. It was all for Marla's happiness."

"You seemed fairly happy yourself," Maggie said.

I was. Willow sniffled again. "I'm happy I can pursue my dreams without anyone doubting me now."

"Who doubted you?" Irritation sliced through Violet's voice.

"It's not important." Willow swiped at her damp cheek.

"Little sister, your heart is broken," Maggie said. "That is very important to us."

And her sisters were so very important to her. But she wasn't about to weigh them down with all her problems. She'd just got her sisters back. "I appreciate your concern. I'm okay, though. But my ribs and knee are throbbing. Can we press Pause on this conversation, please?"

"On one condition," Maggie said firmly.

Violet came to Willow's defense. "Mags, she just got out of the hospital."

"I know. And we are all here for her." Maggie stretched and squeezed Willow's arm. "We are here to help with all the pain. Got it, little sister?"

Willow nodded.

"We will pause this discussion as long as you come to us when you need to talk," Maggie stressed. "Or when you need our help for anything."

"Agreed," Willow whispered, gratitude and love washing over her.

"Now you probably should rest," Violet suggested. "Who knows what we are going to encounter when we get to Mom and Dad's house."

Maggie wrinkled her nose. "I can only imagine."

Willow slipped the hood back over her head, huddled into Nolan's sweatshirt and let those tears finally flow. For the sisters she had found and the cowboy she had lost.

CHAPTER NINETEEN

"WAIT." WILLOW GRIPPED Maggie's shoulder and kept her sister bent down in front of her chair. Two swipes of mascara later, Willow released her hold and said, "You're finished."

"It's too much." Maggie frowned and tugged on the sequined hemline of her long-sleeved top backstage at the Hall of Fame ceremony. "It feels like too much."

"Remember when we wore sequins from head to toe. This is not even close to that." Willow rolled up her makeup brush bag. "It's just a touch of sparkle. And the royal purple color looks terrific on you."

Maggie hugged Willow. "You know just what to say."

"I couldn't believe I let you talk me into white, Willow." J.R. brushed at the fringe on the bodice of her crystal-adorned halter top and checked her appearance in the mirror. "But I'm starting to get it."

"Good." Willow grinned at her oldest sibling. "Because you look stunning."

"I'm in velvet because of Willow." Violet spun around in her vivid blue, deep V-neck jumpsuit. "And it might be my new favorite material."

Iris raised her arms and swayed. "I have hot pink feathers around my wrists, and I could not be happier about it."

Willow could not have been happier. Backstage in a cramped dressing room, helping her sisters transform into the grown-up version of the Belles. The foursome absolutely dazzled. And to know she was partly responsible for their radiant smiles warmed her like nothing had the past few days.

But tonight was not about dwelling on heartbreak and cowboys. Tonight was about celebrating their aunt and their mother, plus the women they were now and honoring the girls they had been. Willow reached for her crutches and suddenly her sisters surrounded her, ready to assist. Same as they had been doing since she came home from the hospital. Braced on her crutches, Willow said, "It's time to get out there and shine the Blackwell Belle way."

"It's the only way we know," J.R. said, repeating the phrase they'd always used at performances long past.

The siblings gathered for a huddle, heads together, arms linked. Gratitude swelled inside Willow for these four incredible women. "I'll be the one cheering the loudest."

"You better be." Iris squeezed Willow tight. "This one is for you, little sister."

The emcee announced the Blackwell Belles to resounding applause from the sold-out indoor arena. The Belles and their horses took to the stadium floor. Willow positioned herself for the best view from the sidelines. J.R. and Iris kicked off the performance, both standing with one foot on one horse and the other on another. The sisters guided the two pairs of horses around the arena at a fast clip.

Willow held her breath as they approached the ring of fire. Her sisters and horses scaled the jump like they had never stopped performing. Iris and J.R. pumped their fists in the air. Willow exhaled on a loud whoop, more excited for her siblings than when she had done the trick herself.

Violet and Flora entered next. Both juggled flaming bowling pins. They transitioned to standing in their saddles and passed the flaming pins to each other while the horses circled the arena. Willow had never seen Violet shine brighter. If only Violet could see herself now. Willow wanted to jump and cheer.

The four siblings returned for the acrobatic lifts and tricks Willow had choreographed. Maggie was a standout, effortless and graceful. It was flawless from start to finish.

Then Maggie guided Stardust into the center of the arena. She notched a burning arrow into a bow and aimed it toward a fiery ring suspended from the ceiling. Suddenly, J.R.'s voice filled the arena. "This performance is dedicated to our fearless coach, Willow. We love you, little sister."

Willow gasped.

With that, Maggie released the arrow. It landed

inside the ring and released a shower of glittery gold and silver confetti all over the audience.

The applause was deafening.

The performance a success.

So much satisfaction and pride filled Willow. Her sisters were phenomenal. And to know she had played a small part in it was more fulfilling than any one of her solo performances. Soon enough, their dad, Flora and Clem led the horses back to their temporary stalls outside the arena and her sisters crowded around Willow in their backstage dressing room. Their collective excitement infectious.

J.R. slipped behind a screen to change. "I can't believe we just did that."

"I can." Willow laughed.

J.R. peered over the top of the screen. "You never did doubt that we could pull this off."

Willow shook her head. "Not once."

Iris embraced Willow. "I wouldn't have believed it, if not for your constant encouragement this past week."

"Your body just needed to remember what it could do," Willow said. "What it was capable of doing."

"Ha! Now I know." J.R. grinned and dropped a cowboy hat on her head. "And if it's okay with everyone, I'm going to go back to trail rides for pleasure."

The siblings laughed and finished changing.

Willow propped her knee on a chair and chewed

on her bottom lip. "Can we talk about what I'm going to do?" She paused and ran her hand over her shin-length suede skirt. "Or not do."

"This sounds intriguing." Iris took the chair beside Willow, tucked her faux leather pants into a pair of distressed red cowboy boots, then opened a gold truffle box. "Now you have my full attention."

Violet shimmed into her forest green sweater dress and grinned at Willow. "Mine, too."

Willow dove in before she lost her nerve. "What would you think if I didn't audition for *Glass Ceilings and Petticoats*?"

The siblings looked at each other. J.R. toned down her stage makeup and met Willow's gaze in the mirror. "Is that what you want?"

"I think so," Willow said. Something about it felt right.

"You'll recover from your surgery." Iris picked out a truffle. "That shouldn't be the reason you give up on your dream."

That was just it. Willow was beginning to wonder if her cowboy hadn't been right after all.

"Look. The important thing is that you are happy." Maggie took Willow's hand in hers and eyed her. "Cowboy heartbreak aside, you are happy, aren't you?"

"I'm tired," Willow blurted. Exhausted, really. Down to her bones. "And so tired of being alone." Willow clenched Maggie's fingers and tried to make them understand. Though she was still figuring it out herself. "Then this week. With you guys." And her cowboy. Her chest clenched. She started again, "It was…"

"Like old times," Maggie finished for her.

Willow nodded, then skipped her gaze from one sister to the next. "I don't mean the training. That was fun. But the other stuff was better. Getting ready for the party and earlier tonight."

"Beating you all quite soundly at charades every night this past week," Violet offered.

That boast drew out their laughter.

"We really did put together a magnificent reindeer display in Nolan's front yard." Iris popped the truffle into her mouth and grinned around the bite.

"I was watching you guys perform," Willow said. "And do you know what I realized?"

"Some cowboys are bad for the heart," Maggie said dully.

"That, too." Willow straightened and confessed, "I realized I haven't been chasing a star, I've been chasing a feeling. The one I get when I'm with you guys."

Her siblings closed in around her.

"I'm not sure it was about performing," Willow added and put her truth out there. "I think it was also about belonging."

"You'll always belong to us," Maggie said.

J.R. added, "We are family."

"I know that now," Willow said.

"Try not to forget it." Iris shoved the truffle box at Willow. "Because there are a whole bunch of things we still have to do, like…" Iris paused and touched her engagement ring, then stammered, "Usual things that sisters do together."

"It's okay." Willow took a truffle out and passed the box to Maggie. "You can say it. We have more engagements to celebrate. Weddings to plan." Willow bit into the chocolate and grinned. "I will be a lovely bride's maid, I swear. I'm really happy for you guys."

"But you're sad," Violet said.

Maggie eyed her. "We want to fix it."

But they could not fix Willow's heart. That would take time and most likely more tears. Still, she said, "You have helped. You've given me a distraction this week and a new direction to consider."

J.R. sampled a truffle and asked, "If you aren't going to audition, what do you have in mind?"

"I'm glad you asked because I'm going to need your help," Willow said.

"Anything," Maggie said. "Name it."

The others nodded.

"I'd still like that introduction to Royce Chaney." Willow smiled. Her confidence in her decision growing. "And I'm going to need your help to keep Flora from interfering."

IT HAD BEEN sixty-two hours and forty-seven minutes since Nolan last held his cowgirl's hand. It had been less than sixty seconds since Nolan flexed his fingers into his palm again that evening and wished that he was holding his cowgirl's hand now, not a silly gift bag.

Nolan worked his way through the arena crowded with rodeo's elite, VIPs and up-and-comers all gathered to honor notable cowgirls past and present. The Hall of Fame ceremony was over, but the celebrations were gaining momentum. He shook hands with promoters and sponsors, stopped briefly to talk to friends from the circuit and took pictures with fans.

But his mind was on a certain cowgirl. And his focus on getting backstage to see her.

A mistake perhaps. But she was close. He had to know she was okay. Had to know... He wasn't sure exactly what he was looking for. Figured he would know when he saw it.

Nolan finished another selfie with a group of teenagers and set his sights on the side aisle that led where he wanted to be.

A blond-haired woman stepped into his path, grabbed his shoulders and flashed a familiar camera-ready smile. "Caught you."

Nolan paused and took in his ex-wife. Her short chin-length hair showed off her blond curls and pronounced sky blue eyes. And her stylish attire only enhanced her showstopping appearance. "Victoria. You look well."

"I look better than that and you know it." Victoria propped her hands on her hips and winked at him. "And I should for what I pay my stylist and her team."

Nolan shook his head and grinned. "Should I tell you that it's money well spent?"

Victoria's mouth twisted, and she tapped her chin. "I can't tell if that's a compliment or not. But I'll take it as one. Although I didn't just chase you through this crowd for a compliment."

Nolan straightened. His fingers flexed around that gift bag. His cowgirl was somewhere close. "If you want to catch up, I'll have to take a rain check."

"Where are you off to in such a hurry?" she asked.

"I'm a friend of the Blackwells." At least, he hoped he still was.

"Those are good friends to have." Victoria's gaze flashed. "I'll tuck that information away for later in case I need your connections."

"You know I won't allow my friends to become possible news stories," he said.

Victoria shoved his shoulder lightly. "Nolan. You know very well that I'm not an entertainment reporter anymore."

Yes, he did. His ex-wife was currently anchoring the weekend evening news in Amarillo and quite successfully. "Are you reporting on this ceremony?"

"No. Like you, I'm supporting friends," she said. "Cowgirls have to stick together."

Nolan glanced over Victoria's shoulder and saw a familiar group of cowgirls making their way from backstage. In the center was his cowgirl, balanced on crutches yet smiling. The Belles surrounded her on either side. Her support. Her team. His cowgirl was in very good hands. Nolan smiled at his ex-wife and stepped around her. "It was good to see you, Victoria."

"Wait." Victoria set her hand on his arm. "I was going to call you next week, but then I saw you here. I have a business proposition for you."

Nolan studied his ex-wife. "What kind?"

"The news kind, of course." She laughed. "Well, not exactly. But I wasn't even sure if you'd be interested in hearing me out."

"Give me your thirty-second elevator pitch," he said.

"Commentator for the TV station for professional rodeo events, including nationals," she said. "Details to be worked out by the powers that be. We have history. They asked me to gauge your interest."

Nolan rubbed the back of his neck. "Why would I want to do that?"

Victoria leaned in. "Rumor has it you're retiring."

"You know better than anyone not to believe a rumor," he said.

"But there's truth in it." She searched his face, revealing exactly what made her a good reporter. "I can see it in your eyes. They always gave you away."

It still wasn't a conversation he wanted to have with his ex-wife at a crowded venue like this one. "I will think about it."

"Not for too long," she said and chuckled. "Believe it or not, these are coveted positions."

"Why me?" he asked.

"You look good on camera," she replied. "And have an even better voice."

He frowned.

"That's all true," she argued. "The added bonus is you have the professional experience, stats and records to know what you are talking about on camera."

That made more sense. He nodded. "I'll text you either way."

"I'm in town tomorrow, then heading to my parents' place on Monday." She hugged him and walked over to join her friends.

Nolan turned, caught sight of his cowgirl and finally started to make his way to her. A dark-haired gentleman and his well-dressed companion stepped in front of Willow. Introductions and handshakes proceeded. Nolan was close enough to hear Willow's bright laughter. He smiled, then caught a name whispered nearby.

He slowed, listened closer to the curious onlookers and heard the name again. *Royce Chaney.* The famous producer.

Nolan tracked his gaze back to his cowgirl but noticed that Flora Blackwell was watching him. She stood close enough to appear to be part of the conversation, yet just enough outside of it to keep an eye out for intruders.

Flora arched one eyebrow and lifted her champagne glass to her lips.

Message received. Nolan dipped his chin, the

slightest acknowledgment. He supposed he had that sign he was looking for after all.

He retreated and scanned the friends and family gathered around the Belles. He spotted an ally propped against the wall and headed over to him.

Clem noticed Nolan and met him halfway.

Nolan shook Clem's hand and asked, "Any chance you could give this to Willow for me?"

"Are you sure?" Clem accepted the gift bag, his gaze fixed over Nolan's shoulder. "Maybe it would be better if you gave it to Willow yourself. And, you know, maybe talked to her."

Nolan saw his cowgirl still in what looked to be an animated conversation with Royce Chaney and his companion. He caught Flora's shrewd gaze again. Turning back to Clem, he shook his head and said, "No. This is better. Trust me."

Clem looked as if he wanted to argue.

Nolan squeezed Clem's shoulder. "Anything you need for your new ranch in Clementine, I'm only a phone call away."

"Appreciate it," Clem said, then added, "Works both ways. Call me if you need anything."

Nolan nodded and slipped out a side door.

Approaching his truck, he typed a quick text to his ex-wife.

Victoria responded immediately and suggested they meet at Jameson Steakhouse near the river for lunch tomorrow.

Nolan liked her text and picked up his pace.

He'd kept his word to Flora. He would let his cowgirl fly after her dreams.

But it also meant he'd have to move on. After all, dwelling in cowgirl might-have-beens would only hold him back. It was past time his boots got going. And it was up to his heart to catch up.

CHAPTER TWENTY

SUNDAY EVENING, Nolan parked his truck in the driveway and stared at the dark ranch house. The Christmas lights were off outside and inside. That suited Nolan. He hadn't been feeling jolly and bright for days now. No surprise there. His cowgirl had brought the sparkle and shine.

Once inside, he dropped his keys and hat on the kitchen table and listened to the thud of his boots echo on the hardwood floors. The house was empty. Annie and Ryan were at Annie's place checking on things now that the power had been restored. Kendall was at a sleepover. And his stepmom was out to dinner with friends.

He was alone. That suited him. He hadn't been very good company recently.

Funny, instead of expecting his father, now he was waiting to see his cowgirl come bustling through the door. A sunny smile on her face and joy in her brown eyes. All that greeted him was more silence. He turned his back to the empty doorway, set his hands on the sink and stared through the window at the shadows outside instead.

The mudroom door opened and closed. "It's so dark around here," Marla chided. The lights flickered on over the kitchen table. "Nolan, I hardly knew you were home."

But it wasn't his home. Not really. He straightened and turned but kept leaning against the sink as if he needed the extra support. Perhaps he did. Letting down his stepmom wasn't going to be easy. He cleared his throat. "I put the house up for sale today." After his lunch with his ex-wife, he'd met a Realtor. "I know this place was Dad's dream and yours, and I'm sorry." *It just turned out not to be mine.* Not now. Not without his cowgirl.

Marla lowered her purse and stood at the island. Her words were measured. "I hate to tell you this. But your father dreamed this house for you and your family."

Good thing Nolan was propped against the sink. "What?"

"Every design decision was about whether it would work for you. Would work when *you* added more horses. When *you* got married. When *you* had kids." Marla eyed him. "Then you got engaged and married so quickly, your father put the build on fast-forward."

"But my marriage never lasted," Nolan said. "Looking back, I think you all knew it at the wedding."

"Well, your father was ever the optimist and romantic." Marla opened the refrigerator and took out the pitcher of her special sangria. "Your father believed as long as there was real love, then the rest could be sorted out."

"That was where Victoria and I fell apart. Right at the core. It turned out that love was not all we needed." That only brought him back to his cowgirl and their secret garden getaway. Nolan shook his head when Marla offered him a glass of sangria.

Marla sipped her wine and studied him. "That's because you and Victoria didn't share the same love that you and Willow do."

That couldn't be true, otherwise his cowgirl would be with him. He had clearly gotten love wrong again. Nolan crossed his arms over his chest.

Marla moved to him and touched his arm. "Your father would approve. And not that you need it, but I do, too."

His stepmom had not wavered in her belief that Nolan and Willow belonged together. He asked, "How can you be so sure that Willow and I have the right kind of love?" Whatever that even was.

Marla touched her chest. "I feel it in here."

His heart. The one Willow accused him of not giving up.

"You can feel it for yourself," Marla said, her expression full of understanding. "You just have to pay attention and listen."

When he slowed down, the silence only reminded how much he hurt. How much he missed his cowgirl. How empty he was. And how he had failed at love. Again.

"When I want to feel close to your father, it's not

this house or the old one I go to." Marla picked up her glass and stared at the swirling ice as if it was a memory forming. "Instead, I walk the same path we used to take between the old house and this one. It's where we planned, imagined, laughed, argued, and stopped more than once to share a kiss. That's where I feel our love."

Affection was clear on her face. So much love, lasting and timeless, still there for his father. His stepmom looked at him, her gaze steady. "But you have to open your heart all the way to feel it."

He had, hadn't he? His cowgirl certainly didn't think so. Nolan rubbed his chest. "You don't have regrets?"

"For loving so deeply and losing it?"

He nodded.

"I would do it all over again. Just the same." Marla toasted him with her wineglass. "To really live, Nolan, is to share a life with someone all the way. No holding back any part of yourself. You do that and you won't have any regrets."

He already had regrets. And a second thought or two now. Like perhaps he had been out before he had ever been fully in. Like perhaps he had lost his cowgirl, not let her go. That made him twitchy and uneasy. And want to avoid that silence. He took a glass from the cabinet. "You know what? I think I will have some wine with you."

Marla beamed. "Come on. We can sip sangria, tell funny stories about your dad and wrap Christmas presents together."

And Nolan could hide from those truths a while longer. He followed his stepmom into the family room and listened to her story about her first date with his dad.

The sunrise woke Nolan the next morning. He had fallen asleep on the sunroom couch staring at the stars. The night had offered more questions than answers. More restless than rested, Nolan got up and tidied. His final task was to carry a bin of leftover party supplies to the storage barn.

He was only a couple of steps inside the barn when that slow dance came rushing back to him. He could feel Willow's hand in his. Her head on his shoulder. The rhythm of their gentle sway. He thought of the cactus garden gate. He heard Willow's laughter. Felt her joy. Felt her imprint on the property.

Back outside, he stopped short and felt his cowgirl's imprint on his heart.

And suddenly, standing in the middle of his yard. Feet away from a lively reindeer team, an overgrown cactus garden, a storage barn turned dance studio, and an empty house, Nolan understood.

It was never about the house. Or the property. Or the land.

He could move to the coast and into a beachfront property.

Or to the mountains for a hillside chalet.

None of those places would ever feel like home. Not without his cowgirl.

Because she was his home.

And his life would never be the same without his cowgirl to share it with.

Because what they had was the right kind of love—the kind worth opening his heart for. The kind that wanted him to play for keeps.

CHAPTER TWENTY-ONE

WILLOW CONGRATULATED HERSELF for making it five minutes without thinking about her cowboy. Progress was progress, even if it was counted in seconds. It was entirely her cowboy's fault that he was in her mind now. She was certain she had seen him at the Hall of Fame ceremony two nights ago. Certain he had been coming for her.

But then she had lost sight of him. And the crowd had dwindled. And her cowboy had never showed. Not at the arena. Not yesterday at her parents' house. And yet her heart waited.

Now she was pretending to read a magazine that claimed to know exactly how to start the new year right. Steps that, if followed, guaranteed she would uncover the best version of herself. Willow closed the magazine, closed her eyes and dropped her head back on her parents' couch. Zinni, her constant companion since Willow had returned from the hospital, jumped onto her lap and curled up.

Willow had felt her best at Sky Canyon. With Nolan.

She felt anything but good these past days without him.

Yet she was moving forward. Albeit tentatively. Thanks to Maggie, she was slowly learning to forgive herself for the arrow accident. But there were still some misgivings. One of which strolled into the family room and set a wrapped present under the Christmas tree. The first live tree the Blackwells had ever put up together as a family. It wasn't perfect, but they had all agreed it was the start of a new tradition and that was what mattered.

Willow set the magazine on the side table and watched her mother fiddle with an ornament. It was time to address those misgivings. "You disagree with what I asked Royce Chaney for, don't you?"

"I do admit I was taken aback." Flora set a bell ornament to chiming. "I had no idea you had a portfolio of your makeup clients."

She didn't. But her sisters were creating one for her with the photographs Willow had stored on her phone for the past few years. And they promised it would be ready in time for her meeting with Royce Chaney after Christmas. "Well, I couldn't very well parade the cast of *The Wizard of Oz* in front of Royce Chaney to show him what I can do."

"Of course you can't do that. I know that much." Flora waved about. "I just did not realize your cosmetology was more than a hobby."

"I went to school for it," Willow said. Although initially she had needed a job to pay her bills and horse costs. And working a makeup counter or backstage suited her skillset. One she had honed while doing her sisters' performance makeup growing up. Somewhere along the way, she'd found both joy and a passion for it. "I have a license. And I'm quite good at what I do."

"If Royce Chaney has agreed to meet with you and his director about working for him as his makeup artist, then I would assume you have talent," Flora said. "He's a busy man."

That was as close to a compliment as Willow was going to get. She should take it and back off. But she was trapped on the couch. An ice pack on her knee. Edgy and punchy. And missing her cowboy something fierce. So she pressed, "But you don't agree with my decision not to audition for *Glass Ceilings and Petticoats*."

"It's certainly not the choice I would have made." Flora propped her hands on her hips. "But then I've always loved the stage." Flora kicked out her hip and smiled. "I've always been happiest being center stage."

Willow had been the happiest being on stage with her sisters. She stroked her hand over Zinni's back. "This is the part when you tell me that I missed my last chance to be a star."

Flora shook her head. "Not this time, dear."

"Why not?" Willow asked.

"That's simple. I thought it would be obvious to you." Flora's eyebrows rose. "It's not your dream. It was always mine."

Stunned and speechless, Willow sank into the couch.

"So now I'm going to keep my word to someone and step back." Flora crossed over to Willow's good side and said, "To make sure you can chase your own dreams." Then her mother kissed Willow's cheek and headed for the kitchen. "But know this, dear. I will be cheering you on all the way."

Willow pressed her fingers against her cheek and stared at Zinni as if the sleeping dog could explain what had just happened. Flora had given her a compliment. An apology in a roundabout, read-between-the-lines kind of way. Then she'd topped it all off with affection and sounded like she was actually rooting for Willow to follow her own dreams now. But did she dare?

Gran Denny walked into the family room and stopped in front of Willow. "You look pale, dear. Do you need something for the pain?"

Willow shook her head. She needed someone to give her clarity. She glanced at her grandmother and blurted, "Am I enough?"

Gran Denny never flinched. She called for Elias, then settled on the couch beside Willow and propped her feet on a pillow on the coffee table. Big E arrived and sat in the recliner beside Willow.

"My granddaughter here wants to know if she's enough," Gran Denny drawled.

Big E pushed himself back into the recliner as if the answer was going to be lengthy and complicated.

Willow clamped her lips together to keep from rescinding her hasty question. She wasn't even certain where it had come from. That wasn't true. Her cowboy was to blame. She was coming to realize he might have been right all along. But following her own career dream was hardly the same as following her heart.

Gran Denny broke the silence. "I supposed Willow realized that living up to everyone else's expectations was going to wear her out something good."

Willow wanted to lift her hand and remind them that she was right there. But she had admitted to her sisters that she was exhausted from feeling like she'd fallen short again and again. Only her cowboy had never made her feel like that.

Big E smoothed his fingers through his white beard. "If she keeps going on the same path, she'll have more than a bad knee. And all before her thirtieth birthday."

Which was in a few months. Willow tugged Zinni closer and admitted, "It's just that I expected I would be at a different place when I turned thirty." And perhaps that was the biggest letdown.

Gran Denny peered at her as if welcoming her to the conversation. "Where was that, dear?"

Willow shrugged. "Maybe not a place exactly. Just not here. Where I am."

Gran Denny pressed on, "What's wrong with where you are?"

Nothing. Everything. Willow bit her lip. Here wasn't with her cowboy. Here was alone because she had pushed away the one person who had believed she was enough. That thought deflated her.

Big E studied her. "I see a cowgirl passionate about her makeup artistry and with the courage to pursue that as her career."

"And someone who's a wonderful cowgirl coach," Gran Denny added, pride and approval in her words. "One who infuses her joy and love for horses into her kids."

Willow adjusted Zinni's pink snowflake sweater. "But is that enough?"

"By whose standards are you judging?" Big E asked simply.

"Because the only ones that matter are your own," Gran Denny shared.

What was her measure of success? *Time to decide, cowgirl.* "But look what you did, Gran Denny, in Wyoming," Willow argued. "And what you built in Montana, Big E. The Blackwell name is synonymous with Elias and Denny Blackwell across the country."

"And we are proud of that," Big E said.

Gran Denny nodded. "We accomplished what we did because we loved it. First and foremost."

"But I think Denny and I are most proud of our family," Big E said, his expression thoughtful. "And what we have built together with the people we love."

"That's stronger than anything we ever built on our own," Gran Denny explained. "When you have that foundation, you can build something together that will be more than you ever imagined."

Willow was stronger with her family around her. She saw that now. And with her cowboy, with whom she had felt so much more. More happiness. More confidence. More like the cowgirl she wanted to be. Always it came back to her cowboy. "What if what I love is not something, but someone?"

Big E leaned closer to her and waggled his eyebrows. "Then we would say you've finally figured out one of the best parts of this life thing."

Willow frowned. "I'm afraid that road might be a dead end."

"You're forgetting, dear," Gran Denny started. When Willow looked at her, Gran Denny grinned and went on, "That you're a Blackwell and part of a team."

"And nothing is impossible with the right people around you," Big E chimed in.

"Family, you mean," Willow said.

"Now you're thinking like a Blackwell." His appreciation and affection were there in his smile.

Perhaps that was the biggest success. Reuniting with her family. Finding those bonds were not so very fragile in the end. That her family would be there for her through it all.

Gran Denny hollered, "Maggie! Get your sisters and get in here!"

Maggie rushed into the room. "Is there a problem?"

Gran Denny shook her head. "Nothing we can't mend together as a family."

Maggie hardly looked appeased by that answer. Willow grinned at her concerned sibling. "I'm ready to talk about fixing that heartbreak now."

"Finally." Maggie clapped her hands together and let out a shout. Within minutes, Willow's sisters and their partners were crowded around the family room.

Big E cleared his throat and the room quieted. "It seems Willow has lost something important and we're going to help her get it back."

Willow worried she had pushed her cowboy too far. Worried there was no coming back from that. "I'm just not sure how to go about it."

"Sorry, Willow." Clem stepped forward, looking slightly sheepish. "Nolan gave me this at the Hall of Fame ceremony. There was so much going on that night that I forgot to pass it on."

Nolan *had* been there. She had not imagined it. There was still hope for her, for them, yet.

Maggie came to Clem's defense and said, "Then we didn't know if the gift would make you feel better or worse. We've been debating about it all day."

Clem rubbed his chin. "But maybe it will help you figure out what to do."

Willow took the gift bag from Clem and the cowboy scooped Zinni up. Willow pulled out the red tissue paper. A note card was taped to the tissue.

You always lifted my spirits in the best way, cowgirl. Now and always. The words were written in bold handwriting. Willow's pulse raced. She carefully unwrapped the tissue paper and touched the sprig of mistletoe attached to a familiar horseshoe frame. Inside the frame was a candid shot of her and Nolan when he'd snuck up and pressed a kiss to her cheek under the mistletoe at the Christmas party. Joy filled her for their perfectly captured moment. And those pieces of her heart started to fall back into place.

Violet leaned over the coffee table for a closer look. "What is it?"

"It looks like a horseshoe." J.R. peered over Willow's shoulder.

What it was *was* perfect. Willow hugged the frame to her chest. It was proof her cowboy hadn't given up on her. She looked at her family. "I've got an idea, but I can't pull it off alone."

"What are we doing?" Clem rubbed his hands together.

"Fighting for my cowboy's heart," Willow said.

"Now, that is my favorite kind of fight." Big E chuckled.

There was agreement around the room.

It was a fight Willow intended to win. After all, if she wanted that fairy tale, she was going to have to write it herself. And wasn't that the true measure of success. A life well lived with the cowboy she loved the most.

CHAPTER TWENTY-TWO

IT WAS CHRISTMAS EVE. Nolan had other places he needed to be and wanted to be. Truth be told, he would have gone to see Santa even for a last-minute wish at the busy shopping mall. He would have rather done anything other than meet a potential buyer at Sky Canyon Cattle Ranch.

But that was exactly what he was doing. His Realtor had left him a lengthy message about a buyer who had requested a personal tour of Sky Canyon. *Today.* A buyer from an important family that his real estate agent did not want to disappoint.

Nolan was desperate to refuse. He had a cowgirl on his mind and in his heart and he'd yet to finalize his plans for Operation Get Your Cowgirl Back as Kendall had named it. But his Realtor hadn't answered his phone call when Nolan had intended to tell him all that.

So Nolan was on his way to Sky Canyon with a simple plan. He would thank the buyer for coming. Apologize for the inconvenience. And send him or her on their way quickly and efficiently. Then Nolan would return to getting his cowgirl back.

Nolan parked in front of the house. No other cars were in the driveway. He checked his watch. He was right on time. He would wait five minutes but then he was leaving. He had already missed his cowgirl long enough.

He climbed out of his truck. Better to intercept the buyer. If he or she never got out of their car, they could be on their way even faster. Nolan paced around his driveway and glanced at his watch again. Four minutes to go. He walked to the back of the house to check near the garage. No cars there. He headed back to the front and noticed something green glinting in the sunlight on his door.

He barely recognized what it was. A very familiar bit of mistletoe was taped to the door with a note that read *Meet me at our secret spot*.

Nolan hurried down the stairs and headed straight for the cactus garden. *Please let it be her*. He was through the arbor gate and still willing it to be her. He rounded the curve in the path and slowed.

There. He finally released the breath he had been holding. On the couch in the middle of the cactus garden was his cowgirl. Her knee wrapped and braced on the edge of the round table. Her crutches within easy reach. A blanket on her lap and her cheeks an appealing rosy color.

He wanted to run to her. Apologize and promise to make her every wish come true. Promise to love her like she deserved. Instead, he forced himself to wait. There was a lot to say. He wanted to get it all out properly. This time he had no intention of dumping his heart on her and running off.

He made his way over to the table and stopped. "Willow. What are you doing here?"

"Trying to inspire you." She motioned to a big cookie tin open and loaded with baked goods. A tall thermos sat beside the tin. "We know my favorite holiday drink. We don't know your favorite holiday dessert."

Not exactly the direction he thought this was going. But he was playing for keeps, so he would go along with it for as long as he had to. "And you want to figure out my cookie preference now."

"I want to figure that out and more, cowboy." She patted the cushion beside her. When he was settled, she dropped a section of blanket over his lap and grinned at him. "I'm the buyer from the important family."

He blinked at her, at a loss for words again. She had arranged all this. He always appreciated a clever cowgirl.

"You didn't think you could list Sky Canyon for sale and I wouldn't fight for it, did you?" She frowned at him, as if seriously offended.

"You want to buy Sky Canyon," he said, his words a slow, incredulous drawl.

"I was thinking more of a partnership arrangement." She picked up a snowflake-shaped cookie, covered in the thickest blue frosting and what looked to be an entire bottle of silver sprinkles.

"Taste this. It's a loaded sugar cookie. Violet's favorite growing up."

He took a bite. "Not bad." Setting the cookie on a napkin, he got back to the point. "Now, about that deal."

Willow broke a piece off the snowflake and popped the cookie in her mouth. Chewing, she said, "It's good. Not my favorite, either. Let's move on."

Yes, back to that partnership. The one that intrigued him and tugged on those heartstrings. But Willow handed him another cookie. He stared at the gingerbread man in his palm and said, "Maggie's favorite?"

"No, Iris's favorite." Willow picked up the peanut butter cookie with the chocolate candy kiss melted on top. "This is Maggie's."

"I don't need to try these." He set the cookies back in the tin and brushed the crumbs off his hands. "Where is your favorite?"

"Why?" She eyed him.

"Because you are my favorite Blackwell." He scooted closer to her and dropped his arm around the back of the sofa. "You are my choice."

Her gaze flashed, but her smile lifted as if she had a very good secret to share. "That should make the negotiations about our partnership easier."

"Negotiations." Nolan couldn't help himself. She was close, but still too far away. He took her hand in his and smoothed his thumb over her palm. Just a slow caress across her skin.

She sighed and leaned against him. "Hmm, I have conditions, as it happens."

"Is that so." He tucked himself even closer to her, careful not to jar her injured knee, and kept up that light caress across her palm.

"I want Christmas." It was the first he'd heard hesitation in her words.

He had none. "Done."

She shifted to look at him. "You didn't let me finish."

He tipped his chin and waited, let that love inside him finally flow through him.

"I want Christmas with you." She covered their joined hands with her other one. "Every single one. We spend every Christmas together. No matter where we are or what we are doing, we come back here for Christmas. No excuses."

"Done." He lifted her hand, pressed a kiss to the back of her fingers and met her gaze. "What else?"

"Just like that?" she asked, a catch in her words.

"Just like that," he repeated. His heart was open. There was no turning back now.

"Then can we have a live Christmas tree each year, too?" She linked her fingers with his. "That we pick out together."

"Definitely." He curved his arm around her shoulders and tucked her against him as gently as possible. "Anything else?"

She lifted her head and said, "I wasn't sure we would get past Christmas."

"I have one condition." Now it was his turn. For

those right words. "Your heart. I want your heart." He flattened her hand on his chest. "You already have mine, Willow. All my heart. Every bit I have to give. It's only fair I have yours in return."

"You've always had it." She held his stare, her brown eyes expressive, her tone honest and earnest. "Nolan, I loved you back then. I'm in love with you now. And always."

"I'm going to love you, Willow Blackwell, like no one ever has." He cupped her cheek and leaned toward her. "That's my promise to you."

"No more pushing away." She curled her arm around his neck. "Only holding on to each other."

"You have my word," he vowed and paused to confess, "My first marriage didn't fall apart because love wasn't enough. I didn't love enough." He stroked his hand across her cheek to the back of her neck. "But I love you, Willow, with my whole heart. And I promise to prove it to you every single day."

Their lips connected. Their kiss anchored them. Tethered their hearts together. And there, in an overgrown cactus garden in winter, love took root and bloomed.

Willow slowed the kiss and pulled away. "Is it too late for one last condition?"

"Depends on what it is," he said, his words playful. His heart full.

She pushed him lightly. "I want that first date."

"Only if I get the last one," he countered.

She kissed him. Just a brief press of her lips to his. "You can have that and every date in between."

"Deal." He tugged her back for another kiss. A longer one that spoke from his heart. That gave more than it took. That left another deeper imprint on him. Regretfully, he ended the kiss and set her away from him. "As much as I want to keep making deals and sealing them with a kiss right here in our secret place, we have to go."

Willow sagged back against him. "Where do we need to be exactly?"

He chuckled and said, "It's Christmas Eve, Coach."

"Oh my gosh. The parade!" Willow straightened and reached for her crutches. "You kiss me, and I forget about everything else."

"That's nice to hear." Nolan tugged on her to draw her back to him.

"Do not kiss me, Nolan. We can't be late." She pressed her fingers over his mouth to stop him. "I'm not telling everyone we are late because you kissed me breathless and senseless."

"Fine." He caught her hand and pressed his lips to her palm. "I'll tell them that you kissed me, but it wasn't quite breathless."

"Just a quick one." She was laughing when their lips met again but she ended the kiss as swiftly as it started. "Now let's go. You can leave the cookies."

"No way." Nolan pressed the lid on the cookie tin. "You need snacks at a parade."

Willow laughed.

"And I'm still deciding my order of preference." He stood and picked up her crutches.

She shook her head and accepted the crutches, adjusting them under her arms. "You can't play favorites. We are all equally special."

"Sorry, I'm already partial." He lifted his eyebrows, dropped a kiss on her lips, then polished off the overloaded sugar cookie he had left out of the tin. "But I have to say. This extra thick frosting and these crunchy sprinkles are growing on me."

"Violet will be delighted, I'm sure." Willow made her way slowly along the gravel path.

Nolan stayed right beside her.

For the first time ever, Nolan was not in a rush to get anywhere. He had his cowgirl, and she had his heart, now and always.

EPILOGUE

Christmas Day

"QUITE AN ADVENTURE we've had together." Denny stood beside Elias at the large bay window in Flora's house. She chuckled. "I couldn't have imagined it."

"Something tells me it's only just beginning," Big E mused.

He watched Flora introduce Willow to her Christmas gift. A pair of geldings from the same bloodlines as their original performance horses, Skylark and Wildfire. Big E had a hand in securing the quarter horses that would help Willow start her trick riding training program. Even Flora had agreed to become a coach. Willow hugged her mother and then the horses. After that, she returned to her cowboy, who embraced her openly. There might be unexpected ups and downs ahead for the couple, but they would handle them together and be stronger for it.

"I can feel it." Denny leaned on her cane. "The start of something really good around here."

"We'll have to come back from time to time and check in on them," Big E suggested.

"Absolutely." Gran Denny chuckled. "Someone needs to make sure they still have things in hand. And haven't lost their way again."

Willow and Nolan walked back to the house with Barlow and Flora, their arms linked tight around each other. Big E nodded, satisfied and a bit more thrilled. "They're going to build something special here. Something that lasts."

"Together." Denny squeezed Big E's arm, met his gaze and added, "As it should be."

Bursts of laughter and animated shouts came from the kitchen.

Denny pursed her lips. "Quite a ruckus they're making in there."

Big E nodded. He'd never minded a ruckus. He grinned at his sister. "I suppose we should go see what all the fuss is about."

Denny nodded in turn and started for the kitchen. "Can't leave 'em alone for a minute."

Willow and the others were just making their way inside the back door. Big E and Denny paused to take in the commotion. There was a turkey waiting to be stuffed and popped into the oven. Potatoes needing peeling on the counter. And all sorts of other fixings were ready to be assembled for Christmas dinner. No one was working on dinner preparations, though. They were all staring at Annie with a mixture of amusement and not a touch of mischievousness on their faces.

"Wait. Time out." Annie turned off the vintage radio on the counter. Her gaze skipped around the crowed room. "Chase... Blackwell." Annie swirled her finger at them. "Is Chase Blackwell, only one of the best singers out there I feel the need to mention, a Blackwell like you are all Blackwells?"

"Of course, Chase is one of us." Big E pushed his shoulders back, lifted his eyebrows at Annie and added with pride, "Chase is my grandson."

Willow motioned to her siblings gathered around the kitchen. "Chase is also our cousin."

Annie speared her arms out. "How did I not know this?"

Ryan smiled at Annie, and she smiled back.

"Will wonders never cease?" Annie said, grinning and joining her cowboy by the island.

Kendall rolled her eyes and chewed on a cookie. "Mom knows every single Chase Blackwell song. She's a huge fan."

Violet picked up a snowflake cookie and aimed it at Annie. "We could probably introduce you."

Annie's eyes popped wide.

"I can do you better than that," Big E offered. "Chase is performing on New Year's Eve in Las Vegas."

Annie gripped Ryan's hand so tightly, he winced. "Do not tell me this is all a joke."

"We don't joke about family," Gran Denny stated, but her smile softened her rebuke.

"Who wants tickets?" Big E asked.

Every hand in the kitchen shot up.

Gran Denny laughed. "It's going to be a Blackwell holiday to remember."

"Seems like the perfect start to the New Year." Big E's grin was wide. "A road trip with family."

* * * * *

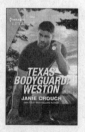